INVERCLYDE LIBRARIES

D0273260

Little Sister

Carol Birch

virago

VIRAGO

Published by Virago Press 1999
This edition published by Virago Press in 2011

Copyright © Carol Birch 1998

The moral right of the author has been asserted.

Acknowledgements to International Music Publications Ltd (IMP) for
permission to reproduce lyrics from: 'Nobody Knows You When You're
Down and Out' (Cox), 'Red Sails in the Sunset' (Williams/Kennedy),
'The Donkey Serenade' (Friml/Stothart/Forrest/Wright) and
'She Wears Red Feathers' (Merrill).

A CIP catalogue record for this book
is available from the British Library.

ISBN 978-10-84408-799-0

Typeset by M Rules in Bembo
Printed and bound in Great Britain by
Clays Ltd, St Ives plc

Virago
An imprint of
Little, Brown Book Group
100 Victoria Embankment
London EC4Y 0DY

An Hachette UK Company
www.hachette.co.uk

www.virago.co.uk

Little Sister

1

I was in work, in Connor's, under the slatted ceiling of
dried flowers. I served coffee and toasted tea-cake, oozing
thick salty butter. There was the murmur-murmur going
on, and in Patacake Alley the people passed, turned fluid by
the small google-eyed panes of the handsome bay window.
For a moment I looked up, dizzy with it all, remembering
that it's the last day of the month, the day my money goes
into the bank, and I said I'd do it on the next payday if
nothing had happened to alter the situation. And nothing
had. Then Mrs Crowe called me into the back and asked if
I'd sorted out my holidays yet, and I rearranged all the
flowers, it's my job to do that, I've trained, I can do sprays,
wreaths, garlands, head-dresses, the lot. I've done the flowers for the Town Hall. I walked home through the old
stone town, and the early summer evening was coming
down on me so soft the way it does, like sleep. I knew it
was going to rain, it was there in the air, a homoeopathic

dose of it. I stood on the bridge and watched swans on the canal. On a painted barge, a small dog lay twitching in sleep beside a green metal bucket bursting with geraniums, blood-red. I crossed the bridge, came through the rising backs, the cobbled alleys where some children were playing. The sky under the arch was pearlised and the ting of the bell on the door of the little shop seemed to come from very far away, like cowbells from the other side of a mountain, and there was my street, and the long ginnelled terrace stretching up and over the hill, and my neighbour passing in her stone-coloured padded jacket, and I was terrified.

'Nice,' she said very seriously, nodding. 'Nice evening.'

She was so sudden and vivid, every pore of her skin a shaded crater, every hair of her head a separate wire.

'Lovely!' I smiled brightly in my existential terror, falling into the house like someone falling on to the Raft of the *Medusa*.

2

My best performances are always behind closed doors.

Living alone you get ridiculous; my hands should be cupped around a wine glass for this swaying stroll about the room, a mug of tea isn't quite the thing. I had the radio on but that didn't quite do it, Bobby Vee and 'Rubber Ball', I mean really. So I put on this old blues thing and here's Bessie Smith, full of drowsy longing:

> Once I lived the life of a millionaire,
> Spent all my money, I didn't care.
> I carried my friends out for a good time,
> Buying bootleg liquor, champagne and wine . . .

Sometimes there's a great appeal to the idea of taking to the wine. In a nice way, of course. The Blanche DuBois syndrome, woman alky as beautiful loser. I wouldn't have the rotten bits, hanging over the toilet looking like hell at five o'clock in the morning. Oh no.

Ooh . . . nobody knows you when you're down and out,
Ooh . . . not one penny, and my friends I haven't any . . .

I take hairpins from my little box on the mantelpiece and start pinning up my hair. I can move like a whore, all languid and elegant, though I don't suppose you'd know it if you saw me out there. I turn my head, check the line of my chin, and in the gap between one song and the next I realise it's dark. In the cool house there are sounds, little tickings and clickings. The town hall clock chimes three quarters and a little chill goes down me to my toes, I shiver, remember that there's something I'm supposed to do that I'm trying not to think about because now it's here it's like fire fighting ice inside me.

The old crackling brass cranks its weary way up again into the next number, and I drift upstairs in the dark, turn on the light in the bathroom and run a bath. I hang the towels nicely along the radiator, get undressed and throw my clothes out on the landing. I have a big mirror in here, it tells all kinds of tales. I love looking at my body, full-breasted, white, mythical in the rising mist. I lift my breasts with my hands. I will, I think, I really will go and get myself a bottle of wine, soon as I've had this bath. No I won't, can't. Drinking alone? Drinking alone in the evening, singing 'I hate to see that evening sun go down' naked in front of a mirror, making eyes at your poor self? Come on! But there should be a witness. Or what's it for?

The little lady of Ch'ing–Ch'i, that's me:

> *Her door opened on the white water*
> *Close by the side of the timber bridge;*
> *That's where the little lady lived*
> *All alone without a lover.*

There hasn't been a man in my life in seven years, but that's not why I said I'd do it, that's not it at all. Next payday, I said. It's not even because I'm particularly unhappy. Well, I have these moments of terror but don't we all? No? Let's not make it into a drama, I'm basically OK, I have food, shelter, a job, friends, you know. All those things. Some of the cards I've had seem unfair to me, but some are OK. I think Sylvia Plath had the right idea with the gas oven. I mean, think about the options. I couldn't manage hanging, that final moment when your tongue starts straining at its roots and you know what you've done, and pills are so boring.

The phone rings. I should have put the answering machine on. It's probably just Susannah or Tim or Sally Wilcock ringing for a piano lesson, so I leave it but it carries on, then when I get down there and pick it up someone puts the phone down at the other end. Typical. I hang around a bit waiting for it to ring again but it doesn't so I go up and soak with a couple of drops of Clary Sage I bought from Trish Allgood, close my eyes, and listen to the music drift up from downstairs. My house, old and well-beloved, folds around me its comforting mother hen wings. I drift. A little window lets in distant birdsong, sporadic and discreet. I go away down the long dim tunnels, I half dream, blood, shiny and dark, dripping down in fine strands and getting on a gritty grey ground under my feet. Well, I faint soon as look at the stuff. I'm down at once, head between the knees, trying to hang on to the world. Suddenly it's pouring, noisily trickling, and it's not dark any more but tomato sauce red and running like a river, and I realise with a quiet pang of shock that it's coming from me. Is it my nose? No, not that. I'm a little girl, I can't find the source.

'What is it, Mummy? What is it, Mummy?' I say.

But of course there's no one there.

My eyes pop open. I see only the broken-down Ali Baba basket overflowing its burden of limp clothes through the light grey sea mist that coats everything in a fine sweat. Everything needs a good clean: the tiles covered in bottles of this or that, the flaking blue paintwork on the door, the freckled mirrors. Tomorrow I'll give the poor old bathroom a damn good clean.

Will I? Clean the bathroom tomorrow?

Falling asleep in the bath is dangerous.

I wash my hair in the bath, get out to rinse it at the sink and stand there dripping and steaming. I wouldn't do anything bloody. Not that mess. The phone rings. Sod it. It rings and rings and my hair flicks stinging water into my eyes. Should run. It's all money, can't afford to miss a client.

I wrap a towel round my head and run but the damn thing stops again, and I stand there.

Listen.

It's starting to rain. Whisper, whisper.

My hair's wet now so that's that, I can't go over for the wine. Anyway, the shop's closed. Saved. Saved from a life as a lush.

This old stone house gets chilly, even on warm evenings. I light a fire in the front room, end up in the kitchen in my pink bathrobe with the towel still round my head, nibbling a cracker and waiting for the kettle to boil. I fan out a few thin slices of Havarti on my old saucer with the deep red roses and gold trim, getting them just so. The music's finished but the rain roars and I go over to the sink and lean upon it, looking out. It's teeming out there now, softly falling on the corrugated roof at the back. A single repeating drip from the guttering slowly swells and quivers, bursting as it falls through the glow from the back alley light. The kettle boils and puts itself out, subsiding wheezily like a lung after a coughing fit.

I pull the curtains on falling darkness and sit in the dark by my fire with the tea on the hob, uncoiling my damp hair and rubbing it with the towel, teasing it out before the newborn flames that fight the good fight in the graceful black arch of the fireplace. Red roses bloom here and there on the black tiles. I put a little more wood on just to hear it crack, then stick on an ancient Platters CD from the library. I want a real tearjerker. I want smoke in my eyes. But there's really nothing moving down there in the old beanbag of the emotions, nothing at all as I get up and walk about the room shaking my drying hair and wondering where the comb's got to. *This* is why, you see, something to do with being heavy inside myself and because I can't feel things like I used to, can really only remember feeling things a long long time ago, as if I once had a sense and lost it. I've thought this out. If I'm honest it's not from pain, it's more from a great sense of adventure because I really do think there's something there on the other side and I'm going to jump into it. I wish I could believe in nothing, I really do, it would help at a time like this. What a comfort, a great somnolent pool, Oblivion. You could pray to it for eternal peace.

Susannah now, she said to me (mind you, she's mad) she said there's no point in committing suicide, whatever it is you're running away from, you still have to face it anyway so you might as well just get on with it. No get-out clause. Well, I don't believe all that, that you put this in and you get that out. I lift my hand and look at it. Flesh, my long-time companion. Coming to the window, I lift the green chenille curtain with my poor unsuspecting little hand and look out at the soothing torrent. There's nothing like a rain-soaked terrace for romance. The pavements are black mirrors, the light from the street lamps sparkling in trembling silver splinters.

How old is she now, Veronica Karen? Thirty-five. Thirty-five because I'm thirty-seven.

When we were little we used to look out like this, Veronica Karen and I; I used to tell her: those little silver pocks, those quick kisses on the puddles, they're invisible fairies landing, just touching down with the tip of a pointed toe then off again. She believed everything I told her.

A figure in a long black coat detaches itself from the darkness and walks rapidly through the pouring rain on the other side of the road, hands in pockets. It's looking at the numbers on the houses. It crosses and heads straight towards me like an arrow, and I jump back, scared. Where was I? Drifting again. The firelight flickers becomingly in my cosy little room, the coals sing, and I wonder what happened and why I drifted so far.

When the doorbell rings I'm shocked. It's no one I know: it's the Angel of Death, he's been listening to me and taken me at my word; it's the demon lover, oh where have you been, my long long love, these seven long years and more? It's Robert come back, trailing his tattered shroud, his breath earthly cold.

Well, I won't answer.

I tiptoe to the hall door and stand there half in, half out of the room, listening. My heart races out of all proportion to the event, as if some great thump has galvanised it. I have this fearful imagination because of all the ghost stories me and Veronica Karen were fed by Auntie Pearl when we were still very small. Auntie Pearl's idea of a suitable bedtime story for a three-year-old was 'The Monkey's Paw' or something from one of the Pan books of horror.

'Not a scary one, Auntie Pearl.'

'No, not this time,' she'd say, and smile. The dark red lipstick on the small kissy lips, a deep dimple in each smooth full cheek when she smiled. 'I promise. This one isn't very scary.'

Before she went blonde and blowsy Auntie Pearl's hair, henna-red, swept back in thick, stiff waves from her round powdered face. Her voice was musical, joyful, rich like syrup: 'In *this* house. In this *ve*ry house, a long, long time ago . . .'

The bell rings again. I almost run to the door, adjusting my bathrobe.

'Cathy?' he says uncertainly.

'Yes?' I say, snappish with nerves, 'yes?'

It's not that I don't recognise him, it's that I recognise him too quickly and dismiss the idea. But it is him. Must be something to do with Veronica Karen then. Funny, I was just thinking about her.

He smiles tentatively.

'My God. Stephen Openshaw,' I say belatedly. 'What are you doing here?'

'I'm getting wet actually.' He laughs a little, foolishly.

I only hesitate for a second before letting him in. He's very tall, in the narrow hall he looms, grinning. 'A fire!' he says when I lead him into the warm flickering room. 'I must have died and gone to heaven,' and walks to it with arms outstretched and back straight, long white Nosferatu fingers pointing the way. He flops down into the blue wicker chair with a grunt and an air of profound relief, sudden like a dog. 'No one has a proper fire these days,' he says, 'hardly anyone,' surveying the room with an eager look and the rain dripping forlornly from rats' tails that hang down over his forehead.

This is like a punch in the stomach.

'What are you doing here?' I ask lamely, feeling stupid with my pink towelling bathrobe and uncombed hair. I come up to the fire and stoop to shovel coal up out of the scuttle, holding the bathrobe modestly where it sometimes gapes. 'What is it? Eight years? Ten?' Didn't he come up with Veronica Karen once when me and Robert were living in Dover Road? I shake my head in wonder.

'Seven years and nine months,' he says immediately, getting up and taking off his coat. Under it is a crumpled dark jacket made out of some thin material. 'I was working it out in the car. It was at Andy and Jana's wedding, just before they left for Australia. Remember that?'

'Do I?' I did them all buttonholes, feathered the carnations. 'My God!' I place coal on the fire, very precisely here and there for some action to perform, though it doesn't really need it.

Years in London rush in, a surge of me and Robert, Veronica Karen, Tonto, Andy and Jana and all those people. And him. Why is he here? Why now? He was a funny kind of thing, half family almost, my sister's ex from years back, one

11

she kept in touch with no matter what. He was there in the London years, always somewhere. I had a kind of soft spot for him then, knowing each other as we did from way back when he used to come for tea to our house and talk to our dad about football while Veronica Karen was upstairs getting ready.

His fingers link together, his wrists protruding from the sleeves of his jacket. 'Is Veronica Karen around?' he asks, bright-eyed and smiling, a little awkward, as if he's trying a little too hard to sound casual.

'Veronica Karen? She doesn't come up here.' I sit back, laughing shortly. 'No no, I can't remember the last time I saw Veronica Karen. I thought she was in London.'

'Oh yes,' he says, 'yes, of course, she was,' then there's one of those terrible silences while he looks at me with a kind of expectancy and I wonder if there's something I ought to be saying. Stephen Openshaw sitting there though, it's just not true. He was always around our house. He used to get the train to Altrincham Station when my dad worked there. He has the most amazing hands, I remember them now, enormous and languid and embarrassed. Sometimes he'd curl them sensitively around each other and lean his face on them. I look at him, interested, wondering if he'll do that, and suddenly feel discomforted by the syrup of the Platters track schmoozing a little too loudly between us.

'I thought she was in London,' I say again.

'She was. But she's not there now. I think she's probably in Scotland actually but I thought she might have called here on the way.'

Of course he wouldn't have come all this way just to see me, would he? The last time I saw Veronica Karen was at Auntie Celia's funeral in Shugden and all I can remember is meeting her on the landing in Auntie Pearl's house and getting the giggles and the giggles turning into hysterics and the two of us nearly dying with holding it in, and everybody sitting around in Auntie Pearl and Uncle Vincent's front room. We didn't actually talk to each other though. That was what – seven? – eight years ago? Oh God, I don't know. Last I heard, she was working in a bar.

'Scotland?' I say. 'What's she doing there?'

He shrugs elaborately and gives a sharp laugh. 'Who knows?'

'And you?' I ask him. 'Are you back up here now? Back up north?'

But he shakes his head. 'I'm still in Camberwell,' he says, 'same flat. Bloody Camberwell, it's getting a bit boring. I went to America, you know. Chicago.'

'Chicago!'

I think he had more hair then, yes he did, he's receding at the sides, oh God love him, he was sixteen when I first saw him.

'Yeah, I was on a project. God knows how I did it, I wangled my way on to a research thing and was out there for six months. We were supposed to be checking out this system for teaching the kids from hell. Went to work in a bulletproof vest ha ha. I'm at this crap school in Hackney now but not for much longer, I hope. Got an interview on

Tuesday.' He sounds breathless and nervous. 'You? What are you doing now? I hear about you now and then. Still doing the kiddie books? Old Ambrose?'

He jumps up and looks towards the pictures on the wall.

'No,' I say nonchalantly, 'no, actually. Not any more.'

'You're not? Why not?'

'Oh, I'm doing other things now!'

I sweep his coat up from the sofa and take it out into the hall to hang it up next to my red jacket and old winter coat and hat. A moment of disorientation takes me. His presence is some great anachronism. He doesn't belong in Moorcop, his face fits Manchester and London, the only places I've ever known him. It's all out of joint, I've crossed some weird threshold. I did it, I think, I really did it and now I'm dead. This is some death experience. But why it involves my sister's old boyfriend I just can't fathom.

'So why are you here?' I ask boldly, re-entering the room. 'Is she giving you the run-around?'

He's on his feet still, peering through the darkness at one of the Ambrose the Cat illustrations on the wall, putting his face close. He looks round at me, startled, his mouth open, then he says very seriously, 'You really don't know about Veronica Karen?'

'What's she done?' I ask.

His look intensifies; he gives a sad little snigger. 'What do you mean?' he asks, nonplussed. 'Why did you have to say that? Why do people always assume that if it's Veronica

Karen, she must have done something? So you don't know about her?'

Oh Lord, let's hear it once more for the Veronica Karen fan club.

'Know what about her?'

'You didn't know she wasn't well?'

He sounds incredulous.

'No.'

How the hell should I know? She never gets in touch with me. She cut herself off.

He wilts. 'Oh damn,' he says, sitting down again. 'I was really hoping you'd know all about it.'

He fire-gazes to a string backing. This Platters stuff is just totally embarrassing and inappropriate, I've got to get rid of it, but if I take it off it'll only draw attention to it all the more. I turn it down. 'What?' I say, irritated, 'what?'

'She's got AIDS,' he says quietly to the fire.

Funny how you react to things. A smile spreads itself madly across my face. 'She's not,' I say.

'Yes. She's actually got it.'

I fight with the smile, trying to kill it before he looks up, and oh joy, the music ends. It *is* a death experience. In the lull I think: Typical Veronica Karen. Typical. She would do this, wouldn't she? Oh, Veronica Karen! If she was here I'd get hold of her and shake her into kingdom come.

She never told me.

'How?' I ask. 'How long?'

Oh shameful excitement, life's rippling at last,

something's happening: someone's dying, someone's dying, someone's dying, someone's dying again and it's not me, still not me.

'She started getting sick in January,' he says, 'I mean really quite sick, just before I went to America,' then for one terrible second his face crumples in something like rage and he leans forward in his chair, turning his linked hands inside out like the old finger game, here's the lady's knives and forks, here's the lady's table. 'Oh but years,' he laments, 'well years she's had the virus, you know, but she'd been well – well enough – well it *seemed* like she was well, but . . . I don't see that much of her these days. She was terribly thin. I mean, well, no, it started before then really.' It's guilt his eyes are troubled with. I don't know why people always blame themselves for someone like Veronica Karen.

Out in the street a lone car passes, wheels hissing.

'I think I'd better make some tea,' I say.

His long body sags theatrically. 'Oh please!' He straightens again. 'Mind if I smoke?'

'Go ahead.'

He takes out his cigarettes and leans forward, offering one, but I shake my head and go into the kitchen. I don't believe all this, I really don't. It's just another one of her stunts. I potter about getting the tea, pushing my hair about, looking at my bare feet on the cold black and white floor and adjusting the pink bathrobe, which is thick and woolly and protective, pour boiling water on to the tea bags, thinking: this *should* be wine, why didn't I go over and get some, and I should be in some elegant southern belle kind of thing, all lace upon a white bosom.

'I'm sorry,' he says standing smoking in the doorway, one arm up above his head leaning on the frame, his jacket hanging crooked on him. 'I'm really sorry to have to tell you all this.'

'It's not your fault.' My brain's turning over and over.

'I'd've rung,' he says, 'only I didn't have your number and you're not in the book, are you?'

'How did you get my address?'

He shrugs. 'I don't know, it's been hanging around in my book for years. I didn't even know if you'd be here, I thought you might have moved. Can I do anything?'

'Are you hungry?'

'I'm starving actually.' He laughs apologetically.

I open doors. There's some cheese, half a stick of stale French bread, cream crackers, three ginger cookies; he comes and stands behind me, looking up with interest into my food cupboard with the crumbs and the sticky bits from the marmalade and the bottle of vanilla essence that fell over.

I don't think he's attractive really, it's just me, just the situation. He's certainly improved though. He was nothing much, just a plain, fairly pleasant boy. Funny how people age. There were boys who were lovely and now they're nothing, but he's gone the other way.

'I'll do it,' he says, reaching up. 'Have you got an ashtray?'

I hand him my knife, my good one, hunt for an ashtray. 'The bread's like rock,' I say.

He balances his cigarette on the shelf and begins slicing, precise with the lethal weapon. 'She was in hospital a couple of times, you know,' he says. 'Quite early on she was in.'

My brain turns over and over all the things I know about AIDS: nightsweats, Kaposi's sarcoma, Belsen bones, Benetton, Rock Hudson, Freddie Mercury, T-cells.

'But it was OK and she always came out again.' He crumbles off the soft white cheese with the side of the blade. 'It was just like she was really tired all the time, Cathy.' He stops and stares. 'She could just sleep and sleep. But then she always could, couldn't she? You know what I feel really bad about?'

'What?'

'Going to America. I mean, how can you tell what's going to happen? I got this chance and she seemed OK, she had a bit of a fluey thing, but then everyone did, time of year, and I actually said to her I won't go if you don't want me to. I mean how can you tell? I mean, she just laughs. Oh fuck off, Stephen, she says, you're not my mother. So I went. And then I come back and she's just gone.'

Gone. Dead. She's dead already.

'Gone?'

'Vanished, it seemed at first.' His arms fly out, his shoulders lift in an expansive gesture. A stranger with a waving knife in my kitchen. I always put my knife away at night, always. His eyebrows fly up too, and a wavy line appears in his forehead beneath his straight brown hair. 'Got any pickles?' he asks, and I hand down the jar.

'Thanks. Well, you know Veronica Karen. Never exactly the disciplined kind, not the kind to sit down and do her change of address forms. See you soon, she always says. Could mean this afternoon or the year after next. So I get back and no one's seen her for ages. I go round to her flat but there's never an answer, and the phone just rings and rings – horrible place in Vauxhall, she had, she had some right dives, you know – and whenever you see anyone who knows her it's just Veronica Karen? Veronica Karen? Oh, she's away. Where? Oh, she's in Crystal Palace. She's in Notting Hill. She's gone *crewing*, for Christ's sake, on a boat to Easter Island. Now, come on! No one knows.' He licks his thumb. 'She's been getting people down, moody as hell apparently.'

He glances at me quickly, sharp-eyed, screws the lid down on to the pickles. 'Well, you know what she's like. Just ups and offs whenever she feels like it.'

'Oh yes. I know.' I lead him back to the fire and we sit there, one on either side of it.

'Finally I run into Bobbie quite by chance, remember Bobbie? Million to one chance on the northbound platform at Clapham South.' For one piercing second the northbound platform at Clapham South engulfs me in seedy grey nostalgia. 'Says she ran into Veronica Karen on her way to the bus station and she said she was going to see a lot of people up north and scribbled down this address she might be at. Makes you think how easily a person gets lost.' He turns his face, hollowed by the fire, away. 'She knew a million people and everyone thinks she's somewhere else.' A faint shrug, a turning down of the mouth. 'She'd given up the job, of course. She wasn't with a bloke. There was no one to really notice when she'd gone.' So what? his body says, but here he is, looking for her.

There's a peaceful silence. The fire rustles. I remember going up from Manchester to Cousin Sandra's wedding in Shugden. Veronica Karen brought Stephen, a plain weedy boy, seventeen then, same as me. I remember Grandma saying she can do better than that, our Veronica. I don't reckon much to him. Sniffing with her big fleshy nostrils. He drank too much and threw up in the car park of the Nag's Head, partly over our car. A flurry of bright-coloured aunties rushed to help him; Veronica Karen in a miniskirt looked the other way. She was a sexy little thing at fifteen. I've got the old wedding photos still, we're all there – the aunties and uncles, the cousins, Mum in her pink suit, Dad with his hair still dark, Grandma, poor old Uncle Vincent and Auntie Pearl. I used to feel proud of Auntie Pearl in those days; I thought she really looked like something with her big yellow hat, though of course she was on the edge of fat hagdom even then. That was the first time I saw her get really stupid and pissed, chainsmoking and trying to dance like the young people, blowing loud raspberries, shouting and swearing and trying to get up on the stage with the singer. What am I to do? Shall I ring Auntie Pearl? She always asked after Veronica.

'I've never actually been to Moorcop before,' he says, eating from my rose saucer, 'can you believe? It's nice, isn't it? Not that I saw very much with the rain and it getting dark and everything.' His face keeps changing. Who is it he reminds me of? Is it just himself a long time ago? 'I think I may have gone through it once in the car,' he says, 'with my mum and dad when we were kids, you know, driving up to the moors or something on the way somewhere, but I'm sure we never stopped.'

'Why are you so sure she's ill now?' I ask.

'A feeling,' he says, and then just looks at me in that awkward way again, almost smiling, as if he's waiting for me to say or do something and as if I ought to know what it is. Well, I don't. Hit me with a thing like this, how am I supposed to perform? But he continues very quickly, looking away and making his eyes bland: 'No, not just a feeling, because all the signs were there, she looked terrible, her T-cells were down again, she had a – she had a sore mouth. And this cold, this bad cold, well how many people had a bad cold that time of year? So I just played it down and off I went and of course it was obvious that she might be dead by the time I got back but I chose not to see.'

He reaches into his pocket and brings out a scrap of paper and hands it over. 'This is the address I got from Bobbie.'

I read: 25 Tobin Close, Kilreevy.

'Kilreevy?'

'Little place in Strathclyde.' He lights a cigarette. 'Know anyone up there?'

'Can't think of anyone.'

I hand it back.

'Well, the truth of the matter is,' he says, pocketing the scrap of paper over his breast, 'I think she's in a pretty bad state and I think you ought to know and I thought you might be interested in coming with me to see her.'

I laugh, quite a merry laugh.

For a moment he looks hurt but then a kind of cool distance sets in. 'I'm serious,' he says and goes off into one of those looks again and it annoys me because what I took for awkwardness now seems to me like cheek.

'You're not serious,' I say. 'I can't go chasing about after Veronica Karen, she wouldn't want me to, she knows where I am, she's never tried to get in touch, we haven't even seen each other for years.'

'Oh, the pair of you!' He leans forward intently with his arms twisted together awkwardly on his knees and the smoke coiling up in a graceful silver twist. I hear the rain, a sudden attack at the window, and a lonesome gust of wind. 'She's your sister, for Christ's sake. All the rest doesn't matter. Look, you don't even have to think about it, she's your sister and she's sick and you've got to go and see her. That's all there is to it. You don't have to like her.'

'I can't just dash off like that, I have to go to work.'

'Work? What do you do?'

'I'm a waitress. Part-time.'

'Call in sick,' he says.

'I don't work tomorrow,' I say, 'but I said I'd do Saturday.'

'We'll be back by then, and anyway it's only one day. You'd *definitely* be back by Sunday.'

'They're rushed off their feet on Saturdays.' Me and Annie swearing in the kitchen, Mrs Crowe grandly taking orders.

'Call in sick.'

'I can't.'

'Call in sick. Tell them the truth, for Christ's sake. Your sister's ill.'

'You don't *know* that.'

He turns away, sighing and swaying with exasperation. 'Look,' he says, 'help me out with this one. As far as I know she didn't tell anyone else, only me, that's what she said. She had a thing about not wanting people to know. Do you know what that's like, to carry a thing like that around on your own? OK, she's stupid, OK she's a pain in the arse, but I've known her twenty-one years and she's very probably dying and I don't want to wake up one day and hear that she's dead hundreds of miles away. And I don't think you should either. Come on, Cathy! She's your sister.'

'I don't know.' I shake my head, wanting to laugh, it's so ridiculous. 'I don't know.'

'I thought you'd know where Frank and Tilly lived,' he says. 'I thought there was a good chance she might have gone there. And then if she isn't, we could nip up to Kilreevy and check out that address. We can sleep in the car, the back folds down, you can have it all to yourself and I'll sleep in the front, I've got sleeping bags, honestly I've done it before, it's not too bad.'

Sleep in the car, me and him, oh those days, those days, those sleeping in the car days are gone. I'd look horrible in the morning waking up. Can you imagine? Faded. Dirty eyes. Not even youth on my side. Those days are gone. It's trouble. Always has been. Whenever it's anything to do with Veronica Karen it's trouble, you can stake your life on it: crap flats, mysterious addresses, running round the country, all fairly typical really. And now she's pulled the biggest stunt of all, she's actually going to die.

'Well, I'm just going to have a good ring round of everyone,' I say. 'Someone'll know where she is. Anyway, she's a free agent. I mean, she can still make her own choices, can't she? She obviously isn't that fussy about seeing either one of us, is she?'

He chucks the fag end in the fire.

'No,' he says evenly, 'I suppose you're right. Still and all.'

Poor bugger. Poor besotted bugger, after all these years. The rain hisses peacefully. He looks into the fire, one great hand moving gracefully to cup his neck. Hisss, gentle, those old, old days, car wheels gentle passing our window, and the soft lights shining on the raindrops on the glass, headlights slowly sweeping the ceiling. Hsssssss . . . Mrs Jolly is throwing out the washing-up water, swirling it over the flagstones in the yard. She was scared of storms, those brilliant storms up in Shugden. I told her about the family in the sky, the Jollys, an accident-prone lot who were always moving the furniture about and fusing the lights. Rumble, CRASH! They're at it again. BANG! There goes a wardrobe down the stairs. FLASH! CRACKLE! Albert's fused the lights again.

'I'll come to Frank and Tilly's with you,' I say. 'It's just across the moors. But I'm not going any further.'

What am I, mad? Christ, Frank and Tilly. Of all the people I don't want to see.

He relaxes visibly. 'Give them a ring,' he says.

'You must be joking. They haven't been on the phone for years, they never pay any bills. But I know where they live.'

He smiles. 'Well,' he says, 'what is it? Three-quarters of an hour's drive? What have you got to lose?'

Peace.

'I'll pull down the sofa bed,' I say.

'No no no, don't go to any trouble, please, I'll be fine on the floor, look, I've got sleeping bags in the car, I'll go and get my stuff, shall I? I'm parked just up the hill.'

'Don't be silly. I'll pull down the sofa bed.'

He leans far forward suddenly and says: 'This is just so weird. You don't look that much different really, do you? The hair's different. God knows what I must look like to you, I can't imagine.' He puts his face in his hands for a second then looks up at me and laughs. We both laugh, softly and incredulously because it is laughable, us sitting here drinking tea and Veronica Karen dying out there. Then he gets up and takes his coat from the hall and leaves. The front door stays a little open, letting in the fresh wet night smell, the pleasant summer cold, the soft eager whisper of the falling rain. I get up and put on some music and some coffee, some real coffee to make the place smell nice. Check the milk, yes, enough. Run upstairs past the Ambrose prints on the landing, turn on the radiator in my study, pull out the little sofa bed for him and hunt out a duvet. Sniff it. Little bit musty but not too bad. What will it look like to him in here, my mess, my old books, my antediluvian word processor, my piano with the piles of tattered sheet music on the top?

Why am I nervous?

This changes nothing. There's something I have to do, something I still have to do, stay in control, stick with my decision. I was going somewhere at last, wasn't I? I was practically on my way. Why, it might have been all over by now if he hadn't come.

How did she get it? Who gave it to her? I scroll the pages back through my mind but she had so many boyfriends, the pretty boys and the junkies and the horny-handed sons of toil. I only knew a few. All those people in her life and here's Stephen Openshaw at the beginning and end, still holding his candle.

He's palely loitering on the landing.

'There's the bathroom,' I say.

'Uhuh.' He looks up, arms folded. 'You've got a nice little house here,' he says. 'Are these Robert's?'

'Yes.'

Robert and his camera. Shooting from the hip.

'They're great pictures.' He stands cradling his bag, looking at those old black and white photographs I had framed of the Ribblehead Viaduct and Chesil Beach, Early Morning and Oystercatchers. Veronica Karen had Oyster Catchers up on her wall in Parkway.

'Do you still miss him?' he asks.

'Sometimes,' I say.

Do I? Yes, at moments, profoundly. Like you miss the past, your childhood bed.

He moves on to my Ambrose prints. I don't know, are they a bit twee now? I still love them. I think I was a pretty talented illustrator.

'I love these,' he says, 'they bring back a lot of memories. We always had a few Ambrose the Cat books kicking about the place. I remember that one.'

There's Dame Doolily emerging from her door in the side of the wall, she looks like a little old lady but she's evil incarnate. There's Lorna Lamorna with her extravagant red hair.

'I remember that,' he says, 'and that, and . . .' He smiles. 'Are you really not doing any of this stuff now, Cathy? It's an awful shame.'

'It's hard to make a living that way.'

It's hard to make a living any way. I think of all the jobs I've ever had since I left university and met all that lot and drifted. I've done loads of things. I've done factories, shops, offices, cafés; I've cleaned, looked after kids; I've done tour guides of stately homes, kept records in a hospital, stamped books in a library, pulled pints in a pub, led poor patient donkeys up and down a beach with kids on their backs.

He drops down and studies the decrepit paperbacks on the low bookshelf Robert brought back from Dorset: old university textbooks, English, European History, sci-fi, homoeopathy, poetry.

'Ah – Ambrose!' He pulls out a book and stands, flicking it open. An amused look comes into his eyes.

There are a hundred Ambrose books kicking about. That's what they do, they kick about by nature. They're holding up chair legs, wedging doors open, *Ambrose the Cat and the Silver City*, *Ambrose the Cat and the Wooden Goat*, *Ambrose and Jem*, *Ambrose the Cat and Cloud 49*. Ambrose the Cat was an alleycat-troubadour, coming into and out of people's lives like the Lone Ranger and getting involved in all kinds of magical adventures. He'd turn up at the door in the rain and all hell would break loose. There was a kind of secular mysticism about it all and a faint voluptuousness. People don't read Ambrose any more. Occasionally, very occasionally, you come across one in a cardboard box at a jumble sale, scribbled on, food-besmirched, spineless and unpleasant to the touch.

Stephen smiles, turning a page. 'You know, I got a great

kick out of saying I knew you,' he says, looking up at me. 'My favourite was *The Wooden Goat*. I got quite fond of that one, I remember carrying it around for a while.'

This makes me laugh.

'Of course, I remember the real Ambrose.' He closes the book and stands testing it in his hands as if judging its weight. 'Ambrose was a brilliant cat.'

'I did have an idea for another one,' I say, showing him into the study, 'but they weren't keen on it.'

He follows, puts his bag down by the door and the book on the made-up sofa bed.

'So it goes.' I smile to show how unimportant it is.

When he sees the piano he goes straight to it and runs his hands all over it with delight.

'Do you play?' I ask.

'Not a note.' He glances quickly at me, smiling.

I adjust my pink bathrobe. At the door I turn. 'How did she get it?' I ask.

He sits on the piano stool, folding his arms and stretching out his legs. 'Some guy called Charles,' he says wearily. 'I don't know what's become of him. Could be dead, I suppose.'

'I can't believe it,' I say truthfully, reaching about inside me to see how I feel, like a blind person feeling a face.

'I only met him once years ago. I went to this party and there she was, I hadn't seen her for a couple of years and I found it quite depressing. I mean, the whole thing was quite depressing somehow, it was an awful party, full of really sad old sixties types and I'm thinking got to get out, got to get out, and then I see her sitting in this room with a big brown paper bag full of sinsemilla, all dressed in black lace, you know the way she could look, like something out of a, I don't know, something out of an old cowboy film, a Spanish widow or something. Well, I didn't like this Charles, he had on a leather jacket that was too new. He seemed a bit of a pillock to tell you the truth. But I can't remember anything about him really.'

Veronica Karen has this thing, this great horror, this oh-God-I-hope-I-haven't-got-it-did-I-ever-could-I-ever-have, and what's the reason? Some guy called Charles, Angel of Death, some poor pillock in a too-new leather jacket.

'You know, she's never cried or made a big fuss about it,' says Stephen. 'She's quite brave, Veronica Karen.'

Brave. Veronica Karen brave. She was never brave, scared of the dark, shaking me awake at night to say Cath, I keep thinking someone's going to cut my head off in the night. They won't, will they? They won't really, will they?

Shugden. The black middle of the night.

Course they will, I said. Happens all the time.

No, Cath, they won't!

I used to cry in a ghostly voice on the stairs: 'Veronica! Veronica!' And sometimes for dramatic effect: 'Veronica Karen! Veronica Karen!' But she was only Veronica then, only Veronica, till she was thirteen and started insisting on the full mouthful and refusing to answer to anything else. Who did she think she was? Peggy Sue, Mary Lou, Barbara

Ann, someone worthy of a song – Hey hey hello Veronica Karen, goodbye heart. Doesn't quite trip off the tongue.

'Listen!' His eyes veer sideways. 'It's raining cats and dogs out there.'

Drumming hard on the roof, on the street, on the barges on the canal. All the town will shine.

He flicks lazily through *It's Easy to Play Waltzes*, yawns, moving his shoulders slowly like a cat getting comfortable. 'Nice to think of the fire,' he says, 'dying away down there all by itself.'

3

Lying in bed, I listen for the sounds of Stephen through the wall. He's in there with all my rubbish piled around him, the books, the pictures, the old clothes, the photographs still waiting to be sorted. I have butterflies in the gut. Sleep's miles away.

Well, that's that then, isn't it? Can't do it with him in the house. Well, I suppose I could, there are quiet ways and means, it could be all over by morning. But then he'd find me. Oh, that's altogether too intimate; I'd need to be wearing something nice, my face pale and beautiful on the pillow, hair all fanned out. He'd sit, head bowed, remembering me as a girl.

Funny him remembering Ambrose.

We always had Ambrose.

He was never a kitten, always a big proud noble-nosed creature, all-wise and all-knowing, lying warm and vibrating on the hob, on the stair, on the rug in front of the fire, along a windowsill somewhere. He was the Great Poojah on his throne and she was the Princess Verona. The Princess Verona had to bring offerings to the potentate, fat white Ambrose stretched along the windowsill in the attic, the grim room with the sloping ceiling and the wall only two feet high where I saw the shadow of a man in a top hat. I was Jem the Gypsy Boy and Lorna Lamorna and evil Dame Doolily and Giant Killyloo. She was Tabitha, Annabel, Little Girl Green. I was Mamie, she was Rowena. Mamie and Rowena were orphans who went round the world putting on concerts and righting wrongs. We sang:

> *Red sails in the sunset*
> *Way over the sea.*
> *Oh, carry my true love*
> *Home safely to me.*

We danced in formation, hands on hips:

> *She wears red feathers and a huly-huly skirt,*
> *She wears red feathers and a huly-huly skirt . . .*

Ambrose didn't die till I was seventeen. We brought him from Shugden down to Manchester when we moved. I remember how just before he died he went light. He was a big cat, no an enormous cat, mostly white with the odd little black patch, and one day I picked him up and he was light as a feather, as if all his bones were full of air. He purred in my arms, looking up at me with the pus running out of his old, stoical eyes. Next day he died in his sleep. He was fifteen, very old for a cat. I have a photograph of Veronica Karen posing with Ambrose in her arms on one of the rustic benches in our back garden in Sale. Her head's cocked on one side looking cute, she's making big eyes and holding her lips apart. I remember, I was in the garden with Robin McGeeney who I was going out with at the time, and I was called inside to meet Veronica's boyfriend. Her first; big occasion. She met him in the Twisted Wheel. She was only fourteen, he was sixteen, same as me. We were both pretty, but she was prettier. Robin McGeeney had glasses and was very nice. He worked on the industrial estate at Old Trafford where all the hideous smells came from, but me and Veronica Karen and Stephen were still at school. We went out, the four of us, and sat on the rustic benches and watched the sparrows fighting on the bird table.

Ambrose is buried in that garden. Sad to think of him still there in a garden in Manchester, all alone, with strange people in the house and all of us long gone.

Of course she's come to steal my thunder again, hasn't she? Dying, my foot. She's probably just being dramatic. Dying for dramatic effect. She would.

She never told me.

The sense of time, shocking and irreversible, falling away

over a weir makes me feel quite sick. I was nearly over with it, but this flesh is spared. I was up there on the gallows, facing the crowd, just about to make my last speech.

'Oh, hangman, hangman, stay your hand . . .'

When the reprieve came, the horseman riding over the hill, eyes of his horse straining, showing the red.

Yes, I will, I'll go with him, it's an adventure again, I will, I'll go.

And the maid came down from the gallows.

4

Instead of slopping down to put the kettle on like any old slob, it's necessary to dress carefully, to ruffle hypercritical through my drawers, flinging things to one side, to settle on blue silk, shiny, nice around the waist, my good jeans that fit, to lurk in the bathroom working on my appearance for a little while. I moisturise briskly, put on eye make-up, a considered amount, rub my lips, brush my hair vigorously then tease it about with my fingers. Not bad, I think, peering closely. Well, not for first thing in the morning anyway. Seen it worse.

It's dark and cold downstairs, with that ashy smell from last night's fire and the fug of his cigarettes, but I pull the curtains and rush about tidying up, sweeping away crumbs, making the hearth clean and pretty, hoping he doesn't come down before I've finished. I make toast and tea. There's no sound, so I eat mine and drink some more tea, then pack a few things into my bag, make-up, toothbrush, just in case, who knows, I may change my mind once we get going. Bonny Scotland, here I come. Frank and Tilly, my God, how long is it? I bet they're just the same. Tilly was at my school. I played truant with her sister Jennifer. The school board came round to our house and it was terrible. A man stood on the front step talking very seriously to my mother while I sat on a hard chair in the kitchen and sobbed with my head in my hands, wanting to die. Veronica came up to me and put her arm round me and said 'It's all right, Cath, it'll be all right, it'll be all right, Cath,' which made everything very solemn because she didn't normally do things like that. She was eleven. Even then we didn't get on.

Tilly's very fat, I mean unbelievably fat, not a nice happy fat the way it's supposed to be. The Pullovers, they were called at school because of their name, Paluva or Palova or something. And Frank used to sing the Velvet Underground's 'Murder Mystery' and drive everyone mad. Think of all the people out of the past you'd rather see, all the people you've ever known and all the ones you don't see now, all scattered. Every Christmas we send each other cards and say we'll get together one day. Pale ghosts, Macbeth's line of kings, they pass, Andy and Jana in Australia, Lettie in Ireland, let's see, Bobbie, Simon, Patch, Tonto, and the dead ones, Eamonn, Angela, Jimmy, and the others, on, endless, all is gone gone gone.

I have to sit down for a moment with my hand over my

brow and draw back from the edge of the cliff again, that terrible cliff I come to sometimes, with the waves crashing down below on needle rocks.

Last night I nearly jumped.

'Oh God,' I whisper, 'Oh God.'

Anyway, she won't be there. She fell out with them, didn't she? I check my address book for people who might know her, but really now we have so few people in common, apart from those he's already tried. Of course! Russell and Patti's at Penrith, that's where she'll be. She sometimes did go there when things got too much. Free food. A comfortable bed for a while. Nice views out of the window. They're kind of like surrogate parents, auntie and uncle, nice homey people you can fall upon in times of need. I'll give them a call, sort this thing out. I think about Veronica Karen as I ring, what a pain in the arse she was when we were at home together in Manchester, pinching my money, my clothes, my make-up, how she thought she had a right to everything, how she argued, how she stood on the step with her schoolbag and her bad-tempered eye, saying 'I know what I'm made of,' like a pompous ass. Thought she knew it all. I think if it's really true, as it cannot be, that she is going to die, then I should see her.

The phone rings and rings up there in Russell and Patti's lovely old converted chapel near Penrith. I try to imagine hearing she's gone, not having seen her for so long. No one answers. I go and look out of the window into the front room, out at my ordinary, everyday street, swinging my foot. Now what do I do? What should I be doing today? What's the point in starting anything with him there coming down in a minute? If he hadn't come I could go for a long walk along the canal bank, right up where the houses end and the meadows begin, or drive up to the moors, or play my piano for an hour or two, or take my books back to the library and sit in a café, and maybe I'd meet someone I know, or I could pop round to Susannah's on the way back. Or just read. But I can't do anything with him there. Why has he come here, changing things, changing even the familiar sweep of my old stone terrace? Is he ever coming down? Why should I go? She knows where I am, doesn't she? She never came near when our dad was dying. If she doesn't want to see me, who am I to impose? Oh, wouldn't she just love this, all this chasing around after her!

He sleeps on and on like a teenager.

I go and listen quietly on the landing outside his slightly open door. He's very fast asleep, I can tell by the sound of his breathing. He must feel at ease to sleep for so long, like a cat. I can't sleep well in strange places. I wake up at funny hours, and no matter how much I want to, I can't lie in. Some embarrassable gene keeps shaking my shoulder saying: Quick! Get up! They'll think you're a lazy sod! It was awful when Robert's mum and dad used to come and stay; no matter how much I tried, whenever I got down they were all finished with breakfast, and they'd have left out a reproachful little cereal bowl and spoon for me in the middle of the wiped-clean table.

At eleven, preceded by nothing, he materialises like a ghost at the foot of the stairs, hair swept back severely, a deep blue T-shirt under the dark jacket. Limp-lipped and puffy-cheeked, faintly bashful, he hangs about at the kitchen door.

'Hi,' I say 'want some breakfast? Toast? Cereal?'

'Toast'd be fine,' he says. 'I'll do it. Mind if I make some coffee? I have to have coffee in the morning to get me going. Kick-start sort of thing.'

'I'll put some in the filter,' I say.

'Instant'll do.'

'No, no.'

He slots the bread into the toaster. He says in America they have these loaves that are so artificial you can crush one into a ball in the palm of your hand and when you let go it springs back fully formed like a balloon. 'Makes Mighty White look like health food,' he says, pushing one long-fingered hand backwards through his hair. He has deft hands, respectful of the things they touch: spoons, kettles, the lid of the marmalade. His face is very pale.

'Didn't get much of a tan in America, did you?' I say.

He laughs, a short snigger, sitting down at the table and crossing his legs. I like the little dents that appear beneath his cheekbones. 'Do you remember, Cathy,' he says suddenly, eating his toast, 'when we all went to Daisy Nook? It was an absolute disaster. Me and you and Veronica Karen got the bus back. We were stuck in the fog for hours and we met that creep Alexander.'

Alexander. Oh still, after all this time, I get a little kick. There's always one, isn't there? The inevitable One. The fog was dense. We lost some people. On the bus Stephen had his arm round Veronica Karen, and Alexander was there. Stephen knew him because he was at school with him. Alexander turned round and started talking to us, and when we got off the bus he walked along with us. He had long fair hair and a brown leather jacket and he never looked at Veronica Karen at all. Whenever he smiled, his pale blue eyes strayed on to me.

'Alexander was no creep,' I say.

'Forgive me,' Stephen says coldly, drinking his coffee, 'but anyone who'll do what he did.' He crosses his thighs.

Pointless to pursue this.

'Mind if I use the phone?' he asks.

'Go ahead.'

'It's long distance. London,' he says. 'I'll give you the money. I thought I'd just give Veronica Karen's flat another try.'

'It's OK, go ahead.'

The phone's next door. I hear him tapping the buttons and think how me and Alexander used to go hitch-hiking all over the place, and then when he got his Norton we'd go miles and miles out into the country. Alexander could draw anything, with anything, fast. He was going to art school. He got an A in Art.

He sang 'Peggy Gordon' as we watched the river flow under a bridge in Wales. That's the sort he was.

Alexander the Great.

Veronica Karen's not there. I hear through two doors the silence that is not Veronica Karen in her flat. Perhaps she's dead. Right now.

'Nope,' he says, returning. 'Still not there.' He looks at his watch then at me. 'Well,' he says, 'have you slept on it all, then? You still on for this?'

'God knows why,' I say. 'I don't want to force myself on her.'

'You don't have to,' he says, 'just say hello. That's all. Hello and goodbye.' He shrugs.

If I don't go, when he steps out that door there'll be nothing else to do but go back to yesterday, looking at the rain, starting the whole thing over again but unsettled, restless, spoiled for it somehow.

'We should move,' he says. 'Really.'

'I suppose,' I say. 'I mean –' I make a movement with my mouth, spread out my hands '– dying. It's a big thing, isn't it?'

He smiles. 'Yes,' he says lightly, standing and swaying a little towards me with his hands behind his back, 'I think you could say it's a fairly big thing.'

5

I watch a crow on a telegraph pole, sitting dead still and black against the white sky, like a totem on top of a pole. Its head turns very suddenly as if someone's called its name. When I was little I was always looking for the Roc, for the great bird in the *Arabian Nights*, for a Wonder. I saw its proud wild eye and mighty beak, the flex of its huge knobbled claws like the claws of cockerels but with Saracens' blades curving from the ends. In my mind I saw it flying from afar with its great wings beating down the heavy air, its mass covering the sun and bringing twilight in a second. I heard its terrible cries at the slaughter of its chick and imagined how it would feel to tie yourself to its tree-trunk leg while it slept and be carried away, like Sinbad. I used to think about the Roc when I was sick in bed or just idle, I'd look up and see it there against the white sky, massively alighting on the chimney of the roof opposite. Then I'd blink and it was just a gull or a crow.

The nearest thing I ever saw was a heron. Alexander and I were walking down a lane near Coniston, and it started up in front of us with a great beating of wings and a harsh affronted cry, flying low over the road just above our heads. Time slowed down.

What's keeping him? This is like Veronica Karen, this is, the way she'd keep you waiting stuck in the car like a lemon for ages, as if no one else's time mattered but her own. He's gone for fags, I'm waiting in the car. We've had a genteel argument about whose car to take to Frank and Tilly's. His is better than mine, but I'm a nervous passenger since my big accident, even though that had nothing to do with cars. I have to drive, be in control so I can feel safe. He laughed when he saw my little orange Mini though, stood looking at it for a minute with an uncomprehending smile, shaking his head as if I was asking him to set sail for America in a bath tub.

I open the windows, wonder what it would be like to smoke a cigarette again after all these years, horrible probably. My fingers tap on the wheel and the fluttery feeling swells in my stomach. I think about Alexander and sing softly:

> *Oh Peggy Gordon, you are my darling*
> *Come sit you down upon my knee*
> *And tell to me the very reason*
> *Why I am slighted so by thee.*

I really loved Alexander.

I still catch my breath sometimes when I think of him. He was so beautiful, very gentle and big and totally self-absorbed, with clear blue fathomless eyes and golden hair that hung in careless, unwashed curls around his face. When he was very young he had fits. I used to write poems about him, oh terrible they were! I still remember them word for word.

All alone weeping in my room.

Oh, it's too pathetic.

He was such a bastard really, Alexander; not that he didn't love me but that he didn't love me so charmingly. Of course now I realise that so much he did was just for effect, even the way he came into a room, just like the last time when he was with her. Oh where have you been, my long long love, these seven long years and more? Well, it may not have been seven. I don't know how long it was, years since he'd casually drifted away from me, full of good will, telling me that he really had cared for me. I couldn't believe it when she walked in with him. I was with Robert. We were at Frank and Tilly's, and Tonto was there. No one else knew about me and Alexander, but she did. 'Guess who?' she cried, bouncing in, preceding her prize, smiling full at me. 'Guess who?' and he appeared and it was like a blow in the stomach. I felt physically sick and my heart went badoom badoom, just like it does in the songs: oh heart-beat, why do you miss when my baby kisses me?

'Can you believe it?' she squawked. 'I ran into him at the jumble sale. Can you *believe* it?'

That was the last time I ever saw him.

And that was the year when death's long fingers began to tap so faintly, ever so faintly, on the glass sometimes in the middle of the day.

The crow flies away from the telegraph pole.

I used to think that if I sky-gazed long enough the Roc would turn up, or if not that, then something else. I didn't know what, only that it had to be impossible. I'd open a wardrobe, lift a lid, hear a voice, pick up a strange stone and that would be it.

Stephen appears at the shop door, checking his pockets as he looks down the street. Take your time, dear, do. He saunters across, folds himself carefully into the passenger seat, grinning sardonically, knees touching the dashboard. 'It's like being in one of those Postman Pat cars you get in front of Sainsbury's,' he says.

I drive. He rolls down the window, smoking and looking out on Moorcop's sombre stones. 'I'd forgotten how nice it is up here,' he muses.

We pass Connor's. Annie with her lush señorita looks is doing the outside tables, a little vase of pinks in one hand, cloth in the other. The flowers are gay against her electric blue blouse. Further on I pull up at the lights and who's there but Trish Allgood who works weekends in Cornucopia, crossing with her bags and her buggy laden like an Okie's truck. She gives me a smile and a little wave as she crosses, hunched over in some incredible pushing stance like those pictures you see of children in coal mines in the olden days. Will she tell that I was driving out of town with a strange man? Did she notice? Does she think he looks interesting? I'm famous for having no one, it's part of my image.

'I love it up here,' I say, 'I really do. I like being so close to the moors.'

'Glad you came back then?'

'Oh yes!'

We talk for a while about London in the old stoned days and all the people we had in common. He says he sees Lettie now and then when she's over from Ireland. He saw Patch from the top of a bus going along Walworth Road about three weeks ago. And me? Oh, I haven't seen any of them for ages, not even Frank and Tilly, a stone's throw away. I couldn't be doing with them. You couldn't lead the quiet life around Frank and Tilly. Oh, certainly not, certainly not the quiet life with Frank and Tilly.

He liked America, he says. He wouldn't mind living there some time, but it'd have to be the right place. Not Chicago anyway. And not California because he'd miss the rain.

'I'm looking around,' he says.

'In America?'

He shrugs. I glance at him, a quick glimpse of his high white forehead, his shoulders leaning back against the seat. 'I dunno,' he says, 'I'm just looking around.'

He can't do a thing with his legs, they're just too big for

the car. Chug chug chug, it goes pleasantly, and I'm stricken with conscience for the discomfort I'm putting him through. Moorcop fades back. Pity you can't drive along like they do in the movies, taking your eyes off the road for minutes at a time while you have a conversation with someone. At the big roundabout we pass the Shugden signpost. Me and Robert used to take that turning, going over to see my dad.

'Shugden, ah Shugden!' Stephen says. 'I remember it well,' and smiles out of the window, a mischievous memorising smile.

'Were you only there the once?' I ask.

'Shugden of the puke,' he says, turning towards me. 'Fragrant Shugden. I remember your Auntie Pearl, she was a real goer.'

Shugden where I was born. 16 Shaw Road, Shugden 2, where dust lies thick upon windowsills. Auntie Pearl's still in Shugden, and the cousins. A wreck now, Pearl. Last time I saw her she had a big smelly sore on her leg and Sandra was dressing it.

'Veronica Karen loved Shugden,' he says. 'Childhood's glow and all that stuff. She's got a real thing about her childhood.'

'Shugden was boring.' He's looking at me. I wonder if my chin's got that awful straight line profile I sometimes catch sight of in mirrors. 'Moorcop's nicer.'

Countryside looms, green and woody, riven with valleys. The moors will start soon.

'Did Robert like it up here?' he asks, throwing his fag out of the window and folding his arms.

'He liked Moorcop,' I say. 'He said it had just the right level of seediness to stop it being twee.'

We fall into silence.

We're on the high land. The sheep are heavy and slow as they get off the road. Something's happening, something's happening, at last something's happening. As we cross the moors I'd never thought to see again I am stricken with a needle's prick of raw emotion, joy or grief or something like that. It whistles coldly in me, like a nerve newly exposed to air. I feel free, a sudden dizzying exhilarating thing, as if I'd taken the great leap out into open air and there was no more land but only the boundless horizon, worth the inevitable drop. As if I died. This is part of the process still carrying on from last night, I think, the heather in bloom, the moors and the mountains and dirty old towns. I love the north. When we were young we used to walk up here, we used to come out from Shugden with sandwiches, walk to Moorcop and get the train back. You let kids wander like that in those days; we must have been very young because I was twelve when we moved to Manchester. Whenever we sang at school:

> *Hills of the north, rejoice,*
> *Valley and lowland sing –*

it was the high ground out beyond Moorcop I saw, and the

great sweeping fells beyond. I didn't miss Shugden, but I missed the moors, and I missed me and Veronica singing alone in a carriage with unnaturally coloured pictures of Malham Tarn and Blackpool Tower on the walls and the train wheels going rickety-rack rickety-rack and the whistle blowing when you went into a tunnel:

> *In eighteen hundred and forty-one*
> *Me corduroy britches I put on,*
> *Me corduroy britches I put on*
> *To work upon the railway, the railway,*
> *I'm weary of the railway,*
> *Poor Paddy works on the railway.*

Our father was a railwayman, first in Shugden then in Manchester. Later he retired back up here. Sometimes when we got off the train he'd be there in his dark uniform and cap walking about the little platform with the flower beds as if it was his living room, which in a way it was.

I couldn't go on a train now. I haven't been on a train since the big accident.

'Lost in thought,' Stephen says. He sticks his head forward to light another cigarette.

'Sorry?'

'You,' he says, pushing his hair up with his fingers. 'Lost in thought. I remember that about you. You could be in a room full of people and be all on your own, miles away. Or reading a book. I'd be round at your house and everything'd be going on all round, the telly, the dog barking, your mum and dad and everything, and you'd be sitting there reading a book in the middle of it all and the bomb could've dropped and you wouldn't have noticed.'

The sun sparkles on the surface of a lonely reservoir. The lambs are no more the spotless baby gambolling things of two months back, they are plump and soiled, still following their dams.

'It was like watching the telly,' he says.

'What was?'

'You,' he says, 'you were about as unconscious as the telly is when it's being watched.'

This makes me laugh. He never used to watch me. I glance at him but he's looking out of the window, crossing and uncrossing his long legs laboriously.

'I was thinking about going down to Manchester when I was twelve,' I say, 'and how I missed the moors.'

'They're like the sea.' He blows out smoke.

'I wanted a house on the very top of the moors,' I say. 'I wanted Top Withens. I wanted a horse.'

I wanted to be like Catherine Linton in *Wuthering Heights* riding Minnie to Penistone Crags. I wanted to meet the love of my life dramatically on the way back and not recognise him but despise him at first, so that the consummation would be the more sweet for the rocky road travelled. Of course, when I met Robert it was nothing like that, we just liked each other straight away. At Frank's, as it happened, Notting Hill Gate. I think I was looking for a room. I had on a long red dress with smocking over the boobs and I was drinking a cup of tea. Frank was showing me his pictures, all his photographic gear spread out on an old sofa. He was wearing one of those little tight sweaters the men wore in those days, a dainty, concave-chested little man with a pinched yellow face and a perfect halo of black Afro hair that looked as if it had been done with compasses. Robert came in. Robert was from Guildford. He was doing the lights for a show in the Roundhouse and had a room upstairs. He came in crabwise, staggering under a huge swag load of something on his back. I remember his dark smiling eyes and big mouth. I was twenty-five then, doing Ambrose number four and working in Prima Vera.

Our lady of the flowers, he called me.

'You should write something again,' Stephen says.

I wish people wouldn't say that.

'I had an idea,' I say, 'but they didn't like it.'

'So?' He winds up the window. 'Have another.'

We drive out of the country, through suburbs and housing developments and industrial estates. It's not too far now. Deeper and deeper into dirty littered streets we go. Everything here is just endless Manchester overspill. We get lost, of course, and he winds the window down and calls out to people on the pavement, asking directions. He is very polite. He sits with his elbow sticking out, watching street names carefully. It dawns on me that we are coming to something, that there will be people, that Veronica

Karen might be there. I think about Frank, how he used to sing 'The Murder Mystery' and drive everyone mad. He'd start at the beginning doing all the guitar pieces, then into the whining organ, then the sudden vocals. It was deadly. It went on for about three hours and nothing would stop him. He knew both strands of the vocals and could do both word-perfect, so sometimes when he'd finished one he'd just go straight into the other and carry on till serious violence was threatened.

We had a bet on once about which album it was on. I said *The Velvet Underground*, he said *White Light, White Heat*.

We come upon the place by some strange mystical process, sailing hypnotically through similar streets, round and round, trying this, now that turning, till we chance upon a little road brought up short against a wrecker's yard with decrepit double gates that lean against each other like two drunks holding each other up. On one side is a long brick wall covered in head-high ornate graffiti, on the other the flat-faced terrace of coffee-coloured stone where Frank and Tilly live. Scraps of faded lawn are spread straight on to the pavement in front of the houses as if painted on, arched ginnels go round the back. We prowl along the row of parked cars.

You can tell Frank and Tilly's a mile off. It's the one with the rusting, flat-tyred silver camper van parked outside and the covey of baggy-trousered fourteen-year-old boys smoking tight-lipped in front of it.

I pull in in front of a four-wheel-drive jeep with bull bars. The engine gratefully dies.

'Isaac,' says Stephen thoughtfully, 'the one with the red hat.' He whistles softly. 'Isn't it weird when kids grow up?'

But I don't recognise any of them. Frank and Tilly were always having babies, I remember the odd one from years back but they all looked the same to me. Babies do.

We get out and walk together. He's a lot taller than me. The boys part for us. 'Ey up,' one of them says pleasantly.

'Anyone in?' Stephen asks.

The boys grunt affirmatively and we walk straight across the bald lawn and knock on the bright yellow front door. A pack of hounds bays hollowly as if from the depths of a Gothic keep. He smiles at me suddenly, brightly, as if he knows how nervous I am. Oh God, I am praying inwardly, oh God, don't let her be here, I don't want to meet Veronica Karen here, on her territory. The door opens. I remember Frank at once, the skull-shaped yellow face more lined than before, the halo more ragged.

'Cath!' he gasps at once, shifting a roll-up from hand to hand. 'Cath Cath Cath Cath Cath! Stevie! What a surprise!' He shakes both our hands very affectionately in turn, clutching our shoulders and gripping hard. 'Come in!' he cries, beckoning us excitedly down to the back of the hall and dancing before us, small as a child, into a room on the right from which terrible sounds emerge, as if the pack are being held back by burly retainers and choking on their studded collars. A fat grey Persian cat with wild eyes looks outraged on the swirly-patterned stair carpet.

The room is small and dark and crowded. There's an old-fashioned formica kitchen cabinet with the flap covered in crumbs and slops and a lethal-looking knife. A little boy sits crying and holding his ear on a potty in the middle of the room, and a small brown-skinned girl teeters on multicoloured roller skates. Two big dogs rush towards us and examine our genitals with long eager noses; an indeterminate number of puppies run about in a state of ceaseless neurosis; dark brooding men in overcoats lurk in corners. A billowing chillum is doing the rounds. In spite of the open door leading out into the back garden there is a heavy smell pervading the room, from the chillum, and from the pointed hindquarters, like twin chocolate-coated brazil nuts, of a baby lying on the table having his nappy changed by a young girl with a miniskirt and an emerald in her nose.

Tilly Pullover sits on the floor in front of a bookcase holding twice its capacity of battered books. She's so fat the eye can't take her in at first, like a dizzying drop. She looks heavily pregnant but it's hard to tell because of her normal fatness. On each of her colossal thighs sits a small child like a ventriloquist's dummy.

Frank's little wizened face peers at me through the gloom. 'Look who it is!' he crows. 'Coincidence or what? We were just talking about you! Weren't we, weren't we, Till?'

Actually, I didn't know them that well.

'Hello, Stephen.' Tilly's voice is clipped, her eyes hard and dark and suspicious, very bright and liquid like a little rodent's. She licks her lips, a peculiar, insulting swipe. 'Hi, Cathy.'

I sit down on the settee next to a red-haired woman with a lumpy bandage covering most of her face apart from two technicolour black eyes. For a while we do all the how-are-yous and how's-so-and-sos. Tilly's sister Jennifer, who I played truant with for a week, is still working for the electricity board in Northampton; her husband had a nervous breakdown and her son should have gone to university only didn't. Something loud and aggressive plays from a bank of black hardware; lithe, thin, smoke-blue puppies wash warmly up against my legs, haggling whisperingly in the backs of their throats. Frank subsides into an armchair as if he were getting back into bed. On the broad arm is a huge tin mug of tea or coffee and a plate bearing three cream crackers, an iced bun, a great wedge of cheese and a pickled onion.

A small grey rabbit nibbles something under a radiator.

Stephen sits on a kitchen chair at the head end of the baby, looking at its round soft gingerfuzzed head with open curiosity. 'We were wondering if you'd seen Veronica Karen lately,' he says.

There's a slight, fraught pause, as if we've asked the way to the Count's castle.

'Veronica Karen?' Frank says, picking up a cream cracker

and examining it with a frown. 'I haven't seen Veronica Karen for – ooh – two years? Two years, Till? Yeah?'

'Could be.' A swift hard look passes between them.

Above Frank's head is a shelf for all his photographic gear, a loop of a handle hanging down from a canvas bag, a tripod's legs sticking out from behind a developing tank. It's a stab, the familiar black cylinders with the red and white tops. Robert kept all his in a big cardboard box in the study where my piano now stands. The small black girl, a beautiful child with flower-like lips, climbs on to Frank's lap and slips an arm around his neck. Her roller skates dangle, a silver star glittering on an ankle bone. I remember Veronica Karen telling me how once when she was visiting and she was alone in the living room, Frank came in and stood behind her chair and took his pants down and started whacking her on top of the head with his willy. I see her gesturing, giggling, throwing wide her arms. I hear her squeaky voice:

'I said for God's sake, Frank! Don't be ridiculous!'

We were in stitches.

The red-haired woman next to me hands me the chillum. They always did make me cough. This one explodes in my chest but I keep it down. Oh, well done! I think, expertly done, considering. It's been years. This'll go straight to my head.

'What do you call that bit?' Stephen asks, 'that little hole that bumps up and down.' He points.

'Fontanelle,' I say, 'that's the fontanelle.'

I had a baby once. He was called Johnny.

This one's about three months old, I'd guess, solid and healthy. Its arms and legs wave in silent slow motion. Its eyes look up and back in its head, unblinking, scrutinising Stephen. He stares back. 'Funny things, aren't they?' he says.

'Fontanelles or babies?' asks Tilly.

'Both.'

Johnny had such a small head. The fontanelle was covered with straight wet black hair.

Through the back door the sun glints on a mountain of plastic bottles, grossly swollen tubes heaped against a wall. A large white rabbit lopes by them and in at the back door. The music is full of someone screaming fuck. I remember Andy and Jana's wedding, Brixton Registry Office and a school hall. Frank's mum and dad and grandma were there, and in among all the music someone put on *New Boots and Panties* and it suddenly screamed out: 'Arseholes, bastards, fucking cunts and pricks.' Course, his mum and dad and grandma acted like they hadn't heard. When they showed us the photographs later, Robert was in every one, grinning like Alfred E. Neumann over someone's shoulder. Robert always got everywhere. He was even in the family ones. Somewhere I've got the big group photograph with us all in it: Andy and Jana and Lettie and Frank and Tilly and Tonto and Stephen and Veronica Karen and . . . Gone, gone, gone. All gone into the world of light, ones as young and beautiful as him. But he is not, of course, beautiful, nor

is he particularly young any more. No one would call
Stephen Openshaw beautiful.

'You were doing really well,' says Frank accusingly. 'You
were doing kids' books. Still at it?'

'No.'

'You're not? Why not?'

'I sort of ran out of steam.'

'Oh shame. She never said anything, did she?' He appeals
to Tilly. 'Never told us you'd stopped. You kind of look out
for another one, you know, but you don't see nothing.'

Well, you wouldn't. And *she'd* not say anything. That was
one of the things about Veronica Karen, she never had a
word to say about Ambrose the Cat, good or bad. She
never mentioned the books. It was as if they didn't exist, as
if they were something too embarrassing to touch upon.
Maybe she didn't like me using Jem the Gypsy Boy and
Lorna Lamorna and Giant Killyloo and Doolily and all the
rest. Or maybe she was just pissed off with me for getting
praised and having something work out.

'What you up to, then?'

'I teach piano. I work in a café.'

'No kidding? You teach piano? That's nice.' Frank grins,
playing the air in front of him. 'Pity about the books
though.'

Frank's London. His voice, everything. Frank's the olden
days.

'Well, you know,' I say, 'things come and go.'

'Shame.'

'Should I know you?' asks the red-haired woman with the bandaged face.

'I don't think so.'

'I'm Maida,' she says in a little croaky voice.

'So you're after Veronica Karen?' Frank looks down at his sticky bun, shaking his head like a car mechanic gazing into an engine.

'She's gone AWOL,' I say, watching the white rabbit hop casually across the floor.

Frank laughs. 'She's always AWOL.'

Tilly snorts, shuffling about on her enormous bottom as if it was a floor cushion. 'Veronica Karen! Veronica Karen!' she calls. 'Come out, come out, wherever you are.' Recognising the first line of the Munchkins' song from *The Wizard of Oz*, her eyes pop and she sings it again in a perfect imitation of Glinda, the Good Witch, bouncing her book-end children. The weeping boy on the potty, dressed only in a vest, turns his twisted face and scowls at her.

'He's got earache,' she explains, putting up an arm to adjust her mass of wiry black hair and thereby dislodging one of the children, which falls over backwards, bangs its head a great wallop on the floor and starts to wail. She takes no notice. 'Veronica Karen knows a lot of people,' she says briskly, efficiently rearranging combs, moving her head like Nefertiti. 'She'll pop up out of the woodwork again soon, no doubt.'

'She'll be at Russell and Patti's,' I say.

Stephen looks at me.

'What d'you want her for?' asks Tilly.

Neither of us speaks.

'Ooh,' says Frank, 'mystery,' huffing and puffing with an air of professional skill, creating clouds, a dust storm that obscures his head. As it clears, his face reappears with the small brown perfect oval of the child's nestling under his neck, but only for a moment.

'Shift your wee self, honey,' he says, rising, and the little girl takes a great leap, lands casually on her tiptoes, winging the bead curtain that leads into presumably the kitchen. She totters gracefully to the back door. A sound smites me, the hoarse-throated jangle of the bead curtain like pebbles thrown up the beach by a slow tide. The girl leans forward from her roller skates, holding on to the door frame. Frank barges shoulder first through the curtain: again the swish and rattle. It's not a sound I remembered remembering, but there it went whispering to me and I knew it instantly. Veronica Karen made that curtain out of old clay pipe stems from the foreshore of the Thames near Blackfriars Bridge, where there were millions of them all in little broken bits. She used to go down there collecting and sit for hours soaking the things, washing them, poking the Thames mud out. It's a wonder she didn't catch some awful disease. She thought they were wonderful things. Some of them had names on, bits of raised lettering, little pictures. Samuel Pepys could've thrown this away, she'd say.

It must have taken her about seven years to make that.

Well, she did these daft things. When she was fourteen

she read the Thor Heyerdahl book about the Kon-Tiki expedition and made an entire model Easter Island hillside out of cardboard all over one side of her room, complete with a grotesque family of heads made out of rainbow Plasticine. They sat there in a row for months getting slowly squidged by time and looking like nothing but blobs.

'Veronica Karen made that,' I say eagerly, pointing to the curtain.

Tilly's dark eyes swivel. 'That,' she says flatly. 'She did indeed.'

It was the most useless curtain in the world. It was too heavy. Robert used to do this elaborate mime going through it, forcing it apart as if it was made out of lead. Never hung right, that curtain. The strands are all kinked.

'We got it in payment,' Tilly says shortly.

They shouldn't have it. They shouldn't. I lean down to pet a black and white rabbit. The girl with the emerald in her nose lifts the clean, dry baby, its pink legs bowing out like pincers, the immaculate toes curling under. She sways from side to side, folding the baby deep inside her stick-like arms, her long ringed fingers cupping his soft head. Oh baby. Things come back, you know, things come back for ever. The Roc crying for its slaughtered chick. Her skirt rides up in a sharp V over her crotch, her milky white thighs childlike underneath. Cross-legged, lighting a cigarette, Stephen stares and stares at the bead curtain. It parts unwillingly and Frank brings in the tea and a block of halva on a tray, putting it down in the middle of the floor. 'Garn!

Ga-arghn!' he snarls at the pups. 'Let it stand a mo,' he croaks amiably, sitting back into his chair. From somewhere close and functional he draws forth a hand–mirror and razor and little wooden box, gets out the white powder and starts chopping on the mirror the way my mother used to chop parsley for parsley sauce. He sweeps the powder into expert lines, with a deft little flick of the wrist that gives to the tail of each one a flourish. We take turns with the fiver.

Oh well. In for a penny. Anyway, Stephen's having some.

We gorge ourselves on halva and drink tea. After a while my nose goes numb.

Maida, as in Maida Vale, I presume, starts to talk to me very suddenly, turning bodily and taking a deep breath before saying in a chirpy voice: 'Hello, Veronica Karen's sister!'

I jump.

'Hello,' I say.

This is the past. What am I doing here? What am I doing? I've lost track of the time, look up to get my bearings. Stephen's talking to Frank about the relative merits of Manchester and London.

'What's your name?' demands Maida. 'Would I know you? What kind of stuff do you write? Are you famous?'

'Cathy Wren,' I say. 'No, I'm not.'

She shakes her head with what I think is a sweet apologetic smile but it's hard to tell under all the bandaging. 'No-o,' she says slowly, 'no bells ring.'

'Have you known Veronica Karen long?' I ask her.

'Oh God, years! Years and years and years and years!' She gives a cracked girly laugh, as if that's very funny. 'She came here after the abortion,' she says.

Abortion? What abortion?

'She did? When?'

'Oh, I don't know. Years? She was getting better.'

Tilly laughs without humour. 'What a place to come for a rest,' she says unpleasantly.

She could have had a dozen abortions for all I know.

I get the impression that Maida's quite striking under the bandages and bruising, which are so obvious I wonder if I should ask her about them, but nobody else is saying anything, so I don't. Maybe someone's thumped her in the face. But then she says loudly and humorously, pointing to the centre of her face, 'Do you know what this is?'

'What happened?' I ask.

'No nose,' she says and giggles. 'I cut it off.'

'You did *what*?'

She stands, sweeps across the room to search for cigarettes along the mantelpiece and sweeps back. She is tall, with the bearing and figure of a model. Lush red hair bounces on her back like Lorna Lamorna's, and a long bottle-green dress rustles medievally about her knees as she sinks down beside me.

'Cut it off,' she says cheerfully. 'Only the tip really. Look.' She has a pen, she's drawing a diagram on a box of matches.

'Just a slice,' she says as if it's all a joke. 'There. I've had plastic surgery.'

The sunlight slanting in through the back door, beaming from the dirty bottles, is clean and bright; a vernal outdoor smell has taken hold of the room, and the baby is crowing softly in its mother's arms. Side to side the young girl swings, a smile on her face. Stephen gets up and goes over to the back door and stands looking out for a moment before disappearing.

'You and your bloody nose,' Frank says, aggrieved. 'You and your fucking nose, Maida! Jeez, what a fiasco.'

'I was going to write a kids' book once, you know,' she tells me.

A man appears at the back door, blocking out the sunlight. 'Oh what!' he cries, clapping one hand to his brow, 'oh what! Cathy! Oh what!'

He comes into the room, and it's Tonto, much older, the same warm, hurt, crinkling eyes, beaming like a clown and looking like a gambler with a black silk waistcoat and crumpled black and white striped shirt pushed up to the elbows. I jump up and kiss him and he enfolds me in a heavy-breathing hug, reeking of stale wine. Still a complete piss artist, obviously. He's from her Cretan phase. They were always going off to live in caves there, bringing back pictures of the people they'd met, pictures of Veronica Karen naked on a rock looking like a mermaid with her long hair bleached by the sun. They stayed with me and Robert for two or three nights once, arriving on a motorbike. Veronica Karen was all in black leather with a long fringe that kept falling all over her face. She sprawled on her back on the floor and went to sleep, or pretended to, with her thighs apart and head thrown back and one arm shielding her eyes, a faintly aggressive and definitely erotic centrepiece that we all had to walk around. They did the I Ching non-stop for about two days. I remember all that, the superior man crossing the great water and all that, and I remember Robert's old *Tao Te Ching* with the pale grey photographs, and the jam sandwiches and joints for breakfast.

Tonto was young then and shy, a big craggy handsome thing with a square jaw and vulnerable eyes, already inhabiting his fixed role in life: gentle shambling alcoholic.

'How *are* you, Cathy?' he asks, shaking my shoulders then gripping my hands. 'This girl —' he turns to the room in general, 'this girl is a terrific girl . . .'

He was always embarrassing.

'. . . oh wow Cathy, wow! How far back do we go?'

'Hundreds of years!'

I laugh.

There's a new heaviness about his cheeks, a narrow weatherbeaten look about his eyes.

'I mean, I saw old Stevie out there just now, and I thought . . .'

'They were asking about Veronica Karen,' says Tilly.

A look of terrible eagerness, almost of fear, comes over him. 'Veronica Karen?' he cries. 'Veronica Karen? What? She's here?' He sounds panicked.

'No, no,' I say quickly, 'she's not here. We don't know where she is.'

'Gone missing,' Tilly says in a faintly offensive way, and starts getting to her feet, a ponderous, impressive and rather majestic process like the rising of an elephant. Yes, she is pregnant, I think, though pregnancies get lost in her. She must be so big down there and she's had so many, I suppose they just come swooshing out like laughing kids down a waterchute. When I was pregnant it was me that got lost. I was a helpless head on an invaded sphere.

'What do you mean? She's all right, isn't she? She's all right?'

'She's all right,' I say. 'You know what she's like. She's just gone off somewhere. She's gone to Scotland.'

'She went to Holy Island,' says Frank. 'Remember?'

But I won't think about Holy Island. I just won't.

This has gone too far, I want to go home.

Tonto lets me go, falls down on his knees in front of the tray and pours himself a lukewarm tea. He cradles it, drinking and staring me out over the rim with his flirty eyes, he has them still; the years are giving them that moony melting chocolate quality that dogs do so well. He used to do this look at me over tables in pubs, across stoned rooms. First the long longing stare and then, yes, here it is, the blink, slow and sleepy.

'We must talk, Cath,' he says respectfully, 'we must talk.'

'We must, Tonto,' I say. I lean across and place my palm against his cheek. 'It's so good to see you.'

He lumbers into the space next to my knee.

'Still doing the books, Cath?'

'No,' I say, 'not any more.'

'Really? Why not?'

Jesus Christ, if I have to explain this one more time.

'They've had their time,' I say. 'That's life.'

'C'est la vie, c'est la vie,' he says, kissing my fingers. 'Mmm, I could eat you up.'

For one terrible second I think I'm going to cry. I push him gently aside, go out into the hall, drift up to the first floor landing where the bathroom door stands open on a chaos of laundry and toys and packs of disposable nappies. Frank's pictures are all up the stairs, like Robert's, black and white shiny shots of puddles and old chairs on dumps and interesting pieces of wood. People always do the same things. In the bathroom I lean my back against the door with my heart pounding and that dry hotness in my eyes but it doesn't amount to anything. No tears come. I don't know what it is, something to do with Johnny and Ambrose the Cat and Veronica Karen running away to Holy Island with Alexander and how Alexander went down like the *Titanic* after that. A pink and white marble effect predominates in the bathroom. A high-rise of well-covered clothes horses reaches for heaven. My brain speeds. I drink water for my parched mouth, forgetting for a moment as I dip my head over the tap where I am and why I am unhappy and why I am excited. I don't think the tap is very clean but there's nothing I can do about that. I must live in the moment, that's what you're supposed to do, isn't it? Yes yes, live in the moment. There's no lock on the door and the toilet's too far away to sit and hold the door closed. Oh I hate these people who don't put locks on their toilet doors. Well, I have to go anyway. Present moment, here I am, having a wee at Frank and Tilly's, God knows why. I was supposed to be somewhere else entirely by now but somehow I took a different turning. Restored to equanimity, I go out on to the landing again and see through an open door little cots and home-made bunks, a veritable dormitory. A field of dirty toys covers the ground, like the dead on a battlefield. Spiderman leaps on the wall. I am drawn in by the mobile hanging in front of the window, tiptoe through the room past the filthiest sheets I've ever seen in my life, and set the little fishes dancing on air, slowly round and round. We had a fish mobile over the cot, blue and silver and purple, twinkling with the gloss of Christmas baubles. I look out and see a long sloping garden, wild and grassy, with a shed at the far end, and rabbits and dogs, and Stephen Openshaw with his spidery legs kicking a football around with two scruffy little boys in full Manchester United strip. Six or seven, the age Johnny would have been now.

'Come on,' says Tonto, coming out of the kitchen with a handful of small round cheese crackers bursting through his thick fingers. 'Come and see my little hut.'

I follow him out into the garden. A dog shivers with delight at our approach. Stephen breaks away from the boys and comes over, smiling at me, batting gently with his hand at the wet nose and nibbling needle teeth of a little golden greyhound.

'Want a dog?' says Tonto. 'Nice dog, that. Eighty quid.'

'Not me,' says Stephen, watching the animals, 'I've got nowhere to put a dog.'

I think about getting one, this little golden thing with the mad eyes perhaps. But I haven't got eighty quid.

Tonto, trailing crumbs, leads us to his hut, the shed at the bottom of the garden. It's about four by eight, made of creosoted wood and has a dark corrugated roof and one tiny window. Inside is a single mattress raised up on a low base, a small armchair, a maroon car seat and some low kind of table in the middle covered with smoking paraphernalia and mugs and glasses and a wine bottle full of something very cloudy. We climb on our knees from chair to chair.

'You're living here?' I say.

'Yeah.' He stoops against the ceiling by the door, scratching his head, then sniggers mischievously. 'I'm just sort of hanging out while I dry off a bit, but it's not really working. I made some parsnip wine, see, seemed a shame not to, there was all these parsnips someone brought over from their allotment and they'd have gone off. And the others aren't really drinkers so I've been having to get through it on my own. Want to try some? It's all right. I've just got two bottles left.'

'It looks like a liquidised parsnip,' I say.

Stephen starts to laugh. I've bagged the armchair and he's perched like a grasshopper on the car seat, crossing and uncrossing his legs, shifting them round to the other side then back again.

'Are you all right there?' I ask him. 'You look a bit awkward.'

'Oh, that's normal.' He grins. Nice lad. I remember our mum simpering as she sliced a brick of Battenburg: 'Nice lad, isn't he? Nice lad.'

'Have some parsnip wine, Stevie.' Tonto uncorks the bottle with a loud pop and pours into an empty glass that's standing there. Stephen takes it, puts it to his lips and drinks with amusement in his eyes. Tonto starts to pour one for me but I stop him. 'I'm driving,' I say.

He drapes his long thickening body the length of the bed. 'Veronica Karen,' he says. 'So how is she?'

There's a silence.

'She's all right,' says Stephen.

'I haven't seen her for about seven or eight years,' I say.

'Well you,' Tonto says softly, 'you've been a right little recluse, my darling,' and reaches down and takes a small photograph from a wallet left trustingly open on the floor. 'Oh, what!' he says, gazing at it, 'Veronica Karen, she is so bloody beautiful!' He hands it to me. Veronica Karen in the old days. She's all teeth and hair, laughing, looking down, standing with another girl on a bed in a purple T-shirt and long black skirt. Her face is shiny. She's drunk, obviously, having a good time at some party or other. A picture of the beautiful youth Narcissus surrounded by nymphs is on the wall behind her. She is so young.

'Veronica Karen,' I say, and hand it to Stephen. He gazes solemnly down at it.

'She was the best,' Tonto says vehemently, 'Veronica Karen she was the best. She was – oh! – one of those, you know, one of those classical people you never forget. An original. Veronica Karen, wow! Oh, Veronica Karen!'

Embarrassed, I reach for Stephen's drink, take a swig, gag and put it down again.

Stephen hands him the photograph and sips his awful wine, his serious hooded eyes remaining steadily on Tonto's tragic face. These two never took much notice of each other. Jealousy, I suppose. Is he still jealous, Stephen? After all these years and all the others, all those horny-handed sons of toil, the big rough blokes with muscles and fists in seedy flats with fancy underwear hanging over the baths, her Beauty and the Beast days, can he still feel that? He looked a boy compared to them.

Tonto slips the picture back into his wallet and lets it fall to the floor, sits up and smiles disarmingly at me. 'This girl,' he says to Stephen, pointing at me, 'this girl is so great.'

'I know,' says Stephen.

We all laugh.

'Tonto,' I say, 'you're embarrassing me.'

'We go back so many years, me and this girl,' says Tonto. Then his voice drops a register, becomes ominously soft and breathy and meaningful. 'She thought a lot of you, you know. She did. Veronica Karen thought a lot of you. The things she used to tell me about you. She used to tell me about when you were little girls together and how you looked out for her, how you used to hold her hand when she got frightened going to sleep, you used to share a bed and you told stories. And all the games you used to play. She said you were, you were crucial to her development. You formed her imagination. She said she admired you so much, your brain, she said, was always teeming and it all just came pouring out. Oh yes, she thought the world of you.'

Cobblers.

There is a long silence.

Stephen shifts his legs round to the other side of the chair then back, finally straddles it like a horse, his feet meeting somewhere round the back.

'You OK there, mate?' asks Tonto.

'Yeah, yeah,' he grins. 'This works well for me.'

We all laugh again.

'More tea, vicar?' says Tonto, upending the bottle of parsnip wine. There are tears in his eyes. The look of the wine reminds me of the sweet drink a girl called Bernice used to bring to school every day in a little flask. She used to pour it out into a glass as we sat in the dining room with our packed lunches. Veronica was two tables down. That liquid fascinated me, we never had anything like it at home. I didn't know what it was. I imagined it would taste delicious, fragrant, exotic, like honey, pineapple, peaches, like nectar whatever nectar was. I didn't know Bernice very well, but one day I could bear it no longer and asked if I could have a taste. She raised her eyebrows in faint surprise, pushed the flask across and looked away. I poured a drop into the bottom of my glass and returned the flask. I savoured the moment of that one and only taste. It was OK. Lemony, slightly acidic. Nothing special.

'It's so long since I've seen her,' says Tonto, tears spilling over the rims of his eyes.

I reach over and take his hand.

'When you find her,' he says, wiping his nose, 'when you find her, let me know, won't you?'

He clutches my hand, staring at me with old, desperate eyes. 'So I can – wring – her – fucking – neck,' he says, his grip tightening at every word, and a ripple of winter spreads through me, disintegrating as it goes. And suddenly I remember the sound of him tearing up her clothes, insistently, methodically, after she'd gone away with Alexander.

She brings this out in people.

He stares at me, shaking his impressive head in bewilderment. Tonto could have been a male model. I see his younger self staring out at me from windows in town, wearing the latest thing.

Somewhere distant there are raised voices, a crash, the repeated slamming of a door. Slowly, my brain refigures. Things settle into their outlines.

'Jesus Christ,' whispers Tonto.

Stephen's looking at me.

'What?' I say. 'What?'

Tonto leaps over the table and shoots out the door,

which thwacks back against the garden wall and returns, inch by inch in startling slow motion.

'Fucking madhouse,' Stephen says, getting up with a niggled air and brushing himself down.

Gathering our things, heading for the door in this tiny space, we come close together. Something passes between us, some unavoidable viral thing we triggered, quick, zap yourself with vitamin C or something, head it off. Not Stephen Openshaw, for God's sake, too much trouble. He is vaguely amused, avoiding my eyes, somewhere above my brow. We sway slightly in our befuddlement. Then we're outside in the brilliant silver light of an early rain-threatening afternoon, with a dog jumping at my knees and my stomach all of a sudden collapsing with unfelt hunger as I realise I haven't eaten anything except a chunk of halva since breakfast. He walks ahead of me, his jacket all rumpled at the back, down the garden towards the sounds of tumult coming from the house.

The door is open and a scrubby kid stands jogging philosophically from foot to foot with his hands behind his back. The room is dark, full of raging wraiths.

'Yes, you did! Yes, you did!' Tilly's voice screams. 'You were slobbering all over her!'

'You're paranoid! You're paranoid!' yells Frank from the kitchen.

My eyes clear. Frank emerges heroically through Veronica Karen's bead curtain. Tilly leaps, surprisingly nimble for such a big woman, clamps her leg-like arms

about him and bites the side of his face. He bawls like a
foghorn. She lets go, sweeping through the jangling pipe
stems as if they weighed nothing at all. The Red Sea parts.
Then wave after wave crashes down like an angry torrent,
the smashing of crockery, and her voice deeply roaring:
'Mother naked! Mother naked! Mother fucking naked,
she's walking around my house!'

'You fucking madwoman! You fucking bitch, Till!'
Frank declaims. 'Oh yes, you've really done it this time,
missis! Oh yes! You're going to find yourself divorced!'

Tilly cackles hysterically. 'Artistic photographs!' she bel-
lows. 'Artistic fucking photographs!'

This is just so typical of Veronica Karen's friends.

Maida stands backcombing her hair dreamily before the
mirror. Kids wander in and out. Tonto weeps in the hall.

'I think it's time we were on our way,' Stephen says into
a sudden surprising silence.

Tilly bursts out of the kitchen, making the bead curtain
croak.

'Look, Cathy,' she says, furious and controlled, shaking
with it, her black eyes like pellets, 'there's no fight with you
but I think it's probably best if you just go. We're not very
keen on Veronica Karen round here at the moment.' Her
teeth begin to enunciate her words in an exaggerated way.
'In *fact* if you really want to know the truth, she's a conniving, two-faced little bitch and I wouldn't cross the road to
piss on her if she was on fire.' She leans forward and sticks
her face an inch from mine till I'm studying the shine

between the pores on her nose. 'I worship the ground he walks on,' she hisses. 'No one takes that from me. I was in hospital. Having our sixth child. She's in my house conniving my downfall. She was in every time I was out. Know what I mean? Don't look away when I'm talking to you!'

I'm tired. What do I want with these people, these ridiculous people? What the hell do I want with Veronica Karen?

'You're crazy!' cries Frank, hurling himself into a chair. 'You're crazy! You're crazy, Till! Oh Till, Till, baby, don't do this to me!'

'Stop it, you two,' says one of the kids.

Stephen stands behind me, he puts his hand upon my arm. I am sane, it says. We are in this together. 'Come on, Cathy,' he murmurs.

Frank springs up, pushes Tilly aside and confronts me. Tilly's spit shines on the side of his face, her little teeth have left marks. His hands fan across one another wildly. 'There was nothing,' he says, losing his voice, 'nothing ever ever ever between Veronica Karen and me. I swear it on my mother's grave!'

'Don't be ridiculous, Frank,' says Maida, amused, lighting a cigarette. 'Your mother's not dead.'

He groans. 'They were artistic photographs!'

A teapot full of tea hits the wall. The lid comes off and the mess splatters everywhere, cold little droplets spraying my face.

'Come on, Cathy,' Stephen says, his lips close to my ear, 'no point hanging around here.'

Tonto's contorted face greets us in the doorway. 'Yes, best if you go,' he says mournfully, 'just quietly go.'

We leave. I step on some rabbit shit in the hall. On the stairs one of the little boys in Manchester United strip sits chewing toffee. Drolly, he rolls his eyes.

'That'll never get to Scotland,' Stephen says, standing irritatingly with his hands on his hips, looking at my car indulgently as if it was an ugly dog.

'It's not going to Scotland.'

'*I* am,' he says, sighing as I open the doors. 'Now I'll have to go all the way back for my car.' He looks at me balefully.

We sit in the car looking at the crazy gates of the wrecker's yard.

'Oh, come on, Cathy,' he says impatiently, 'come on, we'll fill the thing with petrol and hope for the best, it's not worth going back now, come on.'

'Don't be ridiculous!' My brain runs and runs.

'I've got a headache now,' he says in a peeved tone. 'I need paracetamol. Got any paracetamol?'

'No.'

'Damn! I've got paracetamol in the glove compartment in my car. Damn! Stupid morons.'

I check the mirror, straighten my shoulders.

'She wouldn't sleep with Frank, would she?' I say, amazed.

'How the hell would I know?' He flounces sulkily back against his seat.

'Surely not!'

I mean, *nobody* sleeps with Frank.

I remember him giving me and Robert a lift somewhere in London once in the dim mists of time. I remember us pulling up at the lights next to a man in a car with a doctor's sticker. All the windows were open because it was hot and Frank looked over and asked the man if his sticker was for real. The doctor nodded. 'Go on, man,' Frank grinned, 'it's a great scam!' I remember bashing him on the head when he did 'The Murder Mystery' one time, and how nice he always was to me personally, in spite of all the things people said about him. Robert liked him. He liked anyone off the wall or perverse in some way. He was impressed by that sort of thing.

'Sad,' I say, 'it's just sad.'

'Sad? It's not sad, it's pathetic.'

'Think,' I say. 'A storm of chaos was caused here even by the mention of her name.'

'Crap.' He folds his arms, turns his legs sideways. 'They carry on like that all the time.'

I want to go home. This is ridiculous, I can't drive like this.

'I want coffee,' he says fiercely, sitting up again, 'I want coffee and paracetamol.'

I start the engine. 'Let's go and find some place.'

'All that stuff about wanting to wring her neck,' he says

in a grim voice. 'Bit much, that. Poor taste, really, in the light of what actually happened.'

'She brings it out in people,' I say.

'Why would anyone want to wring Veronica Karen's neck?'

That makes me laugh. 'Oh, I don't know,' I say, nudging out into the empty street. 'I can see it.'

6

I'm a café-sitter. I can sit for hours in any café, drink coffee endlessly, read the paper, read a book. I've sat alone in greasy spoons and dinky tea shops and honky-tonk café/bars and elegant little places with classical music playing in the background. I love it. I'm OK here in this somnolent tea shop in the middle of a parade of anonymous shops, a quiet respectable sort of place with dusty-pink ruched curtains and nice matronly waitresses who smile a lot. The coffee's too hot to drink, the tea-cake's fine but inedible because I've still got a speed thing and can't eat it. Stephen's face looks pale and gaunt, his eyes large and soulful. The hollow of his throat is a feather of shade above his blue T-shirt.

'Penrith,' I say.

'Wherever. I don't think I should have to do this on my own. You come with me.'

I look at my watch. It's ten to three.

'Stands to reason,' I say. 'It's on the way.'

'I don't even know them.' Aggrieved, he crumbles his scone.

'Oh, Russell and Patti are OK,' I say, 'I'll give them a ring for you. Of course they might not be there.' I look over the ruched curtain and lick my dry lips. Across the road there are three phone boxes outside a betting shop window full of large colour photographs of hounds with fanatical faces.

He sighs deeply and rests his chin on his clasped hands.

'They've got an old chapel,' I say. 'Incredible place, land all round. They've got an organic farm.'

'Oh, I'm just going up to Kilreevy.' He turns a guardedly hostile eye upon me. 'Call them if you want. Just see if they know anything.'

We look at each other for a moment. His eyes, troubled and cold at first, turn intimate by imperceptible degrees. I look slightly away, not wanting to hold his gaze because there's no point. I don't want that again. It's like when your dog dies, you just don't want to put yourself through it again.

'I've come all this way,' he says, 'and it's really good to see you.'

Then his eyes are cold again, a strange light clear brown like acorns, and he leans forward, low and intimate over the table. 'It's not some silly romantic chase I'm on,' he says evenly, 'some forlorn quest. She's just a very old friend. For my sins.'

I wonder if she'd do the same for him. Or would she stick him somewhere in the back of her mind, carry on till the news came through: Stephen Openshaw, remember Stephen Openshaw? He died, poor thing. Then she'd have a little weep, a little reminisce, a little worry at the fragility of our mortal state, pop down to Interflora and send the best she could afford.

She sent flowers every time, always such beautiful flowers they stole the show.

'I'm going to ring Russell and Patti,' I say.

I leave him and go outside, stand blinking in the bright rain glare for a moment before running over the road and into the phone box on the end of the row. I get out my book and dial, looking over at the pink ruched curtains and the steamed patch that covers most of the window and makes a blur of his inscrutably watching head. They'll know something; she checks in with them as if they were her mum and dad. She stayed there that terrible Christmas, the first after the big accident, when my dad was so ill.

Russell's cultured voice smoothly reels off the numbers.

'Russell?'

'Speaking.' Eager and efficient.

'It's Cathy.'

There's a small pause, the burble of comfortable conversation, maybe the TV or radio in the background.

'Cathy Wren.'

'*Good* heavens! *Good* heavens! I don't believe it.'

'Yes, yes, it's me.'

'Good God, I hate to think how many years it is. Patti, you're not going to believe this.'

'I rang you this morning,' I say.

'Damn, we popped over to Carlisle. Patti, it's Cathy Wren. How *are* you?'

'I'm fine. And you?'

'We're very well.' He has the serious, urbane tone of an old-fashioned gentleman. 'You know, I was only just thinking about you the other . . . what are you doing these days? Are you ringing from Moorcop?'

'No, I'm near Frank and Tilly's. Do you remember Frank and Tilly? No? Oh well, never mind, listen I haven't got all that much change. Have you heard from Veronica Karen lately?'

'She left a message on the machine when we were in Thailand. Six months ago. Six months, no five.'

'Did she say anything about Scotland?'

'She did, as it happens. She called twice. She said she was going to Scotland and then to Easter Island.'

'Easter Island!'

'Easter Island,' he says decidedly then laughs. 'She's a case, isn't she?'

Stephen's face is still, watching. The pips start to go and I stuff more money in from my little pile. Time's going. I don't want to lose Russell, Patti's talking in the background, I haven't seen them for so long I don't know them any more. 'Listen!' I babble dementedly, 'I'm with Stephen Openshaw, remember Stephen Openshaw?'

'I don't think I . . .'

I don't want to go back, I want to go on, further north. Not for her but for me, for the motorway cutting through the sweeping green hills of the north one last time.

'Could you put us up for the night, just for tonight? We're on our way to Scotland. I thought you might know what Veronica Karen was doing in Scotland.'

'Is something wrong?' he asks seriously.

'Wrong? No, nothing's wrong.'

'It's just your tone, Cathy, yes, of course, you must come at once. We had a card too. Wasn't from Scotland, I don't think. Now where was it, somewhere funny like Dewsbury or Grimsby or one of those funny places. We've probably still got it somewhere, nothing ever gets thrown out in this place, this is a kind of Sargasso Sea, a great flotsam of the gross material universe. We're drowning in it.'

The money's about to run out.

'She's not well,' I blurt.

The pips go.

'Patti says she thinks she may have . . .'

He's gone.

Why did I say all that? I step out of the box. What have I done? What's all this with Easter Island? Didn't Stephen mention that too? She's mad. Those awful Plasticine heads, once rainbow-coloured, now grey, lined up all along the cardboard hill in the back bedroom in Manchester.

Horrible shapeless listing things. 'Don't touch them!' she said. 'The gods put them there!'

When I tell him I'm coming he smiles, straight at me and with all he's got, not one of those quick furtive little things he's been tossing about. It throws a circle of complicity about us. To smile like that he must really want me to come with him, I think. He lights a cigarette and leans back with one arm cocked up, smoking with an easy air as I sip my cooling too-milky coffee, wishing I'd had a cappuccino like him. Is this all it is, a bit of fun to be with a nice man for a change? Or am I doing it for Veronica Karen, out there wrestling with death?

'Of course we could just turn around and go home and mind our own business,' I say.

He smiles again, touching my hand with the tip of one finger for a brief electric second. 'Don't be silly,' he says simply. 'You know we can't. Your car, though. Are you really absolutely one hundred per cent sure it'll make it?'

'Of course it will!' I don't know why people make these assumptions about my car, it always gets there.

'I suppose it'll do me good,' he muses, gazing at the plates of cakes and pastries all laid out under clingfilm on a long sideboard. 'Your car,' he explains; 'a lesson in endurance.'

Passion cake, muddy slice, chocolate fudge slice, cherry scone. Damn waste not being able to eat anything. 'Did you ever know Veronica Karen to run around after anyone like we're running around after her?' I ask.

'Hmm.' He looks out of the window. People walk non-descriptly by the mad-eyed dogs. 'That's an interesting one.'

She wouldn't taint her free spirit with all that unattractive stuff like care of a sick parent. She says she didn't know how bad our dad was, but she did.

'I do remember once,' he says, 'she got this stray dog from somewhere and she spent about four days tramping about all over the place trying to find it a home. It wasn't a very nice dog so nobody wanted it and she couldn't keep it because of where she was living. D'you fancy one of these cakes?'

'Couldn't possibly. Could you?'

He looks thoughtful. 'Do you know I think I possibly could.'

'You ate all that halva,' I say. 'What happened to the dog?'

'It went mad. Ended up where there was four or five of us all standing outside in the corridor, and every time we tried to open the door to let it out it's hurling itself at the door and frothing at the mouth, eyes all white and everything. We rang the RSPCA and they said put a muzzle on it. Ha! Like belling the cat. Ended up where the landlord came along and just opened the door and out it trots as docile as a lamb and toddles off down the road wagging its tail.'

He stirs the dregs of his coffee. Then he says, 'I think I'm going to have that big custardy one. Are you sure you don't want want one, Cathy?'

I wave my hand dismissively. He gets up, a slow bit-by-bit unfolding, and goes to tell the waitress.

The flowers here look a bit sad. They need me. Veronica Karen sent flowers every time, delicious wreaths that caused everyone to stop and look and cry: Oh, what gorgeous flowers! And on the card was her undistinguished handwriting: *Good night, God bless Dad, with all my love, Veronica Karen*. Why the full bloody mouthful? Wouldn't Veronica do, just this once? She was always Veronica to him. Veronica Karen! More fool me I went along with her stupid airs. *Deepest sympathy, Veronica Karen*. But she never came. He loved getting her letters, I found them all in a box when I was going through the house after he died, all neatly stacked together in date order going back to when Mum was alive. She hardly wrote at all towards the end. She sent me a stupid pretentious postcard once, a crap black and white sub-Beardsley thing. 'A friend of mine did this,' she'd put on the back. So what? Poor old Dad. I remember the fear in his faded eyes. He had a little picture of her on top of the television. I see Auntie Pearl carrying out the commode, silver-blonde hair, double chin, big legs in pink stockings and beige shoes. She got fatter as he grew thinner; all billowy bosom and jabot she was then, all powdery-smelling.

Look at Stephen there, talking to the waitress easily, calling forth smiles from her.

'I'll bring it to you, love,' I hear her say.

'I've ordered some more coffee,' he says, sitting down

again. 'What I mean is, she was crying all night about that dog. Wondering where it was.'

'I meant people,' I say. 'Did you ever know her to run around after a human being?'

His lips curl up in a dry smile, he covers them with a hand bent back at the wrist and gazes out of the window, eyes glazed with milky fondness.

Oh, she's so fucking wonderful. Selfishness is so admired. I open my mouth to speak but the bitterness rising up is too acrid. The waitress brings two more coffees and a round swirl of a Danish pastry the size of a good-sized fris-bee for Stephen, gleaming with gloss, its lattice bulging with hard custard and raisins and starry sugar crystals.

'Cathy,' he says, ignoring it, 'what's the matter?'

I want him to understand this, I want him to know. 'When there was trouble,' I say clearly, 'she never came near. She couldn't stand it when people had the bad taste to get ill or die or anything. She was always unavailable. On holiday. Moving flats. Couldn't be reached. She was never there when the shit hit the fan.'

The big hungry mouth that is the big accident gapes underneath me. Me and Robert were coming back from Shugden to Moorcop on the train. He'd gone to get a bun from the buffet. He was the one in one-person-killed-and-five-injured. I was eight months pregnant. I was OK but it did for poor little Johnny, though I carried him to the end.

'After the accident,' I say, 'she sent me an awkward letter. Well, that's OK, you expect it to be awkward, but you'd think she'd have let on she knew something had happened. She was in Weymouth. She seemed to be in Weymouth for a long long time. See you soon, she said at the end of the letter, as if nothing had happened. Anyway, she always said that but you never did see her soon. I got more from you, you sent me a nice card.'

'Oh Cathy!' he says, touching his temples, putting such tired sincerity into those two words that I'm stopped in my tracks. And then for one slow dramatic moment he throws his arms wide to me across the table, like mother hen calling her chicks.

'It's fear,' he says, subsiding immediately and becoming blasé again. 'You're so much stronger than she is. She blocks things out when it's too much to take. Self-protection at all costs. It's a weakness, an inability to cope, she's always been like that.' He starts on his Danish pastry. 'Oh anyway, look, I'm not trying to defend her. She's not perfect, we none of us are. Of course she's a selfish bitch. She always was. Don't you think I know it?' His eyes open wide. 'She *practised* on me, for Christ's sake.' He laughs.

When I don't respond, he stirs his coffee and says quietly, 'I just think we should do this, you know.'

Such loyalty.

'It's a case of she can't go without saying goodbye, that's all,' he says. 'This time she's not allowed to.'

He crosses himself before he gets in the car, grinning.

For a while we just drive, heading towards the motorway.

He fiddles about in the glove compartment among the tapes, bypassing Bluegrass Heaven, Ladysmith Black Mambazo, P. J. Harvey, the Staple Singers, *Magic and Loss* and *The Humours of Clare*. He goes for the Mozart piano sonatas.

'How's your head now?' I ask.

'Not so bad. The paracetamol's kicking in. Thank Christ.' He closes his eyes, lounging back with his knees sticking up.

We'll be hitting rush hour soon. Friday, everyone knocking off for the weekend. As we join the motorway, he tells me a story about coming up to Morecambe when he was little and getting into trouble for going in the sea with his socks on. He continues to regale me nervously with tales of Butlin's Pwllheli, Rhyl off-season and Blackpool in a week-long force nine gale that swept two people and a dog away. 'My dad always used to sing in pubs and embarrass us all,' he remembers. 'If there was a mike he'd be up there, it was terrible. He always sang "You Were Meant For Me" out of tune. "You Were Meant For Me" and "You, You're Driving Me Crazy."'

My eyes are on the road. I sense him leaning lazily against the side window. He's kind of looking this way but maybe it's not dead at me, maybe it's the speedo he's looking at or something.

'You, you're driving me crazy,' he sings artlessly. 'What did I do? Oh, what did I do?'

How awful the line of my chin is in profile, there's not a

thing I can do about it. Actually I have this way of kind of arresting a swallow halfway through that makes it look a little bit better, but the trouble is you can't hold it.

'This car's making some funny noises,' he says guard-edly.

'Oh, it's all right, it always does.' I concentrate on my throat. I'd thought the car was sounding pretty good. It isn't exactly what you'd call a motorway car but we doddle along nicely with the engine rattling in a cosy way and everything passing us. What must I look like? The woman with the terrible undulating throat.

'What are you laughing at?' he asks. I think I hear a smile in his voice.

'Nothing.' I shake my head.

'Bizarre, isn't it?' he says, 'me and you driving along like this.'

It grows brighter towards early evening. 'Bolero' hymns us on northwards. The land grows wild and high, a massive green Avalonian vale cut through by the motorway. I could've stifled in Frank's, stifled in the past. Far away, little grey houses wisely brood on timeless hillsides, the happy dwellings of people I can only imagine. When night falls, a buttery glow will bleed from their windows under the vast blue-black of the howling universe.

We come off the motorway and drive on quiet roads for a while, then country lanes with riotous hedgerows and pale sprays of wild flowers springing from the verges, down a valley that drops by degrees lower and lower into real old deciduous woods with gnarled boles and toadstools and holly and ivy and moss so thick you could make a coat out of it.

'This is wonderful,' he says, growing eager and rolling his window down as far as it will go.

We glide through dappled tree-shaded tunnels. We're nearly there. I remember this. Me and Robert came up from London a couple of times, Veronica Karen did too. Once we were all three here in winter and we went for a long, long walk in the snow through the woods and up the fells to a pub in the middle of nowhere. Veronica Karen had dropped some acid and it started coming on in the woods. She said it was like Narnia, the snow hanging from the boughs and the birds singing. We'd taken a joint to smoke along the way, but found, of course, that we'd forgotten the matches, so we tried to light a fire with two sticks that were slightly less wet than the others, only of course it didn't work. We were all wearing denim. 'The Denim Kids,' sniggered Robert and we stood in a row with linked arms and laughed at ourselves. She must have been between men. I didn't know then, I didn't know when we all stood there laughing that the next one would be Alexander.

A little stream runs alongside the road. The late sun glints on polished rocks. A sheep and its lamb run from the roadside, cross the stream and head off up the fell, triggering a half-hearted stampede amongst the rest of the flock. We pass a little church and a farm, cross a humpbacked bridge that sends our stomachs flipping like pancakes, turn left and into the long lane where Russell and Patti live, and pull up in the lay-by. The sign, sober green and gold letters on a white board, says PEARL ORGANICS. A gravel path runs from the wrought-iron gate in a long curve to the recessed arch of their front door. Stephen looks at the grey chapel nestling beyond the evergreens, the stile leading over an old stone wall into an orchard, where the black arthritic fingers of trees grasp and tangle together.

'Nice place,' he says with a world-weary air, standing on the verge.

He follows me up the path. Off to the right are long low sheds, greenhouses with pale leaves pushing at the windows, crops in fields, cabbages and sprouts and beans and carrots. Closer, a huge red motorbike leans against the wall of a tumbledown shed.

'Nice bike,' he says.

We stand looking at it. A piano plays in the house, a stoical version of 'Greensleeves'.

'I had a motorbike phase once,' I say.

It was so short it's just quick flashes, frozen images with no thread. Red and yellow stippling on the bulbous breast of a Norton. Terror and joy as we soared, leaning into the bends, death as close as the scrolling roads.

'Was that when you were going out with Alexander?' he asks.

I nod.

'She had a motorbike phase too, Veronica Karen,' I say,

'she bought all the gear.' We crunch through the gravel. 'Black leather. Leather pants, leather jacket, zips.'

She used to take off her helmet with a flourish and shake all her thick hair out like something out of a shampoo ad. Who's the girl with the lovely hair? I'm thinking of this when I ring the bell. The piano is silenced. Deep in the chapel-house, there are voices and the squeaking of boards. When the door opens Russell grabs me straight away and hugs me before I can even get a proper look at him. 'Cathy, how wonderful,' he says, letting me go. His face is more florid than before, a kind of permanent brick red. There are wrinkles in his neck.

'You look fantastic. You look absolutely marvellous, gorgeous as ever.'

The first time I saw Russell was in a tutorial on *Ulysses*. We have all grown older, but Russell, even then, looked like a grown-up amongst a bunch of kids. He was born that way, with his sensible haircut and sensible flannels, loose round the backside and short in the ankle.

'This is Stephen,' I say, 'Stephen Openshaw.'

'Veronica Karen's friend, of course, of course.' A quick handclasp. 'Come in, come in, both of you, Patti's dead excited.'

He's one of those tall, lean, big-bottomed men. Stooped and beaky, he steps along the stone corridor like an odd, ungainly wader. I always thought he'd make a very good Flay though he doesn't have enough of the surly quality.

'Here they are, Pat.' We follow him through a heavy oak

door into a room that has the appearance of a huge, up-market and very cluttered antique shop.

'You old so-and-so!' Patti walks towards me with a mannish gait, tall, arm-swinging, dressed in salmon-coloured cord trousers and an oatmeal jumper. Her hair is a vigorous mop of grey and brown. 'You never get in touch. You're a swine, you really are. What have you been doing with yourself all this time?' She's filled out, grown strapping and hard-bodied.

New windows look out over a sloping green valley towards fizzy green woods; high in the far wall are three arched windows bearing the original stained glass of the chapel, a gold Agnus Dei in the middle. The room is loaded with books and toys and plants and pictures and tables and sofas and ornaments and general bits of junk like garden gnomes and scales and peculiar big stones. Because they have lots of money the scruff and clutter doesn't look a mess, it looks provocative and interesting and invites you to browse.

'Amazing place,' says Stephen, as he shakes hands with Patti.

She has a squeaky laugh. 'Our little collection,' she says.

The three of us sit down, each on a different sofa. Russell remains standing. 'First things first,' he says genially, clasping his hands together. 'What can I offer you? Tea? Coffee? Something harder? Cathy?'

'Coffee for me, please, Russell.' The sofa sucks me in softly like a jelly and my feet leave the ground.

'Yeah, coffee for me too.' Stephen has picked up a small grey replica of a steamroller and is turning it over and over in his hands.

'I thought for a minute you were bringing Veronica Karen,' Russell says excitedly. His smile is long and narrow and crooked. 'We haven't seen her for such a long time. Ages, isn't it, Patti? You know what she's like though, she's the devil for not getting in touch. You both are.'

'Oh, I know, it's terrible, I have all these letters in my head,' I burble.

'Right then. Coffee it is.'

He goes out and can be heard whistling jazz in the kitchen. On an old lace doily on the table next to me are various items: a small silver swan, the mouthpiece of a trombone, a shepherd swain soliciting his Phyllida, a bronze heron and something that could be a Navajo head-dress sitting on an antique brown globe of the world. Stephen looks up to the soaring cantilevered ceiling. 'Well,' he says, amusement in his eyes, 'first time I've been in church since my sister got married.'

Patti leans forward, shoulders square, knees out. 'It *is* funny,' she says. 'Or it was at first. You kept thinking about where everything would have been. You know −' she points, 'there's where the altar would have been, for example. You sit with your coffee and you think: they would have put the coffins here, and, infinitely more pleasant, here's where some blushing country bride must have stood, trembling with apprehension . . .' Her voice is brittle. She chuckles. The pale blue moons under her eyes have grown since I last saw her, swollen with a bloom like health. Her eyes are tired, pink-rimmed.

We got married, I don't know why, most people didn't, it was just a laugh at the time, a literal laugh, we were like kids trying not to giggle in assembly all the way through it. There was me and Robert and Simon and Patch and Andy and Jana and all the rest, and I wore a very pretty dress, long and clingy in varying shades of purple and burgundy. I loved that dress. Our lady of the flowers, me. I carried a very simple bouquet of freesias. It was just a big piss-up really, not a bit romantic. I wasn't even in love with Robert by this time, that's the funny thing, and I knew it; we didn't even have sex much. Well, the sex was never up to much with me and Robert anyway, but then that's not what it was all about. He was just my best friend.

The smell of coffee drifts in.

'You are staying the night, aren't you?' Patti sits back, drawing her long legs beneath herself and squatting comfortably against the cushions. Her face is roundly handsome, with big lush lips customarily parted, or pouting of themselves in a way she doesn't intend. 'Because I'm assuming you are. I want to know all about everything. What are you doing? How's Moorcop? Did anything ever come of that idea you had that you were going to send to the publishers –'

'Oh God, that was ages ago. No, nothing came of it.'

I go through it all again, accounting for myself. Then we

go through it all accounting for Stephen, who she claims to remember, though we can't think how. 'Probably just heard a lot about you,' she says. Then we have to go through it all again for Russell, coming in with the coffee.

'So,' she says, 'you're going to *Scotland*?'

Stephen and I look at each other and laugh.

'We seem to be,' I say.

Everything's always done so nicely at Russell and Patti's. On the tray there is a tall jug of coffee, hot milk, cups and saucers, two plates of tastefully displayed ratafia biscuits and little buns with choc chips on top. Patti probably made them, she makes everything. All the crockery is rare, genuine art deco, old Wedgwood, delicate filigree peacock-patterned china. Russell presents me with a steaming cup and saucer so fragile and genteel my finger and thumb won't fit through the handle, so wide and shallow of brim that the hot coffee vibrates and threatens to spill if I attempt to bring it to my lips.

'So,' says Russell, in a let's-get-down-to-business voice, 'Veronica Karen's not well, I think you said. I hope it's nothing too serious.'

'She's got AIDS.'

It's real, there's no going back. I've told.

Immediately I wish I hadn't.

Silence falls.

'Oh, my goodness,' Patti says. She sits forward, covering her cheeks and mouth, drawing them downwards. 'Oh, my goodness me!'

Russell goes on handing out coffees. His big angular face is dead serious, the mouth a hard slit. 'I'm not believing what I've just heard,' he says quietly, leaning down towards me with the two plates, the biscuits and the buns. Coarse dark hairs show above the collar of his shirt, trying to crawl up his neck from his chest. I take a bun and he retreats, looking uncharacteristically sulky and angry, as if the news is a personal affront to him.

Stephen puts down his dinky cup and leans across to me, clearing his throat. 'I'm not sure we should have told,' he says in a low voice. 'She wasn't telling people. I only told you because you're her sister.'

'People have to know,' I say, face burning. My fault. Put my foot in it again. I pick at the glaze on top of the bun. 'It's real. It's what's happening. In a way it doesn't only involve her. You can't just pretend a thing isn't happening, it won't go away.'

'Oh, poor little Veronica Karen!' Patti's eyes are glossy with tears. They make mine hurt, so red and inflamed are they, as if the tears sitting on the rims were made of acid.

'Oh shit. Shit shit shit,' says Russell in a weary voice, sitting down with his trousers riding way up above his ankles and his big shoulders hunched forward. 'Can you take this in, Pat? Can you?'

Patti shakes her head impatiently, sniffs, wipes her eyes with a brisk sweep of her large, raw, workworn hands.

'Possibly you shouldn't have told us,' Russell says, looking at me with kindly eyes, 'but I'm very glad you did. One can't help – I mean, why – I mean, what a sad thing that she didn't tell us anyway. All these years and years we've been friends.'

'She didn't tell *me*,' I say. 'Stephen did.'

'She mustn't give up,' Russell says; he has an eager air, innocent as a lamb. 'She really mustn't. You know, you hear of amazing things. People who go on for years and years and years. If she just takes care of herself. If she can just keep positive, in the mind, I mean, I know it must be bloody hard but – I mean, if she can just hang on, they're coming up with new things all the time –'

'I think it's a bit late for that,' Stephen says cautiously. 'I don't mean she's got the virus, I mean she's got AIDS. You know. The full-blown thing.'

There is another silence.

'You don't *know* that,' I cut in and Stephen throws me a disparaging look.

'I do,' he says, 'I know.'

'Oh yes.' I sip from the top of the trembling coffee. 'Stephen knows. He's in mystical communication with her.'

He has to go through the whole story again, how, where, when, whom as far as anyone can tell. I watch the feelings flit across their rapt faces, dread, pain, sympathy, guilt, fear: what did we do? Kisses. Could we have? No, no, of course not, but what if – she bites her nails, Veronica Karen bites her nails, bites the skin all round them: blood, what if, that night, did she, what if the blood, what if, she's so sloppy. And even though they know how small the chances are, even though they feel bad for thinking about it, they're all scared except for me because I haven't seen her for so many years there couldn't possibly be any of her in me.

'Was she having anything for it?' Patti asks. 'Any treatment?'

'She was on AZT at one time,' says Stephen, 'but it made her sick so I think she stopped it.'

Patti gets up, scowling at her knees, brushing her hands down over her big high hips. 'I need a drink,' she says and goes out.

'So what's all this stuff about Easter Island?' I ask.

'Hmm.' Russell rubs his mouth, leaning on a crossed knee and staring at the carpet. 'Got a thing about islands, hasn't she? Oh, I don't know, Cathy, it was just a message on the answering machine.'

'St Kilda,' says Stephen, getting up and wandering about the room, looking at the books, the old tins and boxes and curious gem-like stones. 'St Kilda. She wanted to go there once. She talked about it all night. She said she wanted to go somewhere wild, somewhere where it would be like going off into the desert for forty days and forty nights, or the Aborigines going on walkabout, or . . .'

'What's that place?' I say, 'the rock with all the gannets, off Ireland, where the monks used to live on seagulls' eggs and . . .'

'Skellig Michael,' says Russell. 'I've been there. It's magnificent.'

Russell's been everywhere.

'These aren't the kind of places you go and stay, though.' He laughs. 'Actually it's really terrifying. I went there with my brother and his wife, all that way in a small boat on a very rough sea. It was worth it, oh it was worth it but my goodness! You have to go up hundreds of little steps and it's just a sheer drop down into the sea. Let's just say it's a good place to confront the fact of mortality.' He makes sweeping, bowl-shaped gestures with his large knobbly hands; Patti comes in with an opened bottle of white wine and the narrow stems of four wine glasses slotted between her fingers. 'There's a sort of high green – bit – on the top and it's so, so exposed, and so high, and so ancient, you just feel completely blown away.'

'Sounds just the place for Veronica Karen,' says Stephen, turning a small Ganesa over and over in his hands.

'What does?' Patti pours wine.

'Skellig Michael.' Russell stretches full length, leaning back with his hands knotted behind his head. 'We're talking islands. Veronica Karen and islands.'

She smiles, handing out wine.

'You look at the horizon,' says Russell, head back, smiling reverentially at the ceiling, 'and everything is so blue and enormous you feel it's going to suck you off the top. Or a hand's going to come out of the sky and pluck you away like one of those blessed lottery adverts, or . . .' He sighs, accepting his drink. 'People often experience this need to jump off, apparently. I can understand it.'

There's a long silence. I sip alternate wine and coffee.

Stephen stands by an alcove full of books, turning his head to one side to look at the spines. I think I could eat something soon. She's an amazing cook, Patti, I wonder what we're having for tea. He has a nice stance, a neat arse. I wonder if it would be all right for me to go with him? All this will be over in a day or two and he'll be back down south, back to his real life. Could I do it and not go on wanting it again, wanting more till I was into all that again? I wouldn't survive another round. Survive. Ha! That's a laugh. But I'm scared and my heart feels sick. I keep wanting the bitterness of the wine to finish, but there's always a few sips left that I have to keep taking. I see a picture in my mind of Veronica Karen sitting in the middle of a green bowl-shaped sward on top of a lonely rock in the middle of an endless curved sea. She's got her knees drawn up to her chin and she wears a long gypsy skirt the way she used to in the old days.

'Course, she's not really gone to Easter Island,' Russell says reassuringly, leaning back and playing with the stem of his wine glass. 'I mean, think about it. How do you get there? It's not exactly in the travel brochures, is it?'

'She said she was going to try and get a place crewing on a boat,' says Patti.

Russell laughs. 'Don't worry.' He turns to me. 'She didn't last more than two weeks on Holy Island. And that's civilised.'

'Oh Lord!' Patti puts her hand up to her face and laughs. 'I don't know what they expected. Shangri-La. They said the natives weren't very friendly. Still, she says, it got me away from Tonto.'

'We saw Tonto today.'

'No! Not that I ever met him. Just the name, you don't forget the name. She could pick 'em, couldn't she? Blokes. If there was a weirdo around he'd go for Veronica Karen all right.'

Then we are struck dumb, struck laughterless because it breaks in on us: Veronica Karen is going to die.

Russell pulls at the knees of his flannels and turns to Patti, gulping, swishing the wine around his mouth before swallowing. 'When was the last time we saw her?'

Patti says: 'Appleby Horse Fair. Don't you remember?'

'God yes! She stayed about a week, it was about three years, yes it is, three years ago. She slept most of the time.'

She always did. I remember once she came to me and Robert and we hardly ever saw her. Lazy sod, in bed at two o'clock in the afternoon.

'You know what she's like. You get up one morning and she's gone. There's just a note, just thanks for everything, you know, nothing special, see you soon and all that.'

'She always puts that in letters,' Patti says: 'See you soon. And of course you don't see her soon at all, it could be years and years, and you think you've really lost touch with her this time, and then she just turns up again one day. Her little face on the doorstep. Little waif, you know. Or you get a call from the station. Come and get me.'

She smiles fondly.

'I hate her,' I say, finishing the bitter wine.

Everyone looks at me.

'Isn't it terrible, a time like this and I still hate her?'

'But you don't,' says Stephen and a great violence swells in me like a pain and I want to slap his face.

He looks at me and shrugs and makes a wry mouth.

'Do you know what she did?' I say, 'do you *know* what she did?' and though my voice does not tremble I feel fury crawl like scorpions in the pit of my stomach. *They* know what she did. They colluded. 'It was Christmas, the first Christmas after the accident. Just me and Dad and Auntie Pearl, for God's sake. I would love to have gone away. I would *love* to have gone away, anywhere, anywhere at all. Even then, even after all that had happened, she never came.'

Russell comes softly and sits down next to me. 'Cathy. Cathy,' he says in his calm sixties BBC voice.

'She stayed here,' I say, never taking my eyes off Stephen, whose own have become sad and embarrassed and full of pity. 'She must have had to pass Shugden to get here. She said she had to work and couldn't get away. She even went to the trouble of getting Christmas cards and writing them and leaving them down in London for someone to post at the appropriate time. And all through Christmas it's: hey Cath, remember that time when you and Veronica dug up all the flowers, remember this, remember that. He so badly wanted to see her. And all the time she was here. She was *here*.'

Russell takes my hand and leans close so I can smell the clean efficiency of his breath, talking into my face low and serious. 'That Christmas,' he says, 'it was you that was on her mind. We didn't ask her to come here. She just let us know two days or so before that she was spending Christmas with us.'

I keep Stephen's eyes but I can't read them.

'His last Christmas,' I say. 'Of course, I only found out by chance.'

'You weren't out of anybody's mind, Cathy,' Patti says firmly. 'She was really worried about you.'

'She cooked most of the Christmas dinner, her and old whatsisname, old wild boy who went mad.'

'Alexander,' says Patti.

I didn't know. Truly till this minute I didn't know. I thought he just stayed the once, after Holy Island. But it doesn't matter.

'We were *all* worried,' Russell says. 'You should've come. You should've been here.'

'How could I come?'

'We sent you a letter. You never wrote back. We thought –'

'I'm not talking about me! I'm talking about my dad! He wasn't a bad man. What do you have to do to get your kids around you when you're dying?'

Maybe they did write me a letter, I don't remember, it was such a horrible time. Things get jumbled. Patti and Russell look at each other, a strange, half-guilty look.

Stephen comes over and sits the other side of me, drooping forward with his big hands linked. 'It's all right, Cathy,' he says quietly, 'really, everything's going to be all right,' as if I'm some kind of idiot hysterical child and I think: what am I doing? Am I mad? Why am I entertaining thoughts about this man? He's just nothing.

'You look so angry,' he says.

I laugh.

'Oh, come on!' Patti pleads, jumping up with a determined smile and checking the level of the wine, 'we're not all going to fall out. Not at a time like this. Come on!'

'No, of course we're not falling out.' Russell pulls my hand firmly to press against his face, his big red Mr Punch face smiling at me.

'I'm not angry with you,' I say, 'I'm angry with Veronica Karen.'

'The pair of you!' he says, squeezing. 'I love you both and I could knock your heads together.'

I don't care. I don't care. Veronica Karen never cared, why should I care? I hate her. I hate Veronica Karen. Why am I chasing all over the country after her?

'About dinner,' Patti says brightly. 'Is eight all right or are you absolutely desperate? Why don't I sort out a few starters?'

Oh God, I need out. I need cool water.

'Excuse me,' I mumble, getting up and heading for the door. I have to haul on the thick knotted brass ring as if I were hauling up the anchor. They're watching. Jesus, why does everything have to be such a performance, it's only a door, for Christ's sake. In the stone-flagged hall leans one simple besom. Doors stand open. I go into the kitchen and grab a cup, some wonderful two-handled Chinese affair, from the draining board. The water slops into it and I stand looking through the window at a long field sloping down to the woods, thinking about how she brought Alexander down from what he was to this joke I still hear of from time to time, this kind of mad lapdog who ended up exploding.

I feel a little bit sick. That's it, no more wine, who is it that keeps filling up my glass when I'm not looking? Russell. With his genial mine-host air.

Patti follows me in.

'So she was with Alexander?' I say, turning from the window. 'I thought she only brought him here the once.' It's OK, they don't know about me and him. No one does apart from Stephen who goes back all the way. Unless she's told them, of course. Unless they've all sat around the dinner table discussing my affairs. I knock back the water with a hardened drinking gesture, as if it were schnapps. I really should take to the drink, I think I've got the natural style for it.

'Oh, she brought him a few times,' Patti says, doing things at the stove. 'Can't remember. They were on and off for years. Like Liz Taylor and Richard Burton, drama queens, the pair of them. I wasn't surprised when all that weird stuff happened. Funny bloke, Alexander.' She folds her arms, leaning against the fridge, square shoulders cock-eyed. 'What did you think of him? Did you know him?'

She knows nothing.

'Not really,' I say.

'I asked him why they'd gone up there, Holy Island, and he says: "We just wanted to go."' She affects a husky child's whisper.

Not like that, he was not like that, I remember his voice. Soft.

'He was a bit like,' she says, 'like he just wasn't quite all there, somehow. Weird.'

He wasn't weird when I knew him, I want to say. Not really. He was just . . . he was just . . .

'I mean, he just sat there with this vacant look on his face for hours.'

He was just distanced. I read a self-help thing once where you were supposed to walk around visualising a shining egg of protective light all around you. It was like he'd got that, but it had hardened and become impenetrable and every-thing just bounced back from it. You couldn't get in.

'He'd done some lovely little pencil drawings of Holy Island,' she says sadly.

'Yes,' I say, 'he was a very talented artist, Alexander.' I remember his hands drawing. A kiss on a lonely road.

She sighs. 'Poor soul! Bit of a wreck really. Oh, I suppose he was all right! He was OK. Just a bit pretentious.'

I still have three letters from him. So much that he wrote to me in that so tiny writing seems pretentious now.

'Like Veronica Karen,' I say.

I once saw a shopping list written by Veronica Karen. Nutz, she'd written. Kat Food. Her handwriting was very ordinary but she'd carefully remembered to put those stupid round dots, like goblet navels, over the i's.

'I think more coffee while we wait.' Patti flicks open a machine, her hands rough and strong, covered in little scratches from the garden. Something starts to bubble on the stove. 'The trouble with Veronica Karen,' she says sensibly, 'she tried to be too special.'

The past tense, she's using the past tense. We both realise at the same moment.

'Of course he was obsessively jealous,' she says quickly. 'Always accusing her of things. I don't know how she put up with it.'

'Well, she was no saint.'

'Doesn't justify what he did,' she says firmly, spooning coffee into a crisp filter. 'It was the violence I couldn't take. Anyway –' She brushes her palms together, smiling regretfully. 'I'm really sorry, Cathy, really really sorry if that Christmas upset you. We had no idea . . .'

'It's all right, Pat.'

How did he give that impression, that on the inside he was all writhing and twisting in torment, some beautiful existential jungle of profound discontent? It wasn't the things he said. He spoke in a very low voice, radiating tranquillity. He was like a noble lion with a pawful of thorns.

'Patti,' I say, 'do you like Veronica Karen? I mean really like her?'

She pauses, slumping and putting her head on one side while she thinks. 'I don't know,' she says lightly after a while. 'It's not a matter of liking sometimes. It's not as simple as that. It's just that sometimes you can know someone for so long that it really doesn't matter any more, I suppose. They say you choose your friends but –' She shrugs. 'There, that should do!' She taps the machine and it starts to hiss. 'Anyway, you,' she says, stooping to look in the fridge, 'are you and Stephen –' then breaks off. 'Saskya!' she cries, clicking her fingers.

'What?'

'Saskya. Of course! That's where she's gone! Why on earth didn't I think of it before?'

She gets out a tub of hummus, a bowl of salad leaves. 'I'm just heating up a few things,' she says, 'rice won't be long.'

'But that was years ago,' I say.

I remember a postcard of a lovely house, a strange fairy fortress with a mandala over the door, bright against the grey stone.

'But Scotland,' she says. 'Too much of a coincidence. It's worth a try.'

Suddenly I'm very tired.

'Are you and Stephen,' she repeats, shaking a head of celery over the sink, 'you know – are you . . ?'

'No, of course we're not. I haven't seen him for seven years and nine months.'

She bursts out laughing.

'What?'

'You,' she says, 'you're really funny.'

I catch sight of my face in the shiny gold of the tap and it looks terrible, old and gaunt and jaundiced, scraggy-haired. I'll fix it, fix the hair. But when I get up on to the landing with the lozenge-paned windows, Stephen is there eating chocolate drops out of a little bag on top of a bookcase.

'I'm sorry,' he says, 'I found these here and I have to eat them. I'm sorry, I just have to.'

I stand there with my horrible old face exposed and wish him away but he comes up close, staring at my hideousness. 'I was wrong, wasn't I?' he says. 'I shouldn't have come for you. This is just an awful pain for you, isn't it? I'm sorry.'

His brows are raised, causing ripples in his high pale forehead. The shadows under his eyes are deeply etched.

'I'm all right.' I just want to get away from him but when I move he grabs my arms with a curious intensity that comes, I suppose, from all the drink and drugs he's consumed. 'Let's go, Cathy,' he says. 'Let's just turn around and go home. You're right, we should never have come.'

Home? What is he talking about? Damned if I'm slogging all the way back to Moorcop tonight. I'm in this to the end now. To the end.

'Don't be ridiculous.' I step back.

He places a chocolate drop in the palm of my hand. 'You're angry with me,' he says.

'I'm not angry with you.'

He's like a strange animal, giving off heat. I get a terrible urge to fling my arms round him, to hold on to him as tightly as I can, crush his bones. Quick and soft, he kisses me with his warm chocolatey mouth: a wisp of smoke uncoils in my throat, in the cavity of my chest, a delicate stroke. Then he brushes by me, downstairs, and I go into the bathroom and lock the door.

Oh God, my face! I need my bag. The chocolate drop's melting in my hand so I eat it. It tastes of his mouth. Patti, of course, never wears make-up. I poke about and come across a mess of little stubs and bits and pieces about a thousand years old in the drawer of a blue and green what-not. So she rouges her cheeks sometimes; well that's no use to me. Now if this was Susannah's I'd be OK, I'd have my pick. So what was all that about then? Eh? I don't believe it, me fancying Stephen Openshaw. I try to imagine him in my life, in my house, but I can't, and I can't imagine being in his. I know nothing about him. Here's a dried-up navy blue mascara, a smear of grey eyeshadow. I do my best. My mouth is pale, fading into my face. I'd put some lipstick on if I'd brought my bag up, but then again no, don't want him thinking I've gone to any trouble. I bite my lips, up and down, give them a good rub till they're red and healthy looking. Hair. Nothing a brush and a tousle can't mend. Thank God I washed it when I did.

They've had a proper window put in, but here by the side of the bath is one of the originals, a narrow slit at the apex of a wide stone frame, the kind of thing you shot arrows out of in the olden days. I sit down on the side of the bath and wonder what this room was once used for, looking out of the slit at the sky softening towards night. The clouds over the trees hold more rain. I remember that Christmas, the first one without Robert. I wanted to run, I wanted to be anywhere but in Shugden with my dad and Auntie Pearl smoking fags together after the turkey, but I couldn't go. I see us all three sitting in front of the telly watching football on Boxing Day. Neither me nor Auntie Pearl knew anything about football and we didn't care, but Robert did; Robert used to watch with him sometimes His ghost sat between us. I see my father lift up a card to show me, his face pleased and solemn and glowing. It is from Veronica Karen, something rather arty, in her taste rather than his.

She was his favourite. She should have come.

A tap is dripping. Tap tap tap, it goes, like that, like the rain tap tap tapping on the puddle, sweet and low, drip drip dripping from the eaves. The Roc flies down with a slow grasping movement of its wings, on to a branch of Russell and Patti's big horse-chestnut tree. When I was little I was always looking for the Roc. Now I realise I am still always looking for the Roc. And every now and then I think the Roc comes.

But it's always an illusion.

Something smells good in the kitchen. Chin up, deep breath, once more unto the breach. I go downstairs.

'Of course, that's how we met Veronica Karen,' Russell's telling Stephen, 'through Cathy. We were at university together.'

They're sitting talking, drinking more coffee, eating Kettle chips and crudités with hummus and some other kind of dip .

'I rang Saskya,' Russell says to me. 'Left a message on the answering machine. Stephen doesn't seem keen on the idea.'

'It's too far back,' Stephen says. 'She hasn't been up there for years, she gave all that up.'

I grab a handful of Kettle chips. 'I don't know,' I say, 'maybe it does make sense. A retreat, that's what she called it. When has she ever been more likely to need a retreat than now?'

Might be nice to see it, it's supposed to be very beautiful.

Stephen pulls a face.

'Well, wait and see,' Russell says sensibly, yawning a big yawn that shows high shiny gums. 'See if they ring back. Give them another buzz in the morning.'

'Saves us a hell of a journey if she is there,' I say. 'Have you got a map, Russell?'

'I sure have.' Ever helpful, he leaps up and dashes across to one of the bookcases and squats with his ankles showing bony and large, running his long finger along the ancient Penguin classics, poetry, plays, children's books. I'm touched to see, amongst the A. A. Milnes and Arthur

Ransomes and E. Nesbits, the full set of Ambrose books, all twelve familiar slim spines, like old photographs glimpsed in a drawer, stabbing you, pulling at you, stop, stop, look at me! Look at me! Once I lived.

Patti comes in, rubbing her large veined hands down over her salmon-coloured hips. 'Won't be long now,' she says comfortably, picking up the depleted wine bottle. 'Are you all nice and hungry?'

Kneeling, Russell spreads the map on the floor. 'It's a doddle from Carlisle,' he murmurs.

Patti walks about refilling the glasses. 'There are two sofa beds in the library,' she says, 'so you have your pick. Actually, it's the nicest room in the house.'

'That'll be fine,' I say.

'Fine,' says Stephen. His eyes flicker at me but I don't look.

'Well.' Russell raises his glass. 'Here's to absent friends.'

We drink and think of Veronica Karen. Stephen looks at me, gives a little shrug and drinks too.

'Let's *eat*,' says Patti.

117

7

'Are you and Stephen,' says Russell, lowering his voice in the hall outside the library, 'you know.'

'No,' I say, 'no, we're not.'

'Ah. Just my nosy mind. Sweet dreams.' He gives me a warm lingering smile and bounds upstairs.

Stephen looks up from making his bed when I enter the room. 'I have to ring in sick tomorrow,' I say, flopping down on the duvet on the other sofa bed. 'I hate that, having to lie. It'll be awful for them, Saturday, one hand short.' I take off my shoes and socks, wondering, what now? Will anything happen? *Did* anything happen? Do I want it? We've been looking at the road atlas. Kilreevy's just a dot and a smudge and a name on the map. When I looked at it I laughed because it seemed so stupid to be going there, and then I thought Stephen must be completely mad. I'd rather go to Saskya, this lovely house I've heard about. It figures in a border ballad called 'The Death of Willie o' the Side'.

But, of course, this isn't a pleasure trip.

He punches up a cushion and casts it down on his bed. Behind him is a wall of books, and there are books all around us, ancient leather-bound volumes, matching sets. A neat little upright piano stands in the lavishly curtained window. He comes over and sits in a nearby chair, leaning forward with his arms resting on his knees. His eyes are tired. 'They'll cope,' he says. 'Are you tired?'

'Very.'

'I'm not going to drink tomorrow.' He yawns. 'Do you think I'm like this all the time? I'm not. It's seeing you again.'

'Seeing me?'

'Yeah.' He laughs. 'You made me nervous so I had to get drunk and take all those drugs.' He laughs again. 'I'm not like that really. I'm a fully paid up member of society now, you know.' Jerkily he rises, loiters about the place, plays a single note upon the piano. On its ring-stained top a waxy cascade billows from a bizarre candlestick in the likeness of a cornucopia of sorrowing skulls. A water-dropper, a simian madonna and child, probably oriental, sits at the other end. The baby monkey's human hand reaches up and touches its mother's glazed, grey face.

Suddenly I'm terribly afraid, fainting afraid, feeling sick afraid. I jump up. 'This is horrible,' I say, walking about aimlessly, 'us here talking like this and Veronica Karen dying. This is a nightmare. I wish it was all over. I feel strange. I don't know what's happening any more. I don't know why I'm not at home doing what I normally do.'

'And what would that be? Sit down,' he says, coming over to me, 'sit down.'

I can't keep still. What *would* I be doing? Watching telly? Sitting round at Susannah's listening to her moan about Tim? Reading in bed?

If it gets any worse my teeth will chatter.

'Sit down,' he says, 'please,' taking my hand quite firmly. 'If you really want to we can call this whole thing off.'

'How can I?' The nightmare deepens. 'We can't call it off for her, can we?'

We sit side by side on the bed where I will sleep. I am taut and still, like a string. He's looming very close over me and I think that soon one of us has to make a move, and I think it will be him because he's already done it once, but when I look up his eyes wear a distant, cold look and his lips are tight.

'I'm in this nightmare too,' he says, 'believe me.'

I move away, unsure. The terror ebbs.

'Your feet,' he says.

'What?'

'Your perfect feet.'

'What?'

He gives a little laugh. 'No, really,' he says. 'You have the most amazing feet. They're absolutely perfect, look at them.'

I look. He's right and I've never really thought about them before. My feet are beautiful. I laugh.

'Do you know that song?' he goes on, '"Down by the Salley Gardens"? Yeats.' And then he sings, unaffected, unembarrassed, neither poorly nor brilliantly:

> *Down by the salley gardens*
> *My love and I did meet.*
> *She passed the salley gardens*
> *With little snow-white feet . . .*

and stops, and leaves a silence hanging on the air.

I remember Alexander singing 'Peggy Gordon' as we watched a river flow under a bridge in Wales. He's just like Alexander. Doesn't look like him, of course, oh nothing like. But he also knows how to make these sharp illusory moments that stick like burrs in your memory, agonising. I can't look at him.

He says, 'Do you remember Davy Boland's party?'

I was by myself, pretending I was OK, downing cider and dancing alone in the hall. Stephen was with Veronica Karen. She was wearing that funny long navy blue dress she got at the second-hand emporium and thought looked so kooky and original, God, how she primped and preened for hours in front of the mirror that night. All the people in Davy Boland's tiny little front room, Newton Heath, New Year's Eve, round the piano. Schoolboys and schoolgirls. Shades, gone the way of all shades. Veronica Karen was making a big show of being nice to Stephen, she was all over him. Everyone was drunk. She turned at one point, by the piano, and her pointed little elbow caught him a whack on the side of his head. 'Ow!' he said and his hand flew up. 'Oh love!' she cried, all concern, 'oh love!' and held his seventeen-year-old head and kissed it better as tenderly as any mother. I was watching, quiet in the room, in the shadows, Alexanderless. Alexander had gone away to art school. He'd not written for three months and he'd not come home for Christmas. To cut a long story short, he'd left me but without really telling me. How brilliantly I dissembled! All night long a step away from tears and no one ever suspected. At midnight everybody kissed. I couldn't avoid the cold wormy lips of a boy like a vole, and another, fat and beery with a rapacious tongue. I was heading for the bathroom, the bedroom, anywhere to hide, and there suddenly was Stephen.

He was very polite and kissed me in a gentle brotherly way. 'Happy New Year, Cathy,' he said, and whispered close to my ear, so that it tickled: 'He wasn't good enough for you.'

I got a taxi home and cried all night.

'I remember Davy Boland's party,' I say. 'What a funny thing to suddenly remember.'

I was feeling fine, I was living my life, a little suicide maybe, what of it? But this is terrible, terrible. Real danger. I don't want to be needy again, don't want to be like the time it all went to pieces after Robert went, and Johnny went, and then the books went too and I couldn't make any money any more. I hid in my house and read. Once I found myself halfway up the stairs on my knees weeping and praying to God. I didn't know how I'd got there. I got by. I cleaned houses. I worked in shops. I sold cakes, I sold dried flowers. I filed cards, beautifully mindless, I put books in order, I arranged things meticulously on shelves. Give me indexing, filing, the glory and beauty of order. And one day, when I realised I'd survived, I said I'm never going to feel like that again, never again in my life will I have anything to make me worry in the night about losing it.

'You know what I thought when I knew I was coming up to see you?' he says.

'No.'

'I thought . . .' but he doesn't go on.

I would. I know it. Give it a month or two and I'd be worrying about him. Why are we sitting here in this classy junkshop, almost asleep together? If he touches me now, I think, if he touches me now, comfortable, well-fed, coming down from all the excesses and wanting rest.

But he doesn't.

'If you really want to go home tomorrow, Cathy,' he says, 'you can, you know. I don't mind. Just drop me back at the motorway and I'll hitch a lift.'

Oh, spare me! The noble knight, courtly love, still bravely pursuing his honour down the lonely roads of life, ain't no use to sit and wonder why, babe, lonesome fucking hobo, the romantic vision, wandering Aengus after his glimmering girl, fucking Colina in El fucking Paso, fucking

Carmen, Lola-Lola, La Belle Dame Sans Merci.

'Don't be so stupid,' I say sharply, getting up and walking about again. 'Let's just get this ridiculous escapade over with so we can all get back to normal.'

Well that's one romantic moment well and truly stymied.

'Cathy,' he sighs, 'don't be bitter,' and then he says, with a trace of anger, 'it's Alexander, isn't it? That's what's upsetting you. Christ Cathy, it was *years* ago,' and when I look I see him raising his eyes ever so slightly to the ceiling; the lids flicker.

'She ruined Alexander,' I say.

'Oh yes, well, of course he was perfect, wasn't he?' He's jealous. The harshness in his voice surprises me. 'I really do think it's a bit rich to blame her for Alexander's weakness.'

'You always excuse her.'

'You always excuse *him*. What he did was inexcusable.'

'Oh don't be ridiculous! From what I've heard, that was all blown up out of all proportion.'

A saint could have strangled Veronica Karen sometimes. I've wanted to do it myself. All Alexander did really was grab her by the neck and give her a bit of a shake after she'd been driving him mad for the best part of five years. And when she went into her Oscar-winning performance, groaning and choking on the floor, he knew that it was really all over now and ran out of the flat and up to the roof and jumped off. Out of their heads on schnapps, both of them. He got the smashed legs and nervous breakdown, she got the sympathy.

I can't look at him. He doesn't know me any more. Too many years.

'I might,' I say, 'I might go home.'

'*I* won't,' he says, jumping up and walking about the room. '*I* won't. What am I supposed to do? Go home and keep on wondering if she's dead yet?' He stops and stands in front of me. 'No. I can't do that. I just can't *do* that.' He glares and I draw back. 'The way they talk about her,' he laments, 'the way *everyone* talks about her, as if she's dead already, as if she's some kind of joke, some bad penny, but *I* remember her when she was young.'

So do I. Oh, so do I.

'It was different then. We used to go up to the ressers and just sit there and –'

He's off, far away, let him go . . .

'– the big grey water and Veronica Karen in her red coat, sitting there with her toes in the water, sticking pigeon feathers behind her ears. Oh, she was so –' he shakes his head sadly. The anguish in his eyes chills me through, it's like looking at everything she siphoned away from me always, the attention of everyone we knew. 'So pathetic really,' he says, 'putting pigeon feathers behind her ears because she thought it looked – what? – wild and free? Romantic? What? What did she think she was doing? I had no illusions, you know. I remember going for a walk with her once early in the morning in the woods at Alderley Edge, and she goes running on ahead picking flowers, blue-bells and things, and she runs back with the flowers, holding them up for me to smell with this kind of con-trived innocence. Even then I knew. Every single act was contrived, you see, but it didn't matter. The fact that I could see right through her only —'

He shrugs, turns away and flops down into a chair.

'It's just how she was,' he finishes up weakly.

I could go over and put my arms around his drooping shoulders but I won't. I'll sit here, cool now again, and pull my knees up to my chin, and crawl into my corner and hide away my lovely feet.

'We were on our way to a party once,' he says, his voice so low I can only just hear him. 'Stockings she had on. Suspenders.' He gives a cracked little laugh. 'Her dress kept riding up under her coat and her suspenders kept coming undone. I hid her in a doorway while she did her sus-penders up. It was a little short pink crushed velvet dress with a frill down the front. She was such a little girl in it.'

He looks up, full at me. He's one of those hologram things, one of those funny pictures that keeps shifting from one thing to another. Auntie Pearl had one once with the Queen on one side and the Pope on the other, Queen, Pope, Queen, Pope, Queen, Pope, plain man, beautiful boy, plain man, beautiful boy, dark, desirable, chocolate-mouthed, but it makes no odds for I am dead to all that.

'She's *dying*,' he says with horror. '*Dying*, Cathy. That's why we don't just turn around and go home. We used to walk and walk, me and her. We never had any money. We talked about everything in the world. I remember sitting in

Stephenson Square on the top deck of a bus, talking about love.' He lifts his chin, tosses out the word like an old sock he's chucking in the laundry bag. 'I'd told her I loved her.' He laughs. '"You don't know what love is," she says. Woman of the world! Huh! "Do *you*?" I said. You know what she said?'

Some answer seems to be required.

'No,' I say calmly. 'I don't know what she said.'

'She said,' and he seems to be quoting, staring into space: '"Real love is a million miles from this. Real love is as far above this as a mountain above a molehill. When it happens," she says, "your whole life is solved." Solved. That's what she said. Like it's a puzzle. "Then there's no more pain and no more trouble, and nothing can ever go wrong again, because even if it does, if you have real love it doesn't matter, because nothing else at all matters, not even death, and everything just falls into place and all questions are answered and all decisions already made. *That's* what love is," she said. And then she looked at me. "*Now*," she says, "tell me you love me."'

What can I say?

He looks away, linking his long fingers and stretching his arms. For a time there is silence, and the sound of the rain on the window softly beginning again.

'And did you?' I ask him.

'Did I what?'

'Tell her you loved her?'

He says nothing for a while then raises his head. His eyes

are blank. 'No,' he says. 'How could I after that? I just felt scared for her. And I felt sad. And I think I just put my arm round her shoulders and said something corny like: "I'm always going to be around you," you know, something really stupid like that. And mostly I have been.'

Poor Stephen. He only really had her for two years, then it was wild shakings of the head whenever he rang, miming: I'm out! I'm out! in the tiny hall where the telephone stood on its little semicircle of bubbled glass with the wrought-iron legs. Mum got really fed up with her. 'You *are* rotten to your boyfriends, you are,' she said, peeved. Because we all liked Stephen.

He gazes into the dried-flower display in the fireplace for a while as if it were a glowing fire. He isn't going to touch me now, it's too late for that. Oh bed. I want to get into bed and close my eyes. How? Veronica Karen would probably just strip off nonchalantly at this stage, flaunting her wares in the guise of maturity. He stands, walks slowly to his bed on the other side of the room and, sighing, slowly, infinitely weary, strips down to black underpants and blue T-shirt. He takes his socks off before his jeans. He's long and white with very dark hairs on the insides of his thighs, thin shoulders and strong arms. Getting under the duvet, he stares solemnly at the ceiling for a while, arms behind his head, never looking my way, then closes his eyes and throws the duvet back from his chest. He moves his shoulders, embracing sleep, the long fingers of his left hand spread on his chest in a who-me? gesture.

I turn off the light, undress in the dark, put on an old shirt and lie down in my makeshift bed. Why didn't he touch me? So what was all that on the landing? Did I not show enough willing?

Stop. Do you want this or don't you?

Yes I do. Yes I do. Oh please God, please can I have him? Is it possible?

It's very quiet out here in the country, very quiet and very dark. It's noisy on my street at night. All the drunks go past from the pub. The light shines in the window.

'She never found it, did she?' I say.

'What?'

'Love. That kind of love she was talking about.'

He says nothing for so long I think he must have gone to sleep, then: 'No. No, she never did.'

Then the silence goes on and on and at some stage the deep rhythm of his sleep fills it, but I can't sleep in strange places. I think of how Veronica Karen had all those friends and none stuck by her. Such a little girl, he said. That's the way they all still talk about her, little girl, child.

It's about bloody time she grew up then; all the rest of us had to. She had so much and made heavy weather of it all, everyone had to dance attendance on her all the time. Gazing into the fire with a face like a wet weekend, depressed. Oh dear dear, Veronica's depressed, poor darling, take her to the doctor's. Depressed? At thirteen? Everyone making a fuss of her. Depressed? What did she ever have to be depressed about, I mean really? She missed Shugden.

Well I did too, in a way. In that poky little house in the suburbs where every street looked the same for miles and
miles, but the roses and the dusty blue hydrangeas were
lovely. Well, she's never had to cope with anything, not like
me. But I loved getting the bus into town and walking in
the big city. I loved the book stalls on Shude Hill, the big
cathedral, the Old Shambles, the pet shops on Tib Street,
the smell of hot-dog stands on Market Street, the big bright
flower beds in Piccadilly Gardens with all the old dossers
loafing around. Once I walked all the way home from
town, past the Manchester Ship Canal and the docks. So
tired.

I am so tired.

I think about all the dead people I know, so many, I
don't think it can be normal to have quite so many dead
friends. I suppose it must be something to do with the life
I've lived, the fact that I seem to have gone for the kinds of
people who don't look after themselves very well. I count
them up, numbering them on my fingers: Angela,
Eamonn, Jimmy, then on, Mum, Dad, Grandma, Grandad,
Grandma Holly, Uncle John, Auntie Celia. And Robert, of
course. And Johnny. No one ever mentions poor little
Johnny. Auntie Pearl, she'll be the next one to go. I hear
their voices sometimes. Eamonn's Belfast brogue: 'What
about ye, wee girl?' Angela, homely, belying her nature:
'Hello, love.' She had very long blonde hair. Sometimes I
see it in the street and it's her but when she turns around it
isn't.

I wouldn't be surprised to see one of them. Sometimes the phone rings and it's Robert. 'I loves ya, Olive,' he says.

In the long, long night a clock ticks somewhere, the soft, polite, apologetic modern ticking of the quartz clock on the wall in the kitchen. World still turning. If I'd gone like I'd planned the other night – when was it? Last night, my God, only last night – it would still be there, the tick, tick, tick, tick, little whisper of time still bravely battling on, saying yes, yes, yes, like a heartbeat, but I would not be here. The world would go about its business all fine and dandy and though I'd fallen through a crack in darkness, slid sideways out of my head, really it wouldn't matter, wouldn't matter a toss. It's so dark in here, not the tiniest smidgin of light anywhere to tell you you're in the world and not in a black hole on the far side of the universe, a little gnat blown about by a giant, God's playful breath. God's breath. Is it an old oath? It should be. God's in the dark, that's what I used to tell her in the night in the back bedroom in Shugden.

I think I hear the hoot of an owl.

'I'm scared, Cath.'

'What are you scared of?'

'It's too dark. I don't like the dark.'

'There's nothing in the dark, Veronica. Nothing to be scared of. Go to sleep.'

'I can't, I can't, I'm scared.'

I hold her hand in the dark. The window vibrates. She gasps. 'What's that!'

'It's only the trains going over Hog's Head Bridge.'

The trains, the trains. Hear the lonesome whistle blow.

'Not that! Not that! Another noise. Something else.'

'No, no, there's nothing else. Go to sleep.'

'But I'm scared of the dark, Cath.'

'There's nothing in the dark, Veronica. Yes, there is. There's God in the dark. Think about that. That's all there is in the dark. Think about that and you'll be OK.'

Once I turned the light off on her, turned the light off and ran out and closed the door and left her in there all alone. She didn't even scream. I don't know what she'd done, some stupid thing to annoy me. I stood on the landing holding the door handle but she never even tried to get out. I don't know how long. Then I felt bad and opened up and flicked the switch and looked. She was in the corner with her head down, surrounded by the toys, Molly and Rex and Onionhead and the Spanish Lady with the scribbled-on face. She was crying on the shoulder of Jo-Jo the monkey. Her tears wet his Dixie minstrel blue and white stripes.

I loved that Spanish Lady. She had a black mantilla.

> *There's a song in the air*
> *But the fair señorita doesn't seem to care*
> *For my song in the air.*

8

I call in sick and speak to Annie, telling her I've come down with some sort of stomach bug. She's so nice about it I feel awful as I put down the phone.

'You just stay in bed and have a nice rest,' she says kindly, 'I'll tell Mrs Crowe.'

Trish Allgood saw me driving through town in my car yesterday morning with Stephen. What if she goes in Connor's? No, she doesn't go in Connor's. None of that crowd do. What if she says something to someone and it gets back to them? It's bloody awful for that, Moorcop. You'd be hard pushed to have a secret affair, wouldn't stay secret very long. You know, in the olden days I wouldn't have cared a toss, I just used to take days off whenever I felt like it. Sod it, I would have said.

I must be getting old.

'Do you think Stephen'll be getting up soon, Cathy?' Patti shakes the coffee pot. 'Shall I make some more?'

It's nine-thirty. I suppose if yesterday's anything to go by he'll sleep on and on if I don't wake him. I steal into the library and take a look at him sleeping, his high forehead poking out from under the duvet, his hair lying sideways. God knows how he ever gets to work in the mornings. There's something I like about the vulnerability of a sleeping man, all at your mercy, all unaware. I could do anything to him. It's a deep biblical scene, Jael and Sisera, Judith and Holofernes, Samson and Delilah, I'm here with the knife to chop off his hair or his head, to drive the big rusty nail through his temples. They will praise me above all women.

I shake him softly. 'Stephen!' I say.

I shake him four or five times, a little more each time. 'Stephen! Stephen! Time to get up.'

Drive you mad probably if you lived with him.

Finally his eyes emerge and open a crack and squint at me as if I'm shining a spotlight into them. Unwillingly, he rises on to one elbow. A nice, sleepy, slightly rank smell comes up from under the duvet. One of those boyish men he is, with a stubble shadow on his cheeks and round his big, well-shaped mouth.

'What time is it?' he asks.

'Gone half-past nine. Long way to go if we're going. Come on.'

He has a thin drawn white look, stretching his wiry arms and yawning. His long straight fingers rub his eyes, pushing up his hair till it stands on end. The smell of Patti's strong coffee drifts in and he closes his eyes and inhales like a Bisto kid.

He wants to go to Kilreevy. I want to go to Saskya, which consists of one great impassable answering machine. It's not that much of a detour and much closer anyway than Kilreevy. Save us a hell of a journey if she's there. Actually, I don't really think she'll be there, but then I don't think she'll be anywhere. I'm just going along for the ride. And we go backwards and forwards, Kilreevy, Saskya, Kilreevy, Saskya, for a while till he says, 'You always get your own way in the end, don't you? I can tell.'

It's a fine day, threatening rain. The sun is dazzling on the wet puddles in the ditches. Russell and Patti stand together at the gate to wave us off. Russell's big smiling face leans in through my open window. 'When you find Veronica Karen,' he says, 'don't forget to give her our love.'

I start the engine.

'Bye!' we all say, and wave and smile, 'Bye!'

I feel rather than hear the sigh of relief that he gives as we pick up speed round the bend in the lane. The sun's bright on the road, dazzling, yet somewhere up there is a great slatey cloud as swollen and heavy as a bag of blood, its fat puffed cheeks all lined with neon silver. We fill up with petrol. This time he pays. I get out and pump the juice, the petrol cap's funny, you have to turn it just so. I wonder how he's fixed, cashwise. How much am I sup-posed to contribute to all this? I mean, it's getting expensive, we're going to have to stop and eat somewhere later. Probably thinks I'm rich. I hate it when people think Ambrose made me rich. He came here for the wealthy heiress, the southern belle pacing her big front porch, wrapping her shawl closer about her bare white shoul-ders, throwing herself down with a sigh on the swing and swinging, one little foot, one perfect little foot in a silver slipper protruding; there lonely with all her riches in her daddy's big empty house, waiting, just waiting. My house, my turtle's shell, my home, my hole, my corner, my den, my God don't take that away from me. Please Lord, don't take that too. Because sometimes in the middle of the night, when someone's just dropped their piano lessons and the tips have been bad and the gas bill's just arrived and someone on the radio's just been saying how you've got to have a pension or you'll die of starvation in old age, then it creeps into my head that I might lose the house. God, don't take my house away. Some tiles on the roof need replacing. I can't afford to get them done. Please please please don't take my house. I love my house. Robert did the windows and all the wiring. We painted the back room for a nursery, the drawers yellow and white, the first and second-size babygros neatly folded inside, the scratch mitts and doll-size socks, the crocheted shawl, the blankets, the fish mobile, blue and silver and purple, twinkling with the gloss of Christmas baubles, swinging gently in the draught from the window, its shadow slowly turning on the wall.

I go and pay.

The shy boy with downcast eyes hands me my change.

Still, not exactly down and out. Ooh, nobody knows you when you're down and out, ooh, not one penny, and my friends I haven't any . . .

Stephen's put on sunglasses.

Walking across the forecourt towards him watching from behind those black shields, I am thirteen, skinny legs with bony knees, that's me, walking with a hunch and a slouch and greasy hair, about my thighs a little grey pin-striped skirt going shiny at the seams. Where do you look, though? I mean, just where are you meant to look? Come now, girl! Shoulders back! Stomach in! Helium balloon on top of the head. I shall be proud and assertive. I *am* proud and assertive.

When I get in I turn on the radio and flick here and there. We get some kind of a golden oldies thing which is quite fun, 'Tears of a Clown' and 'Runaway' and Sam Cooke and stuff. I get glimpses of him sometimes, his long slim thighs up-pointed, hands firm, hair a mess. Suddenly he's exotic, rather glamorous in a cool seedy way. It's just the glasses. What are we? Just a couple out driving together. Standard issue. Happy.

Down, heart.

We are shy today.

We stick with the motorway till just after Carlisle then

turn off. This being the most leisurely car on the road, the journey jogs along in a kind of slow motion made loud by the jet engine whizzings of the hungry machines pinging past us. 'We could have done this in half the time with my car,' he says but without real malice, and takes some time to sing the praises of his poor abandoned Fiesta.

At lunchtime we stop just before the turn-off for Saskya, at a bleak roadside café with damp panes and a high chrome counter with egg custards and minipacks of biscuits sitting under a scratched dome. We have soup and bread rolls and sandwiches, tuna mayo for me, cheese for him. In the looming silence he starts all over again in a hushed voice about wanting to go straight on to Kilreevy.

'We could be there by half one or two,' he says complainingly.

'But it's really close now.' The air is smoky. On every table stands a single silk carnation in a small green bottle. 'It's only about ten miles, it's nothing. I mean we've come this far. I mean it really is a bit of a wild-goose chase, Stephen, you have to admit.'

He sighs and rolls his eyes sideways and up to the ceiling, showing lots of insolent white.

'No really,' I say, 'if you're in this part of the country you just have to get a look at this house. It's supposed to be beautiful. That's why she used to go, you know, not for the religion, just for the aesthetics, the peace and quiet.'

'So?' Something in my tone has riled him. 'What's wrong with that?'

'What *is* Veronica Karen's exact religious status?' I ask him, sitting back, amused. 'Buddhist? Bits and pieces? Whatever's in?'

'She doesn't have one,' he replies, coaxing a crusty roll in half with his fingers. 'You know that. She just has that kind of believe-in-everything mentality.'

'Essentially shallow.'

'No,' he says firmly, 'not that. One thing Veronica Karen isn't is shallow.'

Sod Veronica Karen, I think but don't say.

'Anyway,' I say, 'Kilreevy's a long way. And what have you got to go on after all?'

'Nothing,' he says sulkily.

'Nothing at all.'

'Go home then,' he mumbles, dipping his bread in his soup. 'Go home or stop moaning, I'm fed up with it.'

I get up and walk out, walk down the road, get in the car and start driving. I wonder will he just go on and on for ever and ever, from town to town, village to village, like Baboushka? Is she here? Is she here? No, he's got to get back, he's got an interview on Tuesday. My face burns and an incipient lump tightens my throat. After all, what did I say? What have I done? OK then, I'll go home. I drive to the end of this quiet little ribbon of street in some quiet little place in the foothills of Scotland where nothing ever happens, pass a grim suburb, see the countryside appear and remember his things are in the car, his bag, his big coat. I slow, pull in, stop.

A black cloud glowers low above. Everything's still. I'm cold.

It takes him seven minutes to catch me up. I watch him in the rear-view mirror, his long, slightly plodding strides, the pale approach of his unreadable face with the big black insect eyes. He's put the glasses on again, though it's really not that bright any more. He comes round to the driver's window and I roll it down. His eyes are hidden but he looks sheepish, smiles sardonically. 'I'm sorry,' he says, 'I'm really sorry, Cathy.'

'It's OK,' I say without smiling, 'get in.'

He runs round and gets in.

'I brought the sandwiches,' he says.

We eat them in silence, on our way again.

Am I really moaning that much? A sense of grievance simmers in my chest. Someone needs to put the other case.

'There,' he says, pointing, 'that's the turn-off.'

The sky lowers as we turn into the road to Saskya. He laughs, looking up. 'You had me worried back there. I was thinking Christ! What am I going to do? I'd better run after her fast and apologise quick or I'm in for it. Look!'

Down comes the rain, bouncing off the road, dashing the windscreen, the wipers unable to cope. We're practically at a standstill and I can't see a thing.

'Tropical monsoon!' I cry.

It's cold. The heater's shot. Hail begins, thrillingly ricocheting off the car like a fall of bullets. Then a deluge descends like the end of the world, locking us into a stillness and a hissing of massed gorgons. The windows enclose us like wild screens, opaque, smoothed out like a stream bed. I stop the car and we look at each other.

All right for him, hiding himself away behind those glasses. His mouth smiles.

'You would have left me out in that!' he says, raising his voice above the maelstrom.

For five minutes we sit in silence, enfolded by the end of the world; till slowly, bit by bit, birdsong returns, and hedges, and the wild wet wavy grey of trees with their glittering green tops. The lane is a thin cascade. I turn the key in the ignition but the car makes a noise like someone choking to death.

Bloody damn thing, I don't believe it.

I try and try and try again. From choking, it takes to a loud elephantine trumpeting.

He's looking at me shocked, his mouth open.

'It's happened before,' I say.

'It has? The perfect car?' If I knew him better I'd clock him. 'What was wrong with it?'

Damned if I know. It was always just around town, near home. Tim always came out and stuck his head under the bonnet and mucked about a bit and sorted it out. Good old Tim.

'God knows,' I say, 'it was something, somebody probably said what, I can't remember.'

'Wow,' he says, sitting back irritatingly with folded arms, 'you're way too technical for me.'

'No really, it hasn't done this for ages.' I twist the key, but nothing.

'Well, you'll have flooded the engine now,' he says mildly. 'We'll just have to sit and wait.'

We sit in the little ticking tin box of a car and I suddenly realise how disgusting and horrible it is, how it stinks slightly of old fruit because there's a couple of apple cores rotting away somewhere, how a screwed-up tissue is sticking out of the ashtray.

'You know, I'm not a great one for I-told-you-sos,' he says, 'but if we'd brought my . . .'

'Can I try your glasses on?' I ask to shut him up.

One corner of his mouth turns up. 'My little car. My little Fiesta,' he says mournfully. 'We'd have been there.' He takes the black glasses off wordlessly and hands them to me. They don't fit. They're too big and fall down to the tip of my nose. I hand them back and he puts them on and we sit there for a bit longer saying nothing and his stomach makes gurgling noises. I try the engine again but it's no better so we get out and stand in the wet looking stupidly down into the engine. He's as bad as me, knows nothing.

'Looks hot, doesn't it?' I say.

We poke about uselessly for a bit, feed the thing water, check the oil, look about us. Over the hedge there's a brown field full of grey-bespattered fat pink pigs with long tubular dugs that quiver like jelly as they move. Peacefully, they grunt and blow. It starts to rain again.

'We should look for a rainbow,' I say, turning and scanning the stricken, schizoid sky.

I realise I haven't brought a coat with me. A toothbrush, yes, a hairbrush, my make-up, even a jacket, but not the sort of coat you could walk down a country lane in with the rain bucketing down. You know when you read these things? She just disappeared, just walked out one day, never said a word to anyone, didn't even take a coat with her . . . and she was never seen again. People vanish all the time. People just go out like candles. I shiver and we get back in the car. I try the engine one more time, then he says he'll go look for a garage, or at least see what's up ahead, and grabs his coat from the back.

'I may be some time,' he says, raising his dark eyebrows drolly as he gets out and plods away.

I sit in the car and listen to the radio while the rain runs down the windows and patters on the roof and the pigs occasionally huff in sodden content, and it grows very cold. He won't come back, I suddenly think. I'll just sit here and wait and wait and he won't come back, and I'll get home somehow and it'll all be a dream, he came like a ghost out of the rain and into the rain he went, a ghost. And one day, quite by chance I'll meet someone and they'll say: Stephen Openshaw? Didn't you know? He died in January. Six months to the day before he turned up at my door.

Idly, I try the engine. It catches first time. We're off. I slide it into second, good as gold it purrs. I laugh. The Animals come on the radio singing 'House of the Rising

Sun' and the sun appears in a dark chasm of the sky, shining through the rain. Two or three miles down the road I come upon him still trudging gamely on, head bent against the downpour.

'What did you do?' he says, getting in. He's soaked, he shivers, shaking himself like a dog and spraying the car with a fine mist of unseasonal winter.

'I just turned the key.'

'Great. I'm soaked.' It's dripping off him. He drags his coat off and wipes his face with the lining. You can tell by the frayed silk how old it is. I drive fast for me, swooping round bends, along lanes, on ahead of the rain, bowling merrily along with all the wet hedges gleaming and the sky a bright glory smudged with charcoal round the edges. Of course, it's much further than I thought but he says nothing. By the time we track down the place it's nearly two. We hug a high curving wall till gates appear, tall and ornate, behind which we see a small octagonal gatehouse, very pretty with rambling roses all over the front, those little wild blood-red ones that used to grow in Grandma's garden in Shugden. Veronica swore one bit her once. We get out and ring a bell on the gatehouse but don't get an answer.

'Some house,' says Stephen.

Some house is an understatement. The gates are not locked so we open them and drive on in, closing them carefully behind us. We park the car in a gravelled car park to the left of a long path that runs across a bridge crossing a reeded moat. Coots and Muscovy ducks glide on its silkily black lilting water or stand preening, one-footed, on its banks. Across the moat a well-kept lawn is bordered by sloping beds of rioting nasturtiums and dusty blue bell-shaped flowers. The house itself is an ancient H-shaped manor house with a long mullioned hall, steep roofs and stepped gables. There are two battlemented cross-wings with massive walls and tiny windows set high. Willie o' the Side was hung from one of those battlements, if he existed. In the middle of the lawn stands a round dovecot, but the doves are nowhere to be seen, and over the door is a huge painted sign, a mandala in reds and oranges, bright against the grey stone. It is an eminently lovable house somehow, with a quality like a person that could make you fall in love with it and want to defend it. I want it. I want to live in it alone till I die, just me and the coots and the Muscovy ducks.

We stand on the bridge, looking down at the lilypads.

'What a fantastic house,' he says. His hair is all over the place, still damp from the rain. The black insect eyes of his sunglasses shine at me. 'It looks like a film set. How old do you think it is?'

'I don't know. Fifteenth century.'

'Earlier than that. Isn't it terrible?' Mild wonder creeps into his tone. 'All the world's a film set. It must be about fourteenth. They stopped building them like this fairly early. Fourteenth, early fifteenth.'

I like the way he knows these things. Unless it's all bull-shit, of course. I wouldn't know in this case.

He walks ahead of me across the daisy-sprinkled lawn, his jeans darker from the knees down where he got wet. 'Yes,' he says excitedly, 'do you see the crow-stepped gables? Look.' We go through an arched passage, cool shadow and flat cobbles, into a courtyard. Out the back there are trees and fields. The dark lead-paned windows watch us. There should be horses and horse dung, an ostler lad, scrawny chickens, colour, lights, action! But it's silent and we see no one. Why should Veronica Karen have had a place like this to run off to? *I* never had a place like this to run off to. Kept pretty quiet about it, didn't she?

There are people in the fields. Close by is a cultivated vegetable garden where a hippified young man with long blond hair and a ragged jumper is hoeing with a dreamily absorbed air, whistling constantly up and down an unplaceable and oddly familiar little tune, slow and sad, seemingly circular and nursery simple. No one notices us. The people in the fields are too far away and the young man so peacefully and totally engrossed in his task and his whistling that it seems a shame to break in on his reverie. We decide to try the house. Back in the front courtyard a big rough-looking man in a crumpled white shirt and old black trousers is emptying a bowl of sudsy water down a drain. A stain of green weed falls down the wall and into the grimy pit, its ends moving gently like mermaid's hair or the hair of a drowned person. He looks up and sees us, stares at me fiercely for a moment then rushes towards us, comes much too close and thrusts his great eager beak of a face into mine, scaring me a little.

'Veronica Karen,' he says through a speech impediment that makes him sound as if the back of his nose is all stuffed up with cotton wool; he almost shouts her name so that it echoes, rolling back at us from the mullioned windows and high stone walls. V'whon'ca K'hown! I back off a little.

Stephen looms beside me. 'No,' he says softly, 'she's not Veronica Karen. This is Veronica Karen's sister.'

The man's mouth is loose and wet, his eyes round and unvariable. He stares and stares into my face.

We could never see it, ourselves, but other people were always claiming to: 'You're *so* alike. *So* alike. You'd know you were sisters a million miles off.'

'Is she here?' I ask him, but he gives no sign of having heard.

'Veronica Karen, is she here?'

A tall saffron-robed monk with shorn head and glasses, elegant in spite of his woolly jumper and big boots, crosses the courtyard. We follow him, and the man in the white shirt follows us, holding his blue washing-up bowl against his side like a flower-seller. We follow the monk through a green door, leaving the man outside. There's a wooden table with a visitors' book; the monk, like the White Rabbit, is disappearing head down along a dim, school-like corridor. Where are all the people? Out in the fields? Meditating somewhere? I have that tune in my brain, the one the boy outside was whistling, I know it but I don't know it. Why is the inside of this house such a shock?

Because when you're in here, the outside might as well not exist. You could be in a government building or a bank if it weren't for the distant waft of school dinners. I don't understand it. We walk along the corridor, pass a linoleumed staircase, turn a corner, come upon an alcove where a small Buddha with one naked breast sits serenely on his lotus, touching the ground. Cut flowers in bowls and vases surround him.

'He's rather beautiful, isn't he?' I say.

They're wired up too stiff, those zinnias. Mind you, zinnias are a bugger, I never get them right. You should have seen my mixed summer flowers on the polished table at the bottom of the big staircase in the Town Hall, lilies, golden-rod, larkspur, phlox. We gaze at the Buddha and his blooms for a while, then wander on, hearing laughter and voices from a room somewhere. The corridor opens out into a square space with grimy old pictures on the walls, of sailing ships and teeming quaysides and faint shadowy landscapes, all clouded trees and huge skies and little dwarfed figures. And bang in the middle of them, oddly, a small abstract, just a white dot on a black background, which I walk up to and observe for a moment. It reminds me of what I ran away from, my destiny to jump into the white dot and face that maelstrom, let it take me where it will. I am mad to be here. I must go back to the cliff on which I stood. It reminds me that all this is just illusion, me and him and beautiful medieval manor houses, all front and no soul. Everything I ever had was not mine to keep, nothing ever will be. Not even my life. Fear hits me a blow, sudden, cowardly, drenches me like ice-water down the back, skinning my teeth. My toes curl up. It's just fear, just fear, that's all, just like all the other times. Suicide is jumping to meet it as it hurtles towards you like the bottom of a bottomless well, irresistible as sleep after long labour. Oh, what a long, long labour! Here, the kind midwife said. You hold your baby. You just hold your baby for a little while, my darling.

There. His little dark head.

'I'm going out,' I say.

'What?' Stephen looks startled, turning from the sailing ship with the air of someone accosted in an art gallery.

'This house,' I say, looking round and shivering, 'I wouldn't want to share it with a load of strangers. She isn't here. I know she isn't. I feel it in my bones.'

He rolls his eyes again. 'Christ,' he says, and starts walking on.

'I'm going out,' I call after him, 'I need some fresh air, I'll wait outside. You let me know if you find her.'

He's turning back, but I don't wait, I just wave him on and go back, hurry, hurry down the corridors, oh my ears and whiskers, floating like a ghost, till I'm outside in the fourteenth century again, breathing that sweet fourteenth-century air, smoke, leaves, more rain to come, herb-rich grass. My teeth chatter. I wish I could have a certainty, just one. I never had one in my life, I suppose it's too late to start now. I never had less certainty than when death was an hour down the road. Death is always an hour down the road. Well, aren't you supposed to live your life like that? I have for years. Fat lot of good it's done me. Anyway, as I keep telling myself, all this is extra time, death's ante-room. Stop being scared and just keep on keeping on as the man said. See what happens. Curiouser and curiouser, said Alice. I breathe that fourteenth-century air deeply, drawing long breaths again and again till I'm calm and can walk out of the courtyard, cross the lovely lawn, stand on the little bridge over the moat and watch minnows hovering under the lilypads below. I whistle that tune, up and down, up and down like scales. 'Puer Nobis', sixteenth century. Our boy. I used to play it on the piano out of the *Oxford Book of Carols* a long time ago: unto us a boy is born.

A small track leads away into a copse that runs round the side of the house, so I follow it through the trees till I come to a grey wall, where a stone stile leads into a long field that borders the house and its grounds. One solitary tree, elder I think, casts shade over a wooden shed, a hen house and a long wired chicken run. I sit on the stile for a long time and sing up and down, up and down: 'Unto us a boy is born unto us a boy is born' until I am hypnotically calmed, purified, still.

I hear a footfall and start. It's the man with the white shirt and speech impediment, standing so still against the trees and watching me so unblinkingly I get a sense of the supernatural.

'Hello,' I say.

He nods. I suppose he's quite young, not much more than thirty. His wits are scrambled, you can tell at a glance. 'I thought you were Veronica Karen,' his mouth full of glue says.

'No,' I say, shaking my head, 'Veronica Karen's my little sister.' Why did I say that? I've never called her that, at least surely not since I was about six. He clambers over the wall and sits upon it about three feet away.

'She's my girlfriend,' he says. I *think* that's what he says.

I look at him. His hands are powerful and horny, dirt-engrained. She might. She just conceivably might.

'Is she?' I say carefully.

'She's my girlfriend.'

'Oh.'

He doesn't look at me now, his brown eyes slightly troubled as they scan the field this way and that. Then he says – I think he says – 'Her sister?'

'Yes, I am.'

He jumps down into the field. Knee-deep in long ragwort and cow parsley he stands, a tall heavy man, leaning slightly towards me. 'I've got something to show you,' he says.

I draw back. 'No thanks,' I say briskly, 'I've got to be going now.'

He gives a high, childlike laugh, yodelling slightly like an adolescent. The corners of his lips are frothy. '*You'll* see,' he says, 'something about Veronica Karen. *Come* on.'

'What?'

'*Come* on.'

He beckons with his head towards the single tree, the shed, the hen house.

'What?' I ask, getting up, unsure which way I'm going. 'Tell me what it is first.'

'It's Veronica Karen's!' His voice is teasing and overly familiar.

Something of Veronica Karen's? What? Some family heirloom? A suicide note? Here is your next clue. What's he got? I don't like this story. He's killed her, of course. He's a madman, simple, Quasimodo, Boo Radley, Lennie in *Of Mice and Men*, the somnambulist with the freaky eyes in *The Cabinet of Doctor Caligari*. He's killed her out of frustrated passion and buried her under the hen house, and now he's going to show me her knuckle bone or something. Or her earring.

He starts off across the field, looking back once and beckoning with his arm. I look from left to right then climb down from the stile and follow him. His old trousers, black and shiny, hang baggy round his backside and knees. At the open door of the shed he waits for me. The hens are out of their run, pecking and strutting about, sucroo sucroo like the pigeons under the eaves when we used to play in the attic of our old house in Shugden, and a proud fierce cockerel flicking his feet as he steps.

'Do you have trouble with foxes?' I ask, drawing near.

Up in the tree a fat white hen sits ignoring the world like an old lady on a bus.

He doesn't answer but goes in the shed, so I stay by the door, leaning in a little to see what there is to see. There's a table and a very old chest of drawers, painted blue. He opens a drawer and for a moment sifts something gently through his big finger ends, something like sand, no it's grain of some sort, for the chickens. Then he pulls the drawer out further and takes from the far back a yellow Kodak envelope.

Photographs.

He grins bashfully as he flips it open and hands me the first picture. Fuzzy. Veronica Karen, full face on, round-cheeked, chestnut-haired, smudgy-eyed, not really smiling but looking winsome. A look I know, one that's always annoyed me, one that says: Hey, I'm really a nice person to know, I'm so interesting and really rather special and far above you all.

I am so sick of Veronica Karen.

'She gave you this?' I ask, surprised. It's not a picture I've ever seen before.

'She's my girlfriend.' He smiles and hands me another. Oh Jesus. Her large round white boobs shoved at the camera. She's holding them aloft, offering them like a pushy fruit-seller, come on now darlin', you won't get better'n them anywhere, lovely and juicy, come on now. Her eyes are bold and wry and amused. He hands me another, and another. Veronica Karen sticking her pale round bottom in the air, black high heels and nothing else. Who's behind the camera? Frank? Some greasy slob with a paunch? She's soft and meaty and slim, she knows what she's doing and she isn't shy, not even on this one where she's sticking her fanny in your face, plucking its lips apart with her delicate fingers.

She's enjoying herself. *Loving* it.

My face is hot. I look at him, but he's leerily innocent, a sniggering little boy.

'She gave you these?' I say.

'Yes.' He nods proudly.

'Are you sure?'

He rocks about on one foot, his brawny arms folded round one another hungrily, smiling his loose-lipped smile, never quite dislodging the spots of dribble at the corners of his mouth. I look at him and think: Veronica Karen, how could you? How could you do it? I sheaf the photographs, hand them back. 'Have you shown these to anyone else?' I ask him.

'No-o!' He laughs and rocks about. 'No-o! Get into trouble!' And he laughs and laughs, eyes flashing, putting the pictures back into the Kodak envelope and stashing them at the back of the drawer again. Someone's coming. Stephen, plodding across the field with a disgruntled look on his face. I wake up and see him as a stranger.

'There you are,' he says. 'I've been looking for you.'

'He was showing me the hens,' I say, stepping outside. The man in the white shirt comes too, and the three of us stand there looking down at the birds clucking and pecking and scratching under the tree. From the house a gong-like sound reverberates.

'What's that?' asks Stephen. 'Tea?'

This makes the man laugh in a high, cracked, undisciplined way. We leave him closing the shed and shaking the tree to get the fat white fowl down.

9

She's not here, of course.

The last time was about five years ago, but she moved on by mutual consent because, according to a woman he's been talking to, she kept smoking and drinking on the sly. We stand on the bridge with the house behind us like a watching face.

'I knew she wouldn't be here,' he says. He's just aching to say I told you so, but that's the nearest he'll come to it.

'Ha!' I laugh without humour, 'I knew she couldn't stay straight for long. Amazing she lasted even a couple of days in a place like this.'

'You know what she's like,' he says, strained and tired as he looks at me; 'she was just behaving normally for her,' and then he turns and walks off abruptly, but not to the car; instead he crosses the lawn and disappears through an open door in the high outer wall. After a moment I follow. The door leads on to a rough sloping river bank, with trees overhanging the stream which flows out of Saskya and on down the shallow rocky gorge. He's walking quickly along the bank of the stream with his head down, looking at his feet; coming to a place where it widens into a large deep pool fed by fat waterfalls, he stops, sits down on a rock and stares out at the water.

Oh, a moody one. Was it something I said? My tone of voice, perhaps? Must be wet, sitting on that rock, and the grass is wet, he'll be soaked. I'll give him a few minutes. I lean against the wall, contemplating the house. Two doves have come down to peck at the lawn. Madness, Veronica Karen thinking she could be a Buddhist. I bet she didn't know anything about it really, I bet it was just the trappings, the idea of it. She could never go straight. Lettie came over from Ireland once; she told me Veronica Karen had been at her place for a while and ran out of dope and spent the whole time grazing like a cow on the side of the mountain, looking for magic mushrooms. She said they used to watch her from the back window, working her way meticulously down the mountain, covering every inch. She couldn't be straight to save her life. I keep seeing those pictures, Veronica Karen all shameless like that. Artistic photographs indeed! I wonder if she did it for money? Shall I tell him? Shall I?

No.

I give him ten minutes then pick my way down through the long grass, wetting my legs to the knees. I stop not too near. The place is lovely, full of the bashfully hanging orange of montbretias. He looks up, a strange, clear-eyed appraising look, cool but not unfriendly.

'You must be so wet,' I say.

'Doesn't matter.' He looks away. 'I was wet anyway, a bit more can't make any difference.'

We have to lift our voices above the bubbling of the pool. He says something I don't catch and I cup my ear.

'She talked about this river,' he calls across the roar of water. 'Whenever she came here she used to bring a big bag of dope, enough to last the whole time, and she'd go out and smoke it in the fields or by the river. She told me.' He leans closer, speaking in little dry disgusted bursts. 'Five years ago. It must have been just after she found out she was positive. She must have come up here for a rest. Come to terms with it. She must have been going crazy. No one knew. Even I didn't know then. She had it all to herself.' His face darkens into anger. 'I mean, what gets me about all these places, they're not really for ordinary people. You have to be so fucking perfect, for Christ's sake.'

Suddenly I get a vision of Veronica Karen sitting there in the lobby, smoking her cigarette in that smokeless zone, proud, staring them all out. She has smudged mascara to prove that she's a suffering beauty, nothing too gross, just enough to prove the depth of her emotion, the depth of her soul. I may not be pure, her eyes say, I may not have what you've got but God, aren't I interesting? Aren't I far more interesting than you lot? *Rule*-abiders. Ha, I laugh at rules! The Princess Verona laughs at rules! The Princess Verona brings offerings to the Poojah on his throne, white Ambrose stretched along the windowsill in the attic. Where I saw the shadow of a man in a top hat, I did, I know I did. Well, who do you think you are, Veronica Karen? You may have been the Princess Verona but who made the games? *I, I* made the games. I was all of them, the Princess Verona, the Poojah, Tabitha, Annabel, Little Girl Green, Mamie and Rowena and Lorna Lamorna and Giant Killyloo and Jem the Gypsy Boy and evil Dame Doolily too. If you hadn't had me, Veronica, what would *you* have done, with no one to spin worlds like plates for you?

'When in Rome,' I say lightly. 'If you want to stay in a place like this you just have to take all of that on board. But you know Veronica Karen. Always has to be special. What are they supposed to do, make a special case for her? Oh sure, Veronica Karen, go ahead, go out and get pissed every night. Pick up a few fellas, why don't you? Bring them back here, why not? We could have a party. Don't forget the dope. Drape a few streamers round the Buddha. Use his hand as an ashtray. Why not?'

He jumps to his feet and stands in front of me. 'I can't believe you!' he shouts. 'You know, the trouble with you, you've just got this big down on her because she's not like you. The pair of you, you drive me up the wall. Why are you so nasty? You're sisters, for Christ's sake. Why are you so hard on each other? Why are you so hard on *her*? She never had what you had. You were the one that had it all. You were the one she couldn't live up to.'

The unfairness of it infuriates me. 'Me!' I cry. 'Me! Hard on *her*? Me the one that had it all? What did *I* have? What the hell did I have?'

'I'll tell you,' he says, bringing his pale bony face close to mine. 'You had the talent. You had the career. You had the success. You had the relationship that lasted. You had the –' He was going to say the kid, but he breaks off, stepping back and blinking rapidly at his awful blunder, mutters something and stomps away.

The rain's coming again, you can smell it, you can see it in the way the grasses stand to attention and all the leaves quiver. I lean against the car looking at the beautiful house which will never be mine. A lovely soothing thing, it looks back. What did she think, coming here? That something would be revealed, some strength bestowed to deal with the sword hanging over her head? Walking across the lawn goes the hippified young man who whistled in the garden. He's still whistling, still the strange slow familiar little nursery tune, 'Puer Nobis'. He has a strange white little face and hair of spun gold, like a fairy princess, and his jumper hangs limp round his knees, a long ragged knitted affair of many colours, carried elegantly like a lady's train.

'You should paint it one day, Cathy,' Stephen says tonelessly, looking at the house. 'You could do a really good job.'

The air grows stiff.

'I'm cold,' he says, getting into the passenger seat, huddled up in that little space. I get in. 'I'm freezing,' he continues, 'I need to dry out in front of a good warm fire. I need a cup of tea. *And* I'm hungry. We must be completely stark staring raving mad to have come all this way.'

The car noses out into the lane.

'I've probably caught something,' he murmurs.

I drive fast on the lanes. My little car is rattling. I suppose we're going to Kilreevy, I suppose we have to now we've come this far. This is no fun. I can't speak, I feel awful, I just look stonily ahead. I'd go home if I could. I change down angrily as a tractor turns out of a field in front of us, and we crawl fumingly along behind it for mile after mile. Occasionally he sighs. You know, this is nothing to me, I'm not supposed to be involved in all this stuff any more, all this suffering stuff. I have to keep out of it. One more punch and I'm down. I'm not even supposed to be here.

'Let's find a pub,' I say placatingly, 'let's just sit down for a bit and you can dry off and –'

'Pub!' he says, as if I've suggested just dropping into a casino. 'Out here? There won't be a pub for miles and miles and miles.'

Sod you, then. Only trying to be friendly.

At last we pass the tractor. My car perks up, probably the novelty of passing something, and purrs along enthusiastically till it brings us to more populated parts. The rolling green countryside is punctuated by small towns, vague standard places of housing estate ambience that erupt like brown blebs here and there. I can't imagine what people do here all day. We get out at one such place and walk, his thin body shivering. We find a bar that's open in a hotel, but they don't do food yet apart from crisps and nuts, so we only stay for one drink, long enough for him to dry off and warm up a bit. We're the only people in there apart from the barman and a sulky girl reading a magazine, and the silence is so profound that the sound of our crisp packets opening is like an explosion.

We find ourselves whispering, heads together.

'We're going to have to think about tonight,' he says, looking me in the eye for the first time in ages. 'What are we going to do?'

He keeps asking me these things, as if I should know, as if this wasn't all his idea in the first place.

'First let's eat.'

'I mean,' he says, 'do you want to try and get straight back tonight? After Kilreevy, I mean. Or shall we just pull in somewhere and sleep in the car for a bit? What do you want to do?'

He doesn't meet my eyes.

'We can play it by ear,' I say, 'just keep going till we feel like stopping. Go back to Russell and Patti's. I don't know.'

He smiles quickly. 'How anyone could possibly sleep in that tin pot anyway, I don't know,' he says and pats his pocket. 'I'm out of fags. Got any change?'

I push my bag towards him, yawn. 'Have a look in my purse.'

He tilts the bag. Out falls my purse upside down with its beak gaping and all its insides sliding smoothly out as if it's disgorging its dinner all over the table. There's my loose change and a million cash machine receipts and my library card and video card and cash card and the picture of Johnny. Stephen picks up Johnny and looks at his dark spiky hair, the two small fingers poking out of the white blanket, the soft, ancient troll face with its tiny lip sucked in, its brow raised in perpetual perplexity. Stephen's face is pale under the darkness of his hair and eyebrows. A heavy worried look comes over his cheeks.

'Your baby,' he says simply.

The great pain comes again, like an iceberg to wreck me. I have not felt it for so long, I have not felt a thing, and now it comes, an eyeful of acid and a punch in the throat.

He looks at me.

'Sometimes I wonder what he would have been like,' I say. I'm OK, I'm OK. Please, stand back, don't crowd.

Don't look at me as if I'm a freak.

He puts everything back in my purse all wrong, scoops up change and goes over to the cigarette machine.

Outside the air teems with invisible rain. He stops as we walk to the car. 'Come here,' he says, though I'm there, right there, and puts his arms round me and yanks me against his chest and holds me there for a long time, his heart beating under my ear.

When he lets me go we don't speak.

We find a Co-Op and buy pre-packed sandwiches and blueberry buns and eat them in the car, then drive on towards where the sun is already beginning to think about setting somewhere behind the bushy dove-grey clouds. The towns get bigger as we draw nearer to the coast. Kilreevy, when we reach it, proves to be a fair-sized bleb, a place of very little character clustered round an old market cross and old stocks that stand on a small cobbled hump in the town centre. There are two banks, a Tesco, a Save the Children shop and a Superdrug. We park and walk back to the cross where there is a town map with a You Are Here arrow. Seagulls sit in disgruntled muttering rows all along the spines of the rooftops.

Stephen reaches into his pocket and takes out a scrap of paper and reads out: '25 Tobin Close, Kilreevy.'

It's not on the map. We cross the road and hang around outside the banks; he shows a man the address and asks the way. In between the banks there is an empty shop with whited-out windows and the remnants of a couple of stickers for local pub events. A pavement artist has been at work on the flagstones in front, though the flags are still dark at the edges with the rain of three hours ago. The artist has chalked a mandala in orange and brown and red, and a fair copy of Van Gogh's *Sunflowers*, and a white-blue bird that may be a crane or a heron, spreading its wings and stretching its legs as if about to take off.

'Tobin Close. You've got to go back over the hill a way,' the man is saying.

A mandala in the sand. Tonight when it rains it will all be washed away.

Tobin Close is a street of grey semis in the middle of a lot of other streets of grey semis. Number 25 is standard, with a green wrought-iron gate, a tiny patch of bald lawn and a couple of borders with snapdragons and weeds. In the window stands a wicker basket of artificial flowers and a small pottery ornament of what looks like a leprechaun reading a newspaper. This place has nothing of Veronica Karen, not the slightest feel of her at all. Obviously a mistake. Stephen's face admits it.

Teatime's an awful time to go knocking on someone's door. Furtively, we steal up the path, closing the gate with exaggerated care.

'Go on,' he says, nodding at the door.

'No, you.'

He moves his mouth ruefully and rings the bell, which launches into a jaunty chimed version of 'The Skaters' Waltz', distant and interior. We look at each other and smile in sudden foolish truce. Nothing happens immediately and he's about to ring again when there is a soft sound of movement inside, and then a fat man answers the door. A startled look, almost of fear, appears in his eyes when he looks at me.

'Hello,' I say, 'we're sorry to disturb you but . . .'

'Alexander,' says Stephen.

The fat man has a bald pink head with a rundown

melted kind of look and a few bits of straggly colourless
hair growing out of it here and there. The quick look of
fear is gone; only a blank friendliness remains. 'Hello,
Cathy,' he says. 'Long time no see.' His voice is small and
breathless.

I open my mouth but nothing comes out.

'Come in, you two,' he says, stepping back from the
door. 'Come on in, you folks, and sit down,' and we step in
and follow his fat buttocks, gracelessly swathed in a low
droop of dirty grey flannelly material, as he bobs lopsidedly
before us down the hall. An acute limp jerks his whole
body with every step. We go into a small neat sitting room
with a mustard-coloured three-piece suite and bright crocheted covers on the small round cushions. It smells
comfortably of tea and smoke, and a cat's bowl with milk
sits under the TV. 'Go on,' he says, sinking into an armchair, 'sit down.'

Stephen and I perch side by side on the settee as if we've
come for an interview.

'Alexander,' says Stephen, actually sounding pleased, 'we
didn't think we'd find *you* here.'

'Didn't? Why not? I live here.'

We laugh stupidly.

It's not him. It's not. This is a nightmare. His podgy
white hand, broad-sided, fans wide on the arm of the chair.
Not Alexander. A portly layered neck, a swollen nose, fat
bags hanging under his eyes. His bare white feet are flat and
wide. He looks pregnant.

'So,' he says, not smiling, 'to what do I owe this terribly unusual occurrence?'

Normal as anything, Stephen says: 'Sorry about all this, Alexander, bit of an intrusion. We were just wondering if you had any idea where we might find Veronica Karen, she's gone AWOL again.'

Her name causes not a flicker.

And then I remember something about him having a Scottish grandmother. Yes, she used to sing 'Peggy Gordon', that's where he got it from, he said, although it might have been a lie, he could just as easily have got it out of a book. A kind of paralysis comes over me. It isn't him, he doesn't even look familiar. For a moment I think that this is all some elaborate plot to drive me out of my mind, got up for some peculiar reason by Stephen and this stranger, who gives a little laugh and says, 'I might have known it was something to do with her. Trouble, eh? No, no, I don't know where Veronica Karen is. I don't *wanna* know, my man. I haven't seen her for a hundred years and that's fine by me.'

The front door opens and someone comes in from outside and stands for a while puffing and blowing, taking things off in the hall, then a little spiky brown woman with tightly curled hair and a sad face comes into the room. She looks sharply and suspiciously from me to Stephen and back again, then at Alexander for an explanation.

'Some friends of mine, Mum,' he says. 'This is Stephen, you remember Stephen, I was at school with Stephen, Stephen Openshaw.'

167

She peers at me and the look in her eyes is pure hate. I never met the woman. I never knew anything about his parents, never even thought of them. He said he hated his father once, but that was about it.

'It's not her, Ma,' he says. 'This one's Cathy.'

She nods. 'We'll be having tea in half an hour,' she tells him in an anxious, hectoring way and goes out, obviously perturbed.

He starts to roll a cigarette. 'I didn't know you had my address,' he says, pulling apart the strings of tobacco.

'Veronica Karen gave it to someone,' Stephen says. 'Bobbie. Remember Bobbie? She told Bobbie she could be reached here.'

Alexander's mouth is a sour line. Perhaps it was always on the thin side but who could have foretold this dearth, this flabby crack? He looks seriously at the cigarette paper for a moment or two before licking it with a pale tongue. 'She's not coming in here,' he says indifferently. 'She just isn't getting in, that's all. She shouldn't even have this address. My mum's address. I don't want her coming up here upsetting my mum. What's she wanna come up here for? She don't let go of anything, do she? Did you know my mum moved back up here, Cathy?'

'No.'

'Moved back in 1975.'

'Ah.'

He smiles at me. There is a flicker of the old kindness in his eyes.

'So are you living up here permanently now, then?' asks Stephen.

'Yeah. Does me OK. Do you want a cup of tea? I'll get her to make a cup of tea. Mum!'

'It's all right,' we both say, but he goes on shouting: 'Mum! Mum! Put the kettle on, Mum! I mean, it's OK.' He smokes reflectively. A heavy placidity, it seems, has settled on his soul, though his raised hand trembles slightly. 'I'm on the sick. It's not bad, you know.'

Clinkings and clankings come from the kitchen. A small black and white cat walks into the room, stretching its back legs. His mother mumbles briefly but formidably outside the door and the sense of nightmare deepens.

'She's all right,' says Alexander. 'She's just not very keen on visitors, but she's all right.'

I gaze upon the corpse of my lover. For Balder the Beautiful is dead, is dead, the beauty of Israel is slain upon the high places and the mighty are fallen. Lost and gone for ever. And I call up, like an image from the underworld, the shade of a slim boy in brown leather jacket and jeans, soft eyes, thick fair hair, turning on the bus to smile at me. Now, in his remembered young face, I see the seed of this.

Tea is made. His mother calls him peremptorily: 'Alexander! Alexander now!' and he gets up and lurches out. I don't look at Stephen.

'Who would have thought,' he says in a tone of wonder. I can't speak.

Alexander brings in two mugs of weak milky tea,

holding them totally steady against his limp, and is about to go back for the third when Stephen gets to his feet quickly. He looks very tall and thin next to Alexander. 'Look, no tea for me, Alexander,' he says, 'I've got to go and sort the car out. Have you got the keys, Cathy?'

'No sweat, my man,' says Alexander.

'The car?' I croak.

'The car.' He looks guilty. 'Have you got the keys? I've got to move it, the parking place will have run out. Yes, it will. Have you got the keys?'

Mad, I hand them over.

'I can find a better one, bring it up here a bit. I've got to sort it out. It needs a . . .'

He's abandoning me, that's what he's doing. I stand up.

'No, you stay, you stay.' He's firm. 'You have a cup of tea with Alexander and I'll go and sort the car out and then I'll come back for you. OK? I won't be long. Promise.' He's out in the hall, he's going, he's practically running, there's nothing I can do. Because I can't walk out of here. I have to try and understand what has happened to Alexander. I hear the front door close, the creak of the wrought-iron gate, the sound of Stephen's footsteps growing fainter down the road. Alexander draws on his fag and looks at me very thoroughly and frankly all over and I grow cold. I'd scream if he touched me now. I couldn't stand it.

'So how's things now, Cathy?' he says, looking away. Everything he says sounds the same, as if it doesn't matter.

'Not so bad, Alexander,' I say brightly, 'really not so bad

at all. But you. How are you? It's been such a long time, I can hardly believe how much we've both changed. Are you all right?'

'I am,' he says solidly, 'I'm fine now. I went through some funny times, you know, but it's all over now. I'm OK here.'

'Oh good! I'm glad everything's OK for you, Alexander!'

I can't think of a damn thing more to say. He had a terrible time. He was in an institution for two years.

His mother comes in, frowns meaningfully in my direction, picks up a magazine from a pile on the sideboard and goes out again.

''S all right,' he says after a little awkward silence. 'Don't take no notice of the old woman. It's not you, it's who you remind her of. Know who I mean?'

'I can guess.'

'As you may imagine,' he says, his reedy voice catching as if on a skein of mucus in his throat, 'there's not much love lost there.'

I sip the tea. It's revolting, just how I hate it, lukewarm milk-water with a faint hint of sweetness.

'So what's it all about? All this, then? You and him turning up? What's it all about?'

His voice is all wrong. Not just the reedy phlegmy quality but even the accent. Alexander was a northern lad.

'It's about Veronica Karen,' I say. 'We don't know where she is and we're trying to find her. She gave Bobbie this address. That's all.'

I try looking in his eyes, looking desperately for some trace element. I find only the mild, cold, buried eyes of a stranger, which shift away slowly as he reaches once more for his tobacco. 'You ain't changed, Cathy,' he says. 'Ain't changed a bit. How d'you do it? Drunk of the well of eternal youth, have you?'

'Your voice is different,' I say.

'Ain't the only thing.' He reaches down to scratch the side of a curious yellow ankle bone. His flat feet hug the floor like dropped dough.

'You sound like a southerner.'

'Yeah. Was down there too long after I served my time.' He makes it sound like prison but it wasn't. Alexander was sectioned. 'Horrid place, London. Wouldn't go back. Wouldn't go back if you paid me. Where you living now?'

'Moorcop.'

'Is it nice?' He licks the paper, the same close-eyed attention, the same absorption.

'Very.'

He lights his roll-up. 'What you wanna see Veronica Karen for? Bad news. I'd leave her alone if I were you. Steer round. Makes a mess wherever she goes.'

I sigh. 'I think,' I say, 'she may be very ill.'

He shakes a match, then smokes, looking at the tip of his roll-up closely as if it's conversing with him. 'Oh yeah?'

'Well, I think so, Alexander. I don't really know. Anyway,' I shrug.

I wonder if anything I could say would ever get a

reaction out of him. Why should it? What we were, what all of us were is once upon a time, under the bridge, over the rainbow, east of the sun and west of the moon. We're dust. I should go. He turns his head to the side, blowing out a thin string of smoke, and I stare, fascinated by the folds of skin under his eyes.

'Very ill, is she?'

'I think she may be.'

'Comes to us all,' he says. He's starting to remind me of Charles Laughton in *Henry VIII* and I can't stand it. I long for the chimes of 'The Skaters' Waltz'. Suppose you'd married him when he was lovely and this happened? But maybe if you'd stayed with him it wouldn't have. Where would this one be then, this poor one here? Somewhere in one of the infinite alternative universes. I can't stand it. Oh where is Stephen? I'll kill him for leaving me here like this. He's run away with my car. What shall I do? How will I get away from this awful place? What if Alexander's mad? What if he really is completely barking mad and he's living here with his mad mother: *Psycho* in a little grey council house. He's mad, a strangler, Veronica Karen had marks all over her neck for ages.

'Well, I'm sorry, love,' he says, scratching his head, 'I couldn't give two shits about Veronica Karen. I've got to have my tea in a minute.' He cranes his head towards the door.

'Oh yes! I must go!'

I'll wait outside. I'll go and stand at the corner of the street.

'She was dirty, Veronica Karen,' Alexander says, crossing his fat thighs and looking at me blankly. 'If she hadn't have been so dirty, none of it would have happened.' You get fed up with it.'

'Well, it's all in the past now, Alexander,' I say cheerfully, standing up. 'Water under the bridge. I'm sorry we disturbed you. It's really been good to see you again.'

'Yeah, yeah,' he says, with a moist throaty cough.

'I'll be getting along then. Thanks for the tea.'

'Whatever,' he waves his cigarette, 'you just do whatever. Feel free.'

Out in the dark narrow hall I see his bad-tempered mother carrying a steaming pot across the kitchen. He comes after me. 'What about Stephen?' he asks.

'Oh, it's all right,' I say confidently, 'I know where he's gone.'

Breathing too close at my shoulder, he walks me to the door. 'No well there's a lot of little streets round here, you know, you can get lost.' His limp jerks him against me. I smell sweat and an old stale shirt. Something's cooking, sizzling comfortably in the kitchen. Opening the door I see evening settling over these little grey streets, look up and down but the car is nowhere to be seen.

'She'd do anything for money, your sister,' he says, rubbing one eye ruminatively. 'She had these dirty pictures taken. That's why all that rubbish happened.'

On the step I turn and look at him. He puts his arms straight down by his sides and draws himself up as straight as he can with his crooked legs, pulling back a little into the shadows. His voice is serious and low, in his eyes at last a trace of something, some vague unfocused discontent. 'She tried to tell me I'd imagined them, but I didn't, you know.'

I move out on to the path.

'No,' I say, 'I'm sure you didn't.'

'So don't tell me,' he says, his voice rising a little, 'just don't tell me anything about Veronica Karen. OK? I just don't want to know.'

Hallelujah! He broke through. Everyone always forgave Veronica Karen. But he's not forgiving any more.

I look up and down the street. 'Do you still paint?' I ask.

'I do, as it happens, a little bit. Do a bit of drawing on the pavement now and again.' For a second, belatedly, he is almost affable. 'I done some today, as it happens. Can't be doing with all the mess of the paint though. Not in my mum's house. She's all right, like. I'd ask you to stay to tea but, you know, she's not very keen on visitors.'

10

I stand at the corner of the street with my hands stuck up my sleeves, watching a rogue lamp flicker on and off. I'm standing on a perfectly square modern grey flagstone, but I am falling off the edge of the world into a waking sleep.

'Oh Peggy Gordon, you are my darling.'

The voice that sang sounds in my head, an elegy to itself. If I had known then what I know now. I cried a lot in the past but I'm not to cry any more. I made my mind up and mostly I've kept it together. Yes, I'm still intact. I smell brine, just a tang, an intoxicating dash. The sea isn't far. This'll be one of those little places whose lights you see on shore from the sea at night and feel comforted, imagining the happy townspeople behind their safe curtains before their warm hearths. Oh, happy dream! And those lights will hide whatever is left of Alexander, *my* Alexander, my sweet youth.

I see my car, my sweet chariot, swinging low to me at last.

Stephen studies me as I get in. He looks very plain and tired, the curve of his cheek and chin somehow vulnerable. 'You came out,' he says.

'Why did you leave me there on my own?'

His eyes are sad. The engine idles. 'I thought you'd want to have a talk with him without me around,' he says, checking the mirror.

I turn to the window, leaning back in the seat and drawing up my knees, closing my eyes. I can't stand being in the passenger seat but I couldn't drive. Not now. I want sleep. I want oblivion.

'After all, he is your old flame,' he says.

A huge gulf yawns between us. The length of him and the smallness of the car, he gives the impression of a big boy trying to ride his little brother's trike. 'Light a fag for me, Cathy,' he says.

I reach for the dashboard, light him a fag and hand it to him. Gangster's moll.

He drives without a word, smooth and swift, till I feel that we are out of the town and open my eyes and see fields going past, very fast, and feel the old, old fear of obliteration and laugh within at my fickleness to death. But please, not like this, not smashed to pieces in a car. My old flame. My old flame. His body is the beast, the toad imprisoning the prince. Who now would love him enough to give him a kiss and set him free? He's so far lost in there, so far down there's not a glimmer in the eyes, not an echo of the boy with wide shoulders and narrow hips. Well, he always stood upon his dignity too much. I imagine a princess's kiss upon that pink head: I see the flesh rolling off like wax, the hair springing fresh from his scalp, growing like time-lapsed flowers; I see the eyes growing soft again, full of shame and anger and gentleness.

This is not the way we came. We reach the motorway far sooner than I anticipated, and, wordless still, rattle along southwards in a steady way. There's a feeling of haste and ending and regret. I'll go back to my life now. One day I suppose I'll hear what became of Veronica Karen. It grows dark. Somewhere along the endless manic motorway, something makes me look at him, carefully so that he cannot tell, and I realise that he is crying silently and unobtrusively, wiping his eye with the tips of his fingers from time to time as he peers ahead with a short-sighted look into the darkness and the changing lights.

From outside in the mild, moist evening air, the bar had looked old and picturesque, but inside it's dark and jumping with lights and the jukebox plays loud zappy music. Down the far end there's a stage with microphones and speakers but nobody on it. An old man with a pitted red face roars to us above the noise, 'What's it to be, son?'

Stephen looks at me.

'Just a Scotch,' I say.

I look around. It's Saturday night and the pub is crowded

with lots of very young, bright people with scrubbed faces and undisciplined laughs, but there's a little table wedged in by the side of a fruit machine. I grab it while he gets the drinks in. I'm still half asleep. When I woke in the car the lights blinded me.

'What is this place?' I asked.

Steady, hunched in shadow as he drove, 'Carlisle,' he said.

We'll go no further tonight. We're tired. They have rooms upstairs, he's sorting something out, putting it on his credit card. You can get food at the bar. It was his suggestion. We haven't mentioned sleeping arrangements, it's all been very nonchalant but I'm thinking, will we sleep together? Of course we will. I look for him but he's melted into the crowd. Then I see him at the bar, the ordinariness of the back of his head, the hair a bit greasy, just a bloke in the pub till he turns and my guts twist and yes, I think, I want to, I want to, I will. Don't even think about it. But something in me, some pathetic little voice says sadly, oh yes, after all, it's just a fuck, that's the way things are. It's what people do in these situations. Well, I don't just want a fuck.

He comes back to me bearing the menu. 'I've booked a room,' he says, not looking at me, getting out his cigarettes. 'It's got two single beds.'

So? So?

The whisky goes down like a flame. We sit close sharing the menu, and it begins, a little ticking clock inside, a peculiar force field enclosing us.

'Hey, it's quite posh food,' he says.

Quite posh prices too.

'My stomach feels weird,' he says, 'it's all these little bits and pieces we're having and no solid food. Do you think I'm getting old, Cathy?'

'Probably.'

'There was a time when I could get by for days just kind of skimming. Can't do it now. What are you having?'

The broccoli quiche is the cheapest but I fancy the chicken. I wonder if he's a vegetarian. It was all vegetarian stuff last night at Russell and Patti's, so he might be, I wouldn't know. 'Broccoli quiche,' I say. 'I'm getting old too then. I'm ravenous.'

'Well, *I'm* going to have the chicken.'

'Oh, go on then, get me the chicken too.' I slap the menu shut and lean back.

Dear God, here we go, it's happening, I don't know why now suddenly but it's happening. He goes to the bar to order. I am all alert, like a dog with a rabbit, the music goes thunk thunka thunka badoom doom doom in my head, vibrating in my chest as the whisky burns down. When he comes back with more to drink he gives me a little shake. 'Wake up,' he says.

Oh, but I am awake. I am very very awake.

He takes a drink and says, 'Everything's changed now.'

'What has?'

'Everything.' He turns his head and smiles quickly,

nervous. 'Everything, just everything. Don't you think? Like the weather's changed.'

We watch the lights flashing. One of us will reach out and touch the other, hand on hand, something. Follow the wires, the invisible wires. But he doesn't, so it must be me, I suppose, me. When I do, that'll be it. One step, tiny thing. There were all these sea caves once, somewhere on the Welsh coast where I'd gone with friends, and I wandered off alone and stood in the mouth of one high above the waves, miles down to the viscid grey heave of the sea and the rocks, and put out one foot over the abyss; the day was mild and lovely and the air pure and there was nothing wrong in my life. One more step, I thought, one small and giant step. But I didn't. And I don't, though inside I tremble. The food comes and we fall upon it. When finally we talk, it is of Alexander.

'Poor bastard,' he says, shaking his head and looking genuinely pained.

'I couldn't believe how he'd changed,' I blurt. 'Well, we all have, we all have –'

'I feel bad about Alexander.' He forks his food. 'I used to hate his stupid goody-goody fucked-up image. I remember when we were about twelve he fell down and had a fit right in the doorway just as we were all going into the hall for assembly, and everyone crowded round and the teacher was yelling, "Keep back! Keep back! Let him breathe!" And then this teacher, Mr Anstruther, stuck his finger in his mouth to stop him from choking to death on his own tongue and he nearly got his finger bitten off. I can still see Alexander's body lying there twitching.' He chews, gazing off into the distance, swallows.

I don't want to hear about Alexander. Inside I am trembling.

'He was really slim then,' Stephen says.

You'd think Alexander was dead the way he talks, a ghost, a tall boy walking on before us through the fog as we come back from Daisy Nook, turning to look back over his shoulder and smile his slightly bashful smile. Dear, long-dead, remembered. I don't want to think about him now. Not now. Here is flesh, alive, flawed, subject to wear and tear. A long brownish hand, succulent meat. I have not tasted for so long.

Stephen stops eating and leans towards me with a troubled look on his face. 'You know what I thought?' he says. 'This is awful. You know what my first thought was when I saw him? When I saw how awful he looked, how gross, how old? I was glad. I wanted to laugh. Hee hee, blue-eyed boy bites, the dust!' I can see by his face that he is appalled at himself. 'I was shouting hallelujah, Cathy. I thought I can only benefit from this. I can only look good by comparison to him now.'

The music beats our brains in the pause.

'Were you so jealous of him then?' I ask.

'Yes,' he says and a curious, embarrassed smile creeps over his face.

I shake my head. 'Poor Alexander!' I say softly. 'He didn't

deserve this,' then louder: 'You don't hate him now, do you?'

'I don't hate anyone,' he says, looking down.

Inevitable. Fated. I don't know what I believe, but I do know some things are fated. For good or ill, he's there in the pattern. He kissed me, didn't he? He kissed me last night, I did not imagine it. He kissed me twenty years ago on New Year's Eve at Davy Boland's party, and he kissed me last night.

'We've all changed,' I say.

'Even you, even you've changed,' says Stephen, a nervous gabble, 'and you've changed less than any of us.'

'Have I?'

'Oh yes. Look at you. Incredible really when you think –' but he stops and gulps his beer. We push the plates aside. 'Do you forgive me?' he asks.

'What for?'

He gestures at everything. 'For all this. For dragging you off on this wild-goose chase. Do you wish I'd never turned up?'

'Oh no,' I say, 'I don't wish that. I would always have wanted to see you, Stephen.'

We look at one another and start to laugh for no reason, then just look. He leans close. 'You were terrible, you sisters,' he says. 'You drove me mad.' Our eyes are merry, locked, outrageous. 'I seem to have spent half my life worrying about one or the other of you.'

'Not about me, you didn't.' I smile, turning, emptying my glass.

But he takes my chin and turns me back hard, and now his eyes are serious. 'When I heard about your accident,' he says, 'I kept thinking about you. I hadn't seen you for years and years and then I heard about this terrible thing happening and I couldn't stop thinking about you. I'd be in the pub or going to work or something and I'd think about you, I'd think she must be suffering, right now, this very moment while I'm walking down this road going to work. And there was nothing I could do.' Something like a plea comes into his eyes. He puts out his hand, at last, places the tips of his fingers very lightly on the side of my throat. Some vein there, some vital thread is charged.

'The worst has got to be over, Cathy,' he says.

Now. Now.

The pub is packed to the seams. Broad-bellied young drinking men and girls in Lycra swamp our table, like waves about to burst over a dam. A big black bum squashes over the rounded rim of wood, people put their pints down, crowding ours.

The terror of the fall is upon me.

'Get me a drink,' I blurt, 'please.' My throat's sore from the smoke and having to raise my voice to be heard.

He sighs, withdraws.

'Same again?' he says.

Yes. Better stick to one thing, Scotch, nice soothing drink. Nightcap. He gets up with difficulty and squeezes a way through the crowd to the bar, keeping his shoulders high. I whip open my bag and steal a look at myself in the little mirror I carry around in there. My eyes look very big and black and mad. There are lines under them. Jesus. The women in here, look at them, all dolled up for a night out, glittery dresses and eyes, faces with that awful painted peach look, little black straps on bare shoulders. And me. I look down at my jeans. I want to dress up for him in my subtle way, show him how I can be, show him he could do a lot worse than me. Hell of a lot. Seven years. Seven is a magic number. I fluff up my hair. It's beginning to feel the need of a wash. Well, I'm OK, good as new when the light's right, and anyway he's no great shakes himself, not in the grand scheme of things. Seven years! Might as well be the first time. Might as well be shaking out my wet wings, stepping out from the pupa or is it chrysalis, stretching out my long legs, flexing my antennae. I'm OK. Anyway anyway anyway, he'll be gone tomorrow and this is nothing but an adventure, a strange and rather sad passing thing, something we encountered on a journey that was nothing to do with us and all to do with Veronica Karen.

Just a fuck.

How strange. I had almost forgotten about her, but of course she's been here all the time, sitting between us at this table, laughing and smoothing her hair and being the life and soul as the drink kicks in. I wonder how many times he did it with her and when it was over with them, and the first thing I say when he emerges from the crowd, subsiding back into his seat like a man staggering back into base camp, is:

'What about Veronica Karen?'

'What about her?' he says too quickly, sliding my drink over. He drinks and wipes his mouth. 'What can we do now? Maybe I'll give her flat another ring tomorrow, see if she's turned up yet.'

'Perhaps we ought to inform Missing Persons?'

'Missing Persons?' He looks surprised.

'It's probably easy. They've probably got a list of people with AIDS or something.'

'You can't just go and report someone like Veronica Karen as a missing person, she'd go mad.' Someone pushes in on the bench next to him and he moves closer to me, putting his lips close to my ear so that I feel his breath on the side of my face. 'You know you've got it wrong about me and Veronica Karen,' he says urgently. 'I don't go around mooning about her, desperately hanging on to some long-dead candle. It isn't like that. It hasn't been like that for years. It was once, yes, but that was a long time ago.'

He's pushed closer.

'A long time ago,' he repeats with a nervous air, having to raise his voice once more.

Everyone's drunk. Impossible to speak any more with the noise.

'Let's go up,' he says in my ear.

The drink burns down, too fast. We gather our things and stand, lurch through the lurching crowd, a solid warm mass to be pushed through. At some point we are thrown together with him behind me, his chin above my head. There's a raw bite of desire in my loins. People are dancing. We push on. Near the door we suddenly come face to face and I think for a moment that it might happen now but we are too old for that sort of a kiss in public. Because it will be a real kiss, a soulful one, one that will wither the thorns that bar the way into the magic forest. Only the young can get away with that kind of a kiss in public.

I go into the room first. It is small and beige and ugly, with two army-style single beds with green and blue covers and a brown cabinet between, and an alcove where a few bent metal coat-hangers droop dejectedly. The room is like a bucket of cold water thrown over me. Get on with it, it says, get on with it and get out. Go on. I don't want it to happen in here. I walk at once to the window and look out upon the bright street with the people still walking up and down under the lamps, and a bass beat reverberating through the night, and people spilling out on to the pavement from the pub over the road.

I want to have him at home, with comfort, not here. This is just a shag on the way back from Scotland. One day I'll think, yes, I remember, me and Stephen Openshaw had a shag on the way back from Scotland that time.

He lights a lamp between the beds and turns off the overhead light. A peachy glow suffuses the room. He comes across and stands behind me at the window and there is a moment, still and fraught, full of our breathing, his warm presence like a skin at my back before his arms slide around me, his face pushing into the side of my neck like a cat. A step. A step too low. I am kissing his dark hot sticky mouth, he puts his thigh between my legs, pushing up, and I am held astride, rising on the throbbing pulse, the great soft thrill. Oh, I had forgotten. A kiss like death, like forgetting, a swoon, a seizure of the soul. I had forgot. I am above, down on him, down on his raw mouth, putting it in him like they put it in you. Vicious. Like a bite. I'm on the end of his pin and he's opening me up, probing my shrinking innards. Down and down and down I go and I will never get back, never get back, never get back, and my heart within my breast goes into red raw spasm like a shellfish peeled alive, and I plummet into the pit with terror falling all around me in the darkness, wearing the face of all my losses.

Gasping, I come up for air.

People are staggering on the stairs.

'What's the matter?' he asks.

A kiss, that's all it was. I had forgotten.

He draws his face back and looks at me, smiling, hard-lipped, almost upset. His jacket smells friendly.

I don't just want a fuck.

I kiss him again, fierce, quick.

'This is a terrible place,' I say dramatically.

'Is it?'

It is draining, this moment, I feel the pull and suck of cold air as the plug is pulled. I am pulling it.

'Stephen,' I say, my hands in his hair, 'I don't want this.'

He withdraws, holding me at arm's length, still straddling his leg with my feet dangling inches above the floor, a kid on Daddy's knee. 'You don't?' he says softly, caressing my arms. 'You *don't?*'

'I mean I don't want *this.*' I wave my arms at the room, at the drunks on the street. The beat downstairs has stopped. As if to illustrate my point, someone starts to retch loudly in the toilet across the hall.

I want to tell him and I have no words. A shag is a shag is a shag. I'm losing him, I see it, his eyes aren't with me. He's running down the plughole, my kiss, my swoon is running down the plughole. He sets me down gently as the drunk loses his guts with a flap and a slap on to old cold lino, holds my arms, lowers his face to look into mine. His eyes are puzzled. My throat fills up with tears because he doesn't understand, because a shag is a shag is a shag and he doesn't understand.

'I don't just want a shag in a seedy hotel,' I say.

His eyes go blank, as if a switch was flipped. Oh my God, I've lost him. Cold, I swallow.

'Is that what it is?' he says sadly. 'I didn't know.'

The drunk groans, moans. From outside, the breaking of glass, swaggering voices, wild laughter. He turns away from me and sits down upon the nearest army cot. 'Are you rejecting me?' he asks in a not unfriendly voice.

I kneel beside him, taking his hands and laying my head down on them. 'No,' I say, 'no,' but the mountain cracks, my throat is stuffed, I gasp and choke and find myself weeping all over his hands. I don't cry. Not any more. But I fall, and fall, and fall again, my head is under water and I'm drowning and will never see again, I am weeping like Niagara all over his hands. He murmurs, 'Sweetheart,' he murmurs, 'sweetheart, sweetheart,' and lays me down and presses his body close the length of mine, and strokes my head. His lips drift here and there.

11

Here I am, Jael, Jezebel, Judith again. I wonder is there something of a devil in me that I get these savage visions, man beheaded, man at my mercy. I could bind him while he slept. I could do anything to him. How smooth his throat is, how naked his shoulder, how long and straight his fingers lying firmly together on the pillow.

How beautiful he is.

I'm glad I woke first. The bed is so narrow. Now I am sober, filled with wonder and sorrow and what-have-I-done; I could lie here for ever swooning over his sleep but I have to get up and think and think and be alone.

I am not sure of him.

I am not sure of anything.

People hover ominously outside, their mumbled voices rumbling on like cartwheels over cobbles. I have to get him out of here, get him home. I have to clean my teeth. I have to wash my hair. The other bed is unused, straight and stiff as a soldier at attention. I stumble against it when I pass, like a drunken bee that's been on the nectar too long. Sleep was fluid, a lawless place full of voices and murky strife, of pissed Glaswegians falling up the stairs. In and out, in and out I fell, while he slept on, close pressed, turning with me. Sometimes in the cocoon of the dark I thought he was like some wonderful bloom pouring forth his sweetness on the night air, his pheromones like night-scented stock. Once a lone drunk woke me, bawling 'Delilah' through the reaches of the night.

My clothes lie sprawled, spent upon the field of shadows.

At the top of the stairs a fat man and a fat woman are arguing in tones of bewildered righteousness. Seeing me, they lower their voices and put their heads together.

There are still a few faint flecks of sick on the wall by the toilet. The place reeks of pine disinfectant. I locate a shower and stand there shivering in the grey cubicle, almost screaming when the ridiculous spray suddenly clouts me with a faceful of freezing water. Just what I needed. Thank you, God. My chin is sore from his stubble. I start laughing, faffing about with the water dripping about me like particularly miserable rain, get it fairly lukewarm in the end and stand there soaping my hair with a bar of Dove soap I brought up from Moorcop with me. I didn't bring any shampoo, I thought we'd only be gone for one night. I don't know what I thought. Oh, it'll be all right for now,

I'll wash it properly when I get home. I *want* to be home. Moorcop. Red geraniums in a green bucket on the canal. I want to go for a walk up on the moors. I want to play my piano, get out my bashed-up *Community Songbook* and work my way through: 'Sweet Genevieve' and 'I Dreamt that I dwelt in Marble Halls' and 'Way Down Upon the Swanee River' and 'Killarney' and 'Lowlands Low', deep into the night.

Alone. The little lady of Ch'ing-Ch'i.

Shivering, drying, I look in the mirror. My cheeks are flushed, my eyes wild. Cathy, Cathy, they say, staggered, hopeful, filling up, I did it, I did it, I did I did I did.

Poor thing. I laugh at her. 'It was only a fuck,' I say aloud.

She tries to contradict me but I place a finger against her bruised lips.

When I go back he is serene, contained, sleeping somewhere millions of miles away. If I lived with him, I suppose I'd have to wake him every morning. I look around for something to bind him with. Silken cords, leather. I will stretch out upon him. I sit on the other bed, doing my face in the hard window light, waiting for him to wake. I'll bind him, and when he wakes and tries to rise with growing bewilderment and alarm, I'll stuff something in his mouth.

My face is calm now, eyeliner, mascara, a little lipstick, a face to show to the world. I hang my head over and rub away at my damp hair.

I keep him in this room, bound, mine. Naked.

Years go by.

He's awake.

He rubs his eyes, gets up on one elbow and reaches towards me with his other arm. His cheek is wrinkled by the pillow, his eyes uncertain.

'Hello,' I say. I smile.

At the door he puts his hands around my face and pulls me in for a kiss, a hot sweet tongue one, magic Turkish Delight. Twice more we kiss on the way down, little explosions of lust. In the street the sun is shining on the cars. There is a shyness between us as we get into the car. I drive. We stop at the first services and get coffee and scrambled egg on toast. The motorway whizzes crazily past.

'Do you remember Davy Boland's party?' he says, leaning low across the table. 'You were in the hall. You were miserable over Alexander. No one else knew, but I did. You were being brave. You were pretending really well, but *I* knew. I thought, at midnight I'm going to kiss her, one way or the other I'm going to do it, get her now while she's all weak, and I went looking for you. Everyone was kissing everybody else and you weren't anywhere and I started to panic because I knew I had to find you before all the furore passed because I'd never get the chance again. And then I saw you in the hall, and I just did it. And it didn't mean a thing to you.'

I smile and touch his face. 'You do talk bullshit, Stephen Openshaw,' I say. 'You didn't fancy me then.'

That night she was in her navy blue dress, all gauzy layers, her round bare white arms showing through; and further down, daring, the almost visible white of the creamy solid handles of her heart-shaped hips. How she sat in that dress with her knees up, amongst all the people round the piano in Davy Boland's front room in Newton Heath. She caught him a whack on the side of his head with her elbow. 'Oh love!' she cried, all concern, 'oh love!' and held his seventeen-year-old head so tenderly.

He leans even further towards me, shaking his head slowly. 'That's all *you* know,' he says.

I don't even remember what I was wearing.

We fall silent on the motorway.

I think.

God, I really laid myself open last night, didn't I? Please, please! Let me bleed on you! I must be practical. I'm OK now, I've pushed and kicked and thrust my way back to the surface, I've sounded, filled my lungs again. Three days ago I was in a boat that never rocked and life was simple. A little light suicide maybe, a little grief, well I could handle that. But this? I was overboard there for a while, wasn't I? Practical. Practical. We live in different parts of the country. He's got an interview on Tuesday. Would I want to live in London again? I like Moorcop. Would he want to live up here?

Oh, turn it off, turn it off, why make such a fuss about what everyone else does all the time. Only a fuck, isn't it? Only bodies.

'I'm glad I'm going home,' I say, and it comes out like a challenge, 'I like Moorcop.'

His hand comes over and strokes my leg. 'So do I,' he says.

We drift down the motorway, through the green lakeland valleys, down and down and down with the Sunday drivers and the sun going in and out and him changing the cassettes and singing along with some of them. There's a lightness to everything, a kind of gladness coming from him, because, I think, we are finally free of Veronica Karen. Because we've given up on her.

We turn off and follow the old familiar roads up the moors and down through the valleys of stone villages and towering green crags, and cross the high tops by the reservoir till we come to the first of the Shugden signposts. I find myself indicating, pulling over, slowing down.

'Cathy,' he says with mild surprise, 'are we going to Shugden?'

'Land of my fathers,' I reply, swinging the wheel round.

The roads around Shugden are familiar as old boots. I don't know why I am getting so excited. 'I want to see if my house is still there,' I say, 'it won't take long. There's a nice route back from that end of town. The scenic route.'

'OK.' He seems happy enough.

'Every now and again,' I say, 'say once every three years

I go and have a look, and every time something's changed, something else has gone, and every time I expect our house to be gone because everything else is going all around it, but so far it's always been there. One of these days it won't be, of course. It's weird going back to houses you've lived in.'

He nods. 'When was the last time?'

I think. The last time I didn't feel excited like this, it was just old Shugden, boring and a bit seedy, a bit more run-down like it is each time I see it, and I just drove into it without a thought and went to see my mother's name written ornately in the Book of Remembrance at the crematorium, and put the flowers in one of those wide-necked plastic olive green vases and went outside and looked at the cellophaned bouquets all laid out under the names on the little plaques in the square pink concrete bit like a wide tunnel. The wind blew across the bouquets, shivering their ribbons. There was one name that didn't have any flowers, a woman called Edith, so I went back inside and picked one flower here and there from all the other vases and made a paltry little bunch, and laid them under Edith's name and said a little prayer for her, whoever she might be. And then I went to see Auntie Pearl.

'Two years ago,' I tell him.

We wait at the lights at Hog's Head Bridge. Straight on into town, or turn left for Auntie Pearl's. She's in a new bungalow now. I suppose I ought to go and see her, she'd go mad if she found out I'd passed through town and not been. Last time she had a big smelly sore on her leg and my cousin Sandra was changing the dressing. Pearl was on the cheap sherry, disgusting stuff. She's one of these gruesome old lady drunks that insist you join them and won't take no for an answer, bad as a pub bully really. I had to keep pouring mine away slyly bit by bit into the potted plant.

The lights change. Oh, I'll go next week. This is not the time. I cross the lights, straight on.

All the sadness and glory of the vanished past I get from these streets, even the ones that don't look anything like before, the hard-edged masks over the old soft grey remembered thing. Somehow I have to see it now and then, my shrugged-off skin. And today is Sunday; it is Shugden on Sunday, raising my hackles delightfully, the ugly old place. There's the station where my dad worked, they've dolled up the front with a new pink and grey floor and automatic doors. The bit where the old Woolworth's used to be is covered in precinct, echoing and almost empty because of the day. A big gold sculpture of a treble clef rises from a profusion of pale greenery, creamy smooth, and the traffic lights wink on and off, on and off, reflecting in the black obsidian side of the National Westminster Bank. More lights. I swing obediently out into the middle lane and turn right and go up the hill past the po-faced splendour of the Nag's Head with its car park spread around it like a bride's train.

'That's where you were sick,' I tell Stephen.

'Oh God, I remember!' He laughs. 'I didn't half feel

stupid.' He peers back over his shoulder out of the window, shading his eyes.

We thread through the little streets. All round here used to be big shabby old houses with little front gardens, long straight stern-faced terraces with red-raddled doorsteps. But it's all new now, a flat terrain of square redbrick houses with little back yards enclosed by tall fences made of something that looks like giant basketwork, fox-coloured and highly polished. And here, miraculously, haughtily surveying the upstart mess, is one rare and threatened row of fine tall grim old houses, two by two, their bricks crumbling, the ancient paint withering about their dusty eyes like the images that curl up prior to death in a burning book.

My old house is the one on the end, boarded up. We park in front and sit there looking at it.

'So that's it.' He takes out his cigarettes.

16 Shaw Road, Shugden 2, 16 Shaw Road, Shugden 2, 16 Shaw Road . . .

'Have you never seen it?'

Well, how do I know? She may have brought him here, all those years and years when they were like brother and sister. They may have sat here like this, side by side, and she would have looked wistful and soulful and talked of her childhood.

'No,' he says. 'I never did. Heard all about it though.'

We had pansies in that little patch of dry dead earth at the front. I used to edge up the long sloping wall with the rounded top, playing it was a giraffe's neck and I was riding on its back across the African plains. There was a high black gate at the side but that's gone now and the alley down the side of our house is full of rubbish, rotting cardboard, bloated white heavy-duty sacks of old builders' rubble. There are three bells at the side of the boards that cover the front door.

'Come on,' he says, opening the car door.

For a moment I watch him, his tall figure unlikely on the pavement of my distant past, a coil of smoke going up from the end of his cigarette. It's as if his dark square shoulders are superimposed on an old snapshot. He turns and motions with his head, come on, so I get out and lock up and stand beside him.

'Don't you want to have a look round the back?' he asks.

'I want to go in,' I say. 'I'd love to go in just once before it's gone.'

He takes my hand. There we stand.

'I keep thinking it must be gone,' I repeat. 'Every few years I sneak a look, sure that this time it'll be gone, but somehow it's always here, hanging on. Just.'

He smiles and his hand tightens round mine. 'Not for much longer, I'd say.'

We walk up the path, three or four steps at most, and stand on the big front steps. This path was very long to me then. When it snowed I jumped from the very top into a pure fluffy bed of white, took giant steps to the gate. My mother's hand, in a red glove, was always there. But there's nothing here to see, no door, no windows, it's like the bandaged face of a mummy, or a victim gagged and blind-folded. They should put it out of its misery, turn off the life support. Or I'll buy it. I'll get rich and buy it, mend it, put in new windows and a door, shore up the sagging walls, replenish the roof, install central heating, paint it, be kind to it for the sake of the long life it's had and the indelible imprints it's laid on my soul. Give it a good retirement.

'It's so small,' I say. 'I used to jump off this step and it seemed enormous. I used to psych myself up to it because it was so high.'

He stands on the step below me, puts his hands on either side of my waist and lifts me towards him. Now I'm a head taller than him, I enfold his head in my arms, holding it against my breasts. Over his shoulder I see the sides of those endless boring houses over the road, each one with a satel-lite dish and a cod-rustic door and a small green rectangle like a thin rug under the uPVC window. I lift his face to me and kiss his lips with great tenderness, then walk away from him, across the front of the house and through the gape of the absent gate, down the thin grey path that leads to the back. He follows, past the swaybacked dirty khaki-cream yellow of the high windowsill where, legs dangling, I used to lean on my elbows after hoisting myself up to look in at the dark playroom. From outside it always looked ghostly. If I could see now through the damp splintering board that covers it, if the ghost of glass presented me suddenly with a black mirror, would I see two little girls, their hair in bunches, playing in a room of boxed rubbish and dust and lost things? All the toys are there, Molly and Rex and Onionhead and Jo-Jo the monkey and the Spanish Lady: I am holding her by the waist, making her dance, we are singing, me and Veronica:

> *There's a song in the air*
> *But the fair señorita doesn't seem to care*
> *For my song in the air.*

Out of the shadows they come: the Princess Verona, Jem the Gypsy Boy, Lorna Lamorna, evil Dame Doolily, Giant Killyloo, the Poojah, Tabitha, Annabel, Little Girl Green, Mamie and Rowena high-kicking their way through the dust-softened motes.

> *She wears red feathers and a huly-huly skirt,*
> *She wears red feathers and a huly huly skirt,*
> *She lives on fresh coconut and fish from the sea . . .*

It's like coming back to haunt yourself.

The back yard is just rubbish, nameless spiky black rubbish, piled high so that you can't even get in, can't even see our back door that was the mouth of another world when I first crawled over its lip. We stand looking up, craning our necks back. The attic window is open, a black hole.

'I saw a shadow on the wall in there.' I point. 'The shadow of a man in a top hat.'

'Did you?'

He reaches for me and grabs my head and pulls it towards him as if it were a pair of lapels, kissing my mouth in a total, almost vicious way, his eyelids fluttering. The world is distant, dank, rotting, smudged around me from the corners of my eyes. A touch of rough wooing he gives me, a promise.

When we leave, we are leaning together like drunks.

We drive, skirting through the town towards the road south, looking for somewhere on Sunday to buy food. On Manchester Road the old blind Essoldo sign is gone, with its patches of weeping rust bleeding down from its sockets. We used to go there with Mum and Auntie Pearl sometimes in the afternoon when Dad was at work. We saw everything. We saw all Montgomery Clift's films because Mum had a crush on him. Mum and Auntie Pearl were always horribly embarrassing at the pictures, endlessly shuffling about and changing their seats and whispering loudly and offering round toffees with crinkly wrappers. People used to look round and tut. Sometimes you could just sink through the floor.

'There's a shop,' says Stephen.

It's a Spar, opposite the church. We park down one of the side streets, buy stodge food, which is all there is, pasties and Eccles cakes and a bottle of Appletise. The sun is nice, so we cross at the Pelican and climb the little hill which leads into the churchyard where there are benches to sit on and eat your food opposite the long stained-glass windows. This is where my cousin Sandra got married. The church is old. It stands on top of a mound that was once some lovely thing in the middle of the countryside but now towers over the gritty bone-rattling road that is busy and loud even on Sunday. Some of these graves looked out over fields and hedges and sheep with their dangle-tailed lambs. The shade of what it was remains, like eyes still beautiful in a faded old face. There is a cedar from the time of Charles I, and the trains go by on the other side, low down in a cutting.

Inside, a congregation sings weak and thin, a hymn tune so banal it evaporates on hearing.

'I want to be buried when I die,' I say. 'I want to have a grave with a stone and flowers and weeping cedars and a rookery and the tolling of the bell.'

I don't want to be just a name in a book.

He looks thoughtful for a moment, then says, 'Do cedars weep?'

We pass the Appletise back and forth, sharing the bottle.

But what if they forget me and I'm the one with no flowers? I remember going to see Sylvia Plath's grave in Heptonstall. It was hard to find amongst the straight rows, and when I did, it was neglected, bare, and all you could do was sit there feeling sad.

'You know one of the things I always found attractive about Veronica Karen?' he says, screwing up his pasty wrapper and stuffing it in his pocket.

I don't want to hear it.

'You,' he says, when I don't reply.

He turns his head and looks at me with a full, frank look. Oh, he cultivates the artless approach, but it's all a front. He's good at this game. I recall the names of various women I've heard associated with him. There was an Erica, I think, and a Jane.

'I couldn't believe my luck,' he says. '*Two* gorgeous girls. Course, I was mad about Veronica Karen then, but *you* were like a bonus.' He smiles. 'Of course, you were always with someone.'

I remember sunlight on the apple tree and Ambrose stalking across the lawn. I remember the four of us on the rustic benches, me and Robin McGeeney and Veronica Karen and Stephen.

'You know, I never had any illusions about Veronica Karen,' he goes on, leaning back and looking up at the sky. 'I always knew that there was no way me and her were ever going to be – what? – you know, just normal. You know. You didn't settle down ever with someone like Veronica Karen, it just wasn't in the scheme of things.'

Even now, see, even now he can't stop talking about her.

'She got really annoyed with me once because I said I thought you were attractive.'

'Oh, she would.' I don't care. I get up, brushing Eccles cake crumbs on to the ground, the stuff gets everywhere. I wander down the path a little way, looking at the graves.

'I don't know why it should have bothered her so much,' he says, 'because we weren't even going out together at that time, it was well past. She wasn't like that with everyone, it was just you.' He stands with the empty Appletise bottle, looking round for a bin. 'It was one day when we were just messing about, the way you do, and we got on to each one trying to guess who the other one fancied, and I was getting them all right and she was getting them all wrong, and it was all just a laugh until I said that actually I quite fancied you. And then she went all funny.'

He walks to the gate and bins the rubbish then comes back. A terrible feeling comes creeping: revenge, gladness. He stands not too near. 'Love among the tombs,' he says.

'My great-grandparents are buried here,' I tell him.

'Really?' He looks at me as if I've just said something amazing.

I nod. 'Over there.'

'And are your parents buried here too?'

'No, they were cremated.'

Their ashes are gone, scattered by a stranger over the Garden of Remembrance. We put our arms around one another's waists and walk among the graves, reading the old stones. Husbands and wives lie side by side. Once they walked like this, entwined, amazed at each other. My parents aren't together in death, their ashes blew away, they're nowhere now. So many dead, a multitude. Now and then the grave of a child, still breaking hearts after all these years.

'There,' I say. We stop at the twin stones that mark my great-grandparents and stand there looking down.

'Did you ever think of having another child?' he asks in a casual voice.

There is a small silence.

'Sometimes I did,' I say. 'Sometimes I did, but . . .' and I pause, and shiver, 'but no, not really, I never really thought . . .' and trail off because I can't explain about not wanting to want and wanting anyway, and the vows I took that I would never allow for the possibility of loss like that again.

'Have one with me if you like,' he says, as if he's suggesting we share the cost of a taxi. I don't say anything because what can you say? But then he laughs in a kind of stifled, astonished way. 'It'd be all right.' He leans his head against mine. 'I think it's what we ought to do really, it'd work out. I wouldn't leave you or anything. You know me.' He laughs again. 'Fundamentally faithful. Boring as hell. You'd be stuck with me.'

So many dead people and us alive. It seems a miracle. I kiss him.

A train goes by.

> *Down in the valley, valley so low,*
> *Hang your head over, hear the train blow.*

Inside they're singing 'A Safe Stronghold Our God Is Still'. The trains, the trains, hear the lonesome whistle blow. But trains don't whistle any more. He lifts my palm to his lips like some old-time gallant. How I love him, among the graves, among the dead, how I suddenly love him.

We move to the porch.

'Touch me,' he says very quietly, and there is such a plea in it, such muted desperation, that I put my arm around him on the porch seat and touch him there, a feather-light touch against the hardness in his jeans. He puts his face into my neck and raises his thigh and groans. We could do it now. Right now, here, anywhere. The congregation are gearing up to emerge. There are footsteps on the path. We sit up, dazed.

An old man and woman enter the porch from outside and start reading the noticeboards.

We leave. Hand in hand we descend to the road. A truck thunders by. We walk past a bus stop.

'I don't believe it,' says an old, loose-lipped voice, thick with smoke.

I look round, quaking.

'It bloody well is you,' she says. 'I saw you coming up and I thought, no, it can't be.'

I see a fat old lady with too much make-up on and pray to God I'll never look like that.

'It's Auntie Pearl,' I say to Stephen, 'do you remember Auntie Pearl? Hello, Auntie Pearl.'

Oh Christ, how'll we get away?

'I've been trying to ring you for days,' she says loudly and accusingly, then turns to Stephen and speaks confidentially: 'I can't stand that machine she's got. I won't talk to it.'

'Have you been ringing, Auntie Pearl?'

'Have I been ringing? Have I been ringing?' Her voice rises. Her eyes are very pale blue and bulgy, full of yellowish veins. They stare as if they might burst. 'Course I bloody well have! Where've you been? I'm just coming back from the hospital, the buses are terrible on Sunday.'

In my ears, in my mind, a solemn drum begins to beat.

'Who have you been to see, Auntie Pearl?'

'Veronica,' she says, 'who d'you think?'

'Veronica Karen,' says Stephen in a tone of wonder.

12

Walking down these long creamy-green passages, I want to run. I hate hospitals anyway. I hate *this* one. I had my fill. My stomach sinks and flips, my bowels feel watery, adrenalin chases itself through my body, running and running, making me sick.

Three months she's been here, three months and not a word. Well, what can you do, said Auntie Pearl. Time like this she's got a right to do what she wants. Was there ever any other kind of time for Veronica Karen? She ran away to hide. Back to the bosom of her family, crude old Auntie Pearl. Figures, doesn't it? Veronica Karen always put her make-up on first thing, patting herself under the chin and all that. Couldn't bear to be ugly. Of course she doesn't want people seeing her like this. Like this? Like this? Like what? She'd rather fade out alone, do all that suffering alone, than have anyone see her like this. Or is it just denial? Is she still fooling herself that this is not the big one, that she'll get better and come out of here?

Pearl says she just changed her mind all of a sudden. Just suddenly says: Why don't we tell Cathy? Emily Brontë on her horsehair sofa saying she'll see the doctor now. I have a vision of her lying there with her long hair all spread out upon the pillow, white hands clasped, face pale and smudgy-eyed, a Victorian beauty on her deathbed.

Outside the door I stand dithering.

I'm a coward, I've always been a coward. I'll turn around and walk away, avoid Stephen who's loitering somewhere below, awaiting his audience if she'll grant him one. She's considering it, apparently. I'll sink down in the lift, hit that glorious free air out there, run across the road to the Holly Tree Café, drink cappuccino and eat a cherry scone and gleefully hug myself the way I used to when I'd successfully bunked off school. Ha ha, they're all doing double needle-work now.

But I open the door.

Like this. She is like this.

She's shrunk. She's like a baby bird I once saw lying on the pavement on my way to school, dead and pink and broken-necked, fallen from the nest. She's all the starving people, a concentration camp survivor, a tiny old thing with dry white scalp showing through pale wispy locks, curiously flattened and dull. She wears a pretty nightie, the neck edged with roses and a frill and a thin salmon-coloured silky ribbon. It makes her look like one of those wizened infants with thin old faces and frilly clothes you sometimes see pictures of, the ones who age a lifetime in six years. She looks not quite at me, like a blind person, smiling in her skull.

It's not her.

It's not her, she's already gone, it's someone else, a stranger, a poor poor stranger I have to visit. She's ready for me, sitting up against the pillows. I sit down at the high bedside in the bright room with its smell of crisp linen and cleanliness and the lingering hint of shit, as if someone just changed a baby's nappy and took it out of the room. Her breath is a cold whistle, like wind through icicles in the depth of winter. She has no eyelashes and her eyes are sticky with pus. Ashamed and naked after a lifetime of kohl and mascara, they've gone to ground, unlit.

'Hello, Veronica,' I say.

It's the kind of thinness you can't take in, the knobbed protuberant wrists, the curious jutting depths around the collarbone.

'You're not going to tell me off, are you?' she says, in a thin, hoarse voice. Her fingers, resting on an oxygen mask that lies on the turned-back sheet, are snappable.

'Of course I'm not. What are you talking about?'

I look her up and down. The bed is flat, as if a child's skeleton lies under the sage green blanket. Her other hand is obliterated by a heavy dressing with tubes going up to a drip. Oh, Veronica Karen, your hair, what has happened to your hair? What has happened to your eyes? Inside me something sinks and sinks and sinks again.

'Oh, Veronica Karen,' I say, 'whatever are we going to do with you?'

'See,' she says, 'you *are* telling me off.' Her wintry breath quavers in.

'No, I'm not. If you think *that's* telling off.' I look at the room. 'Stephen's downstairs. Did Auntie Pearl tell you?'

'Oh, my dear little Stephen,' she says, and starts to cry weakly, 'he'd hate to see me like this. I don't think I could stand it.'

I don't know what to say to her. How's things? Long time, no see? Fill me in on all the gaps.

'We've been all the way to Scotland,' I say in a tone of amazement.

She smiles, rolling her lips back from her bumpy white gums. Her teeth look very long and a yellowish crust is caked inside her lower lip. Her eyes close. Of course, I suppose she's heavily sedated.

'We've been running about like blue-arsed flies over you.'

'Well, I called you,' she says. 'I got them to bring the phone in.'

'You called me? When?'

But she just smiles slackly as if she doesn't understand me. I wonder if it's when I was in the bath.

'Why did you give Bobbie Alexander's address?' I ask.

'Did I?'

'We went all the way up to Alexander's,' I say. 'We saw him.'

She coughs. Her eyes stream, her breath grinds in and in and in and never comes out. She terrifies me, coughing like this. She'll choke, I think, she'll crack her lungs. But she recovers tremblingly, like an old machine that's been switched off.

'How is he?' she asks.

I pause.

'He's fine,' I say.

'I was going to maybe go and see him,' she wheezes, 'but I didn't.'

She drifts. Her eyelids flutter gracefully down like dying swans.

'Look,' I say, 'Stephen really wants to see you.'

She shakes her head.

'Veronica Karen, you're being selfish. He's come all this way just to see you. At a time like this, don't you think –'

'Don't just write me off!' she says, furious. 'I'm not dead yet!' She starts to say more but coughs instead. She fights for breath, raising the oxygen mask with a trembling hand. Clear and shiny, it sits like a giant joke nose on her face. Veronica Karen draws in oxygen with the frowning concentration she once employed when snorting up coke. She's had fits, Auntie Pearl said, she had one two weeks ago, please God, don't let her have a fit now. My eyes locate the panic button. But she takes the mask off and grimaces.

'I'm not arguing with you, Veronica Karen,' I say. 'Please don't let's argue, I don't want to.'

Not now, I was going to say, not at a time like this, but she might fly off the handle again.

'Are you OK? Do you want me to get the nurse?'

She shakes her head, drifting again. I look around at the little room, the pale walls glossed halfway up, the machines and tubes and shiny chrome, the bag of clear fluid hanging above, flat at the top, fat as an udder below. I wonder if she's going to die in this room. I should take her home with me and make up a bed by my hearth with the red roses on the black tiles that she has never seen, and feed her by the fire, the good broth our mother used to make. But I can't make that broth, I've tried and tried and just can't get it right, can't get it so, the clearest, purest, most delicious broth anyone ever tasted. I asked Veronica Karen once years ago on the phone when we were still talking: did you ever get it just like that? But she said no, it's impossible. I want it, I can taste it, smell it, I can see our bowls with the tree pattern going round inside and a couple of little birds done child-style, Cupid's bows in the sky. I remember how carefully we watched to make sure the level in each bowl was exact to the last drop.

Now and again her eyelids flicker open. I think of this room being the last thing she ever sees. Does she know?

'I was going to forgive him.' She tries to laugh. 'I was in a forgiving mood.'

'Then do,' I say. 'He's here.'

She puts a stick finger to her mouth and runs it over the yellow stuff inside, frowning. 'What?' she says.

'He's here.'

'Alexander?'

'No no. Stephen.'

'Ah.' She's off again.

'Why didn't you tell me?' I whisper after a while, thinking she's asleep, but she opens her eyes and says, 'What?'

'That you were ill.'

'Don't tell me off.' She frowns. 'You shouldn't tell me off.'

'I'm not. Really I'm not.'

She swallows and a spasm of pain crosses her face. Her breast makes a strange high hissing sound and I think she's laughing. 'You've been all over the place, Auntie Pearl said, you and Stephen . . .' and is cut off by a long indrawn whistling breath that breaks into a cough, so that I tense. But she rallies. She picks with a fingernail at the crust inside her mouth and says, 'This stuff is a drag.'

'You're making it bleed,' I say.

'Huh.'

'Do you want anything? Can I get you anything?'

'Where is he?' she asks.

'Stephen? Downstairs.'

She sighs. 'Do I *have* to see him?'

'You don't have to do anything you don't want to, Veronica Karen.'

She drifts again, then comes round. 'He makes such a

fuss,' she says. There's a film over her eyes and she keeps blinking as if they hurt. 'Fussing like a mother hen. I wish I'd never told him.'

'Well, never mind,' I say, 'you don't have to,' but she turns her face away and scowls:

'I suppose I'll have to.'

Veronica Karen,' I say. 'Why don't you want to see him?'

Slowly her head turns back towards me. 'Because he loves me,' she says, 'and I don't love him. But I do love him. But not in that way. I never did.'

Then she closes her eyes and falls asleep, and I sit listening to the pale singing of her breath, the sighing of doors far away, the tiny scattering of rain on the window. I watch a little bubble moving down a slender tube. This time she is really asleep. I touch her hand and it's cold. Oh freedom. Oh life. I shall get up very quietly and go. But as soon as I even think about it she opens her eyes.

'I will see him,' she says. 'I didn't want to but now I will. Don't leave me alone with him though or he'll get all emotional. I know him.'

He goes straight to the bed and takes her free hand, kissing her on the cheek, sitting back and smiling as if this were just any old hospital visit.

'I don't want you telling me off!' she says fretfully. Her arm goes up towards his shoulder, and as he leans forward, eager to please, the sleeve of her nightie falls back. In the elbow crease of her stick arm there are sores weeping through a dusting of powder. I look down at my own elbow, feeling them there, wanting to scratch, to rub. She cannot be like this, no one can be like this, my sister cannot be like this.

Stephen strokes her hand between his two. 'Idiot,' he says.

'You were stifling me,' she tells him. 'You kept coming round.'

He glances at me, sitting by the large cylinder of oxygen. I think that is real merriment I see in his eyes. 'I know,' he says unapologetically, 'well, never mind, you got your own back, didn't you? It was like *Treasure Hunt*.' He laughs. 'We've been from John o' Groats to Land's End after you. You're a right bastard, you know, you ought to keep in touch with your friends.'

'It's your fault,' she says. 'You went away.'

He pulls his chair closer. 'Blame me,' he says sardonically, as if she were not a death's head, then smiles all over her with his eyes, his mouth, his very self. He never looked at me like that. 'It's so good to see you,' he says passionately.

I look down at the polished tiles of the floor, white wisps like cirrus clouds smeared through grey. The light from the window is reflected there. They don't want me here. I start to rise but she turns her head slowly and her hand wafts vaguely in my direction. 'Don't go,' she says.

'Well, it's not the greatest room,' Stephen says, looking round. 'Can't you get some posters up on the wall? Will they let you? Surely they would.'

He looks at me.

'I don't know,' I say.

'We'll get you some,' he tells her. 'We'll get you some pictures to brighten up the walls.'

'Some different music would be nice,' she says. 'I've only got some old reggae with me. You know that old Al Green tape we used to have? Have you still got it?'

'I have,' he says, 'but it's down in London. Tell you what, I've got to go down on Tuesday for an interview, I'll get it then.'

She smiles, closing her eyes, on the lower rims of which a snotty deposit is building up. She drifts away. The sound of her breathing fills the space between us. There is a gaunt drawn look about his cheeks and eyes and when he looks at me his eyes are cold and nervous and defensive.

'I don't think she can concentrate for very long,' I say in a low voice.

He looks into her face, a long searching stare, till her eyes open again, slowly because of the pus. His face is so close, his lips so parted that I think he is going to kiss her, but instead he says, 'Let's get you sorted out,' and goes over to the sink and runs water.

'He's a sweetie,' she whispers sleepily to me, complacently closing her lips, but I have gone, floated slowly away like an escaped balloon to hang high, lamp-like, oblivious, observing.

When he comes back he has warm wet swabs. Like the women on the post-natal ward, cleaning their babies' eyes, he patiently wipes the stickiness away.

'That's better,' he murmurs.

'You have to put it in there.' She waves her hand towards a yellow sack.

'I hate hospitals,' he says, disposing of the swabs. 'When are you coming out?'

She tries to laugh but can't.

'I can look after you,' he says, sitting down again. He leans back over the chair, rakish. 'I can, you know.'

'You couldn't.' She coughs. Her hand, a washed-out spider, wanders restlessly towards him. 'You'd hate it.'

'No really,' he says, 'it'd be fine. Better than being stuck in here.'

'You could not. I wouldn't let you.'

Absolutely serious he leans in low again, putting his face close to hers. 'Why not?'

She coughs again. Her eyes run and she reaches for the mask.

'It's not some stupid modesty thing, is it? How long have I known you, Veronica Karen? It's twenty-one years, do you realise? I could look after you.'

And me. Me. He's known me for twenty-one years too.

'Do you really think that after all that time anything about you could make any difference?' he says.

She puts on the mask and breathes oxygen for a while, her chest heaving up and down and stirring the pretty silk ribbon with its little-girl bow that nestles between the dim ridges of her ribs. Then she sets it aside, reaches up and touches his cheek. 'I didn't want to see you,' she says.

'Why not?'

His hand, huge, covers hers, holding it to his face.

'I didn't want you to see me like this.'

'Stupid woman.'

I'm not here, I'm pointless. I'll go, they don't want me. I'm rising to tiptoe away, but she turns a little and spreads her fingers at me.

'Could I?' she says pathetically. 'Could I come home?'

Where is that?

'Of course you can,' he whispers, glossy-eyed. 'You can do anything you want.' He lifts her tiny bird's claw to his lips and kisses it. 'We could get one of those things,' he says, indicating the oxygen tank. 'We'd look after you. Cathy too. We'd be there.'

She turns her face and looks at me for a long time. Because there is nothing in her eyes to presage it, it comes as a great shock when she starts to cry, a soft sobbing that labours deep within her chest for a while before breaking out of her in long agonised creaks. Her good hand tries to fly to her face, to hide its nakedness from us, but can't make it.

'Now then,' says Stephen, pulling his chair forward, covering her with his protective shadow, 'now then, what's all this? All these tears, little girl?'

'I don't want this to happen!' she manages to say. It sets her coughing again.

Sweet Jesus.

He slides one hand under her head, the other wipes her

face. 'But it is happening,' he says, 'and that's why we're here.'

'I'm scared!' she cries.

'Of course you are.'

'I'm scared.' She sobs it, and keeps on and on sobbing it, I'm scared, I'm scared, I'm scared, I'm scared, and he says 'Yes, yes,' raising and holding her very gently for fear of her little stick bones breaking. She weeps, eyes clenched, lips shiny. 'Now now now,' he slowly croons.

She says something I can't make out.

'Of course you are,' he says, 'of course. Brave girl, Veronica Karen, brave girl.' His great hand clutches the tangled back of her head. Both their faces are hidden.

'Make it go away!' her muffled voice pleads.

'Ssh,' he says, 'ssh.'

He was never for me. I see them through a faint mist of tiredness, locked together, slowly rocking. Perhaps I am asleep. My hands are cold. All of me is useless and cold. This is a terrible dream, dear God, let me wake up.

Their faces part.

'I love you,' he says, kissing her clumsily, laying her down upon the pillow as if she were priceless porcelain, stroking her hair with the back of one finger. Her eyes, closing, sink back into her face like the eyes on an Easter Island head. The waves are crashing in on deserted beaches on all her islands, on Easter Island and St Kilda and Holy Island and Flannan Isle and the Isles of the Blest. She's going walk-about, into the desert for forty days and forty nights, into the dark that so terrified her in our old dark house. I see her there, a child. She was not to live for so very long. I should have been kinder. I should have been kinder. The air drags whining up and down her tubes. Her breath is driving me mad, like a car siren that's gone on all night. I want to shove my head under a pillow, cut off my ears, jump out the window, scream, smash it to pieces.

She opens her eyes and turns to me. 'Cathy,' she says. Already the pus is gathering again.

'Yes?'

'Bring the photos tomorrow.'

For some reason I think of those pictures in the field at Saskya, but then she says, 'Bring that one of Ambrose on the fence.'

She means our family photographs, hundreds of them in an old cardboard box: two little girls in Southport and Blackpool and Torquay, matching dresses, the Whit Week walks, Mummy in the back garden, Daddy in his uniform, Roman-nosed Ambrose sitting on a fence.

'OK,' I say.

'I remember once,' she murmurs, then stops, forgetting what she was going to say, and looks enquiringly at me as if I might know.

'We went and looked at our old house,' I tell her.

'Did you?'

'Yes. You can't look in the windows any more. I wanted to look in the playroom but you can't.'

Our eyes lock. Last night I had him. There are years and

years and years ahead of me and none for you. I should have been kinder. I don't know her expression, there's nothing there to light it, nothing to let you know.

She smiles. 'Do you remember Mamie and Rowena?'

'Of course I do.'

'Do you remember "She Wears Red Feathers"?'

'"Red Sails in the Sunset",' I say.

'They were all red, weren't they?'

Stephen smiles. I meet his eyes, confused; he smiles as if everything's OK, as if the three of us are not sitting here in this nightmare.

'Games we used to play,' I explain.

'What does red signify?' she asks.

'Anger.'

'I remember once,' she says, and a laugh starts up in her throat, getting in the way of the words, 'I remember once, when we were in the back kitchen . . .' She wriggles against the pillow as if she's going to sit forward but it's no good, there's no strength there, and she subsides, laughing still. But then the laugh becomes a cough, and she clutches the mask to her chest all ready. 'Memories,' she gasps, blinking painfully, 'you don't know. They're good even when they're bad. You don't know.'

'*Catcher in the Rye*,' says Stephen.

I look at him. 'What?'

'*Catcher in the Rye*,' he repeats, 'at the end. Something Holden Caulfield says. Do you remember that, Veronica Karen?'

But, I suddenly realise, she's barely aware. She yawns like a child and it sets her off coughing again.

'Put your mask on, Veronica Karen,' Stephen says anxiously.

Suddenly the cough is terrible. In seconds it has taken her over like possession, harrowing her. I grab the mask and place it on her face and she gasps for it, choking and panting like someone half drowned.

'Get the nurse,' I say.

He staggers to his feet and runs. Tears stream down Veronica Karen's face, gathering along the rims of the mask.

'It's all right, Veronica,' I say, 'it's all right, it's all right, it's all right,' because there's nothing else to say even though it's a lie. I think that this, all of this, is like watching myself die. I feel her departure through and through me, as if small lights are turning off throughout my body, a great skyscraper slowly vanishing into darkness, the lights going out all over Europe. The lights are our shared memories, no more no more no more for ever. When I open my mouth to try and say something about this, a great dragging feeling claws through me and a terrible pain explodes in my chest and I know it for grief because I've known it before, and respect it, and take her hand quickly and say, 'Pax, kid.'

The nurse comes in with Stephen looming behind. Calm and brisk, solid as a joint of meat, she walks to the bed. 'There now,' she says in a Scottish accent, adjusting the drip, 'is it a nasty one, Veronica Karen?'

Like a miracle, or maybe just a remission of torture, the attack ebbs. Veronica Karen nods, still coughing but getting it under control. Her breast heaves like the sides of the fish left dying by the fishermen on the canal banks in Moorcop, and a pool of tears has gathered in the deep hollow of her throat. Stephen wipes her face with a cool cloth. Look at him. Did you ever see such love? I become aware of another self, my ghostly doppelgänger lurking at the back of the room, eyes scornful over its folded arms, sending out its contemptuous rays. Look at this! it says, just look. She will have her deathbed scene, won't she? Doesn't she just love an audience? Adieu! Adieu! Adieu!

I shrivel, lonely, a cold diminishing dot.

The nurse plumps up her pillow. 'There now,' she says, 'there. All better now, Veronica Karen!'

'Pax,' wheezes Veronica Karen.

Her eyes close. She falls asleep with the oxygen mask on. We sit in silence for a moment. Funny what your mind will do. I get a flash, so real, I see and taste and even smell a peculiar sticky lolly we used to eat when we were kids. It was shaped like a cup cake on a stick and came in tough fluted silver foil that you peeled off to reveal its rich deep burgundy colour, glittering with crystalline sugar. I'd give anything for some sweet sugar to put in my mouth now, anything at all. I want sweets and chocolate and fizzy pop. I want a Whirligig. Remember Whirligigs, Veronica Karen? Remember when we were little and sneaked out with our nighties under our coats? It was just going dark and the world felt big and dangerous and there were men going home with their hands in their pockets, and we crossed two big roads to the off-licence and bought sticky lollies and Whirligigs, with their swirly chocolate wheels overlapping. You used to break yours up very neatly, keeping the wheels intact.

13

There is a ramp with two posts at the bottom, a dinky town of little pebbledashed prefabs, signposts with arrows pointing to Radiography and Ear, Nose and Throat. Men in white overalls are at work on a scaffold. Stephen deviates to the post at the bottom of the ramp as he passes, nutting it quite spectacularly and almost knocking himself out. He stands back, glaring at the post as if it had accosted him, his body spiky with anger.

'Stephen!'

He looks at me bleakly, sour-mouthed.

'Are you all right?'

'I just hate it,' he says, swallowing, 'I just hate what's happening. I can't deal with it, I don't know what to do.'

'Neither do I.'

He shakes his head bitterly, pulls me in by the shoulders and squashes me into a terrible hug, all fierceness and desperation. The breath leaves my body. Crushed to death, I think, trying to get my face out to the air, but he is smothering me with his chest, it pounds through my head like mallet blows and I can't breathe. I struggle but he only tightens his grip. I have to heave and push to get him off me.

I take his face in my hands. A bruise is coming up on his forehead, right in the middle. 'It's OK,' I say steadily. 'You get through it. You don't think you will but you get through it.'

The men are watching.

His lips curl but it isn't really a smile.

'She wanted to save us all this,' he says. 'She would have been a great memory, just the way she always was. But now she's this. And she'll always be this.'

He turns on his heel and starts walking. I catch him up and we walk back to the car, together but apart. He paces ploddingly, kicking a stone, head down, hands in pockets. How should I be with him? I don't know what we are together any more. I want a sign. But I don't see one. We get in the car and I drive us back to Auntie Pearl's, licking my lips, which keep drying over as if I'd been drinking hard. It's like an illness, the way I feel. That's the nearest I can get to it. My nerves are unpleasantly sharpened, my guts tremble. Stephen stares out of the window. I am aware of all the stupid little things my body does, the swallowing and blinking and so on, all the way back to Auntie Pearl's.

Auntie Pearl used to have a nice little terraced house out

towards Manchester Road but now she's in a modern semi on a kind of open plan development. Parking and walking up her little white path with the bit of grass on either side is a very public affair. She opens the door before we're out of the car and stands there framed: flat slippers, a red apron with white hearts all over it and a great big pocket hanging open at the front like Kanga's in *Winnie the Pooh*. She looks like the Queen of Hearts, Mrs Pig in a story book with that bloated pink look and her hair horribly blonde for her age, sitting on her head like a luminous Belisha beacon, flashing on and off the message: Old Tart. Before we are halfway down the path she has launched herself from the step and leapt upon Stephen, shrieking: 'What have you done to your head?'

He looks slightly taken aback. 'I just bumped it,' he says. 'It's nothing.'

But she drags him into the living room and makes him sit down in front of a blasting gas fire and limps out to the kitchen for butter, talking all the time. Her leg's a lot better than before, but there's still a fairly wide bandage under her pink stocking. Pink. You'd think she'd play it down, what with its pigginess. In the small room, three mismatched armchairs sit in a utilitarian row facing the blue fun-fur rug and the fire. She's put him in the one in the middle, a huge brown cracked-leather monolith with a low seat and high-sided arms, guaranteed to make anyone sitting in it look like the Incredible Shrinking Man. I sit in the one on his left with the red stretch covers. The TV is on, something about the Lake District, and the smell of long slow cooking permeates the air, familiar and heavy as a million Sunday afternoons.

'So what did you think, hey, Cath?' her voice comes through two open doors. 'Looks awful, doesn't she? You don't get used to it you know.'

She's here with the butter, smearing it on his head, dabbing viciously.

'She's a silly girl! That's what she is! There was no need for it, no need at all.'

He looks as if someone just blacked his third eye. Recovering their cool, his other two are clear, looking at me beneath the flabby drip of her arm. 'Cathy,' he says, 'what are our plans?'

I wish he wouldn't keep landing me with these decisions. The overhead light has no shade, it burns fiercely upon the ornate silver frame of the picture of Uncle Vincent and Auntie Pearl and my cousins Sandra and Claire and David on top of the TV.

'I haven't got the faintest idea,' I say.

'I've done stew anyway,' says Auntie Pearl with a resigned air, straightening. 'You *are* staying for tea. You *are*, because I've taken the cake out of the fridge.'

Stephen and I look at each other and he smiles suddenly, his eyebrows dipping down. 'Whatever,' he shrugs.

'Thanks, Auntie Pearl,' I say. I will never see my home again. 'That'll be lovely. We'd better leave about six though, I think.'

'Yeah,' says Stephen.

'Right,' she says determinedly, taking the butter away and stomping out of the room. Stephen's forehead shines like a sucked gobstopper. 'What are we going to do?' he says to me quickly. 'We can't just leave her here like this, what are we going to do?'

For a moment I think he's talking about Auntie Pearl. I give up.

'I don't know,' I say; 'you tell me.'

'We could take her back to your place. We could look after her.'

'Yes,' I say, 'all right,' going numb.

I look at Africa on the screen, the harsh African sun beating down on a lonely tree under which a small pride of lions lazes. It's too hot in here, much too hot. I must drink this cup to the very end. I can't stand it. I want to be at home like before, I want to have Sally Wilcock coming round for a piano lesson, to get up and go to work on Tuesday and for the sun to shine on the outside tables when I do the flowers. I want Veronica Karen to be out there doing her own stupid thing just like she always did.

I wish we'd never found her.

'We could come back in the morning and sort it all out,' he says. His eyes are round and slightly mad. 'Ask your Auntie Pearl about it. Go on.'

'Fancy a sherry?' she calls from the kitchen.

'No thanks, Auntie Pearl!'

But there's no chance, she's here now with the glasses.

'Auntie Pearl,' I say when she hands me a brimming schooner, 'do you think they'd let her come out?'

'She's not a prisoner,' Stephen says. 'She can do whatever she likes.'

Auntie Pearl looks pained, standing with one pale sausagey hand slung into her enormous pocket, the other delicately holding her glass between finger and thumb. 'Oh, she's better off where she is,' she says. 'They can look after her.'

He looks horrified. 'But she's going to die,' he wails. 'She needs to be at home.' His eyes fill up but don't overflow.

Auntie Pearl closes her mouth and shakes her head as if he's said something in bad taste, choosing not to sit in the very flat black armchair on Stephen's other side and make the three wise monkeys of us, but on an upright chair at right angles to us and opposite the telly. We are all silent, drinking. The sherry's cheap, the colour of henna shampoo. 'Well,' she says, legs ungainly splayed, stomach sitting up in front like a toad's croak, 'we don't see much of you these days, Cathy, do we?'

'No,' I say, 'isn't it awful? We ought to keep in touch more.'

'Well, I can't get about, you know. Not with this leg. Not like I used to. You'll find out when you get old.'

She drivels on about her leg and her arthritis and my cousin Claire's mammography, which turned out to be OK, thank God. Then she comes round with the sherry again. Stephen's drinking his with no sign of discomfort.

'No more, Auntie Pearl,' I say, covering my glass. 'I'm driving.'

'Oh, you sit down and have a little sherry,' she says, though I am sitting down already. 'Christ, you need something for your nerves.'

'No really, Auntie Pearl.'

But she shoves my hand aside unceremoniously and sloshes the neck of the bottle over my glass.

Oh well, I don't seem to have much say in things any more. I want to go home. If I just sip this vile stuff very very slowly, make it last, I should be OK by the time we've eaten. Stephen and she launch into a conversation about African hunting dogs, which have now appeared on the screen, running in a pack across the Serengeti. He's very good at keeping things going. Auntie Pearl's warming to him, I can tell. She keeps nipping up and down, topping up the glasses with a relentless beavering senility that brooks no opposition, in and out of the kitchen, no doubt to fill up her own, returning with pockets full of useful things like spoons and little egg-shaped salt and pepper shakers that she arranges very neatly all along the marbled brown tiles round the fireplace.

We're eating off our knees. There is a ceremony of handing round the plates, full of watery, salty stew that tries to run over the edges. Auntie Pearl is not a good cook, not like our mother. We eat with large spoons, scooping up the juice quickly to make it more manageable. The lions are having their dinner too, faces in the red trough of some poor zebra. Auntie Pearl and Stephen don't seem to notice it, but I stare, fascinated, thinking how funny it is that we're all having our dinner at the same time. I wonder what Veronica Karen has for dinner. Can she enjoy anything any more? I wish she was dead. I wish she was anything rather than how she is.

'Eat,' says Stephen to me.

I glance up at him and he smiles once, quickly, looking down immediately. He won't meet my eyes. What are we now, me and him? Just imagine us all together in my house. Me, Big Nurse, Mrs Danvers, mad, lurking around in the background. Them, Humphrey Bogart and Ingrid Bergman, Cathy and Heathcliff, Carmen and Don Whatsisname. Oh, it was all ridiculous, wasn't it? All that stuff. Heat of the moment. He caught me at a vulnerable time. After all, give him the least hint of encouragement, won't a man always try it on?

'Eat,' he says.

Auntie Pearl slobbers her food, smacking her lips as she tells long convoluted stories about the woman next door whom we've never met and probably never will. She puts down her plate and goes round with the sherry again.

'No more!' I cry.

I may even just end up being sick, I'm often sick at Auntie Pearl's.

'Ere, ere, ere!' she bullies, sloshing the damn thing wildly at me.

'No!'

I shout it, louder than I intended.

'Leave her alone,' says Stephen, 'she doesn't have to have a drink if she doesn't want one.'

'No, of course she doesn't,' says Auntie Pearl in a huff, walking away with the bottle.

'I'm driving,' I say.

She snorts softly.

How can I drive? How can I get home now? Oh, the bastard woman, I have to eat all this food to soak up her horrible sherry. My rage is a terrible worm swelling up my throat. I want to scream. Got to get away from here, got to get away. Look at him, he's no good, he's had more than me and he's still got that one there to go. Drinks like a fish. After all, what is he? Telling me to eat; look at him toying with his food. I put down my plate.

'You've eaten nothing,' she says, offended, 'the pair of you.'

We look at our feet like children.

'That's no way to carry on,' she says softly, going to pick up the plates, but Stephen jumps up and insists on gathering everything together and taking it all out to the kitchen.

'Just stick them in the dishwasher,' she calls out. Auntie Pearl isn't the dishwasher sort, but nothing's normal today.

'Lovely stew, Auntie Pearl,' I lie.

'It was always your favourite,' she says, picking at a thread on her sleeve and sighing. 'Is he the one that was sick?'

'That's right.'

'Thought so. I've got a good memory for faces. Bet you

never thought I could've remembered a lad after all those years, did you? Nice lad, isn't he? She should have stuck with him. She should have stuck with him and got married and settled down and had a couple of kids and then none of this would have happened.' Sourly, she scours her teeth with her tongue. 'I feel sorry for him, I do. She's got no sense.'

He reappears.

'I was just saying,' she says, folding her arms and putting her head on one side, 'she should have stuck with you if she'd had any sense.'

Stephen smiles. 'Oh, I don't really know about that,' he says. 'Things have a way of working out as they should in the end.'

'They don't,' she says darkly, rising shakily and stamping heavily out to fetch the cake. He leans towards me, peering over the massive bulk of his chair. 'What's the matter?' he says.

'What do you mean?'

'I just mean you seem, I don't know.' He covers his mouth and nose as if he were cold and was going to blow on his hands.

I half laugh. 'This is not a normal sort of day, is it?' I snap. 'How do you expect me to seem?'

He turns his face and looks straight at me and his eyes are so cold I know I've lost him. He's about to speak, but Auntie Pearl brings in a large blue and gold plate bearing a vulgar chocolate gâteau with a finish like a choppy sea of pale glutinous peaks, all shiny and granulated. Sweet stuff to gorge on. My eyes and tastebuds sting. Hunger and nausea wash up against each other like Hokusai waves. She deposits the plate with an efficient air right in the middle of the bright blue fun-fur rug and draws from her great apron pocket her terrible swift sword, a monstrous weapon all gleaming and vibrating like a maniac's blade in a horror film close-up. For a moment I expect her to turn like a robot and plunge it into me, I always knew she was mad, but instead she says, 'You'll have to do this, Cathy, I can't kneel down.'

I take the knife, get down on my knees and start cutting, turning the plate carefully, taking great care to get every slice exact as if someone's life depended on it. The fire's burning me up and his eyes are on my face. At last I sit back.

'Wow,' says Stephen, 'what a work of art.'

Auntie Pearl's dithering about with the bottle, a fat pink presence. The level in the bottle's getting low but no doubt she's got another stashed away somewhere. She actually has the cheek to refill my glass but I ignore it. I look at my watch.

'We'd better make a move after this,' I say.

'She's always in a hurry,' Auntie Pearl complains to Stephen, helping herself to gâteau. It's sickly and sticky, the kind of thing that returns to its original condition in your hand. Though my stomach shivers, as if tomorrow was my execution, it is hungry for this. I must feed it, stuff it, pack it like a punishment. I should not eat, I should not want to eat at a time like this. She doesn't provide plates, so we all end up licking cream from between our fingers and off our palms like meticulous cats. All the time she keeps up a monotone, an endless background drone of stories about people you've never heard of, their weddings and ailments and births and redundancies.

'Go on!' she urges, 'have some more! Go on! Put a bit of meat on your bones.'

What the hell. I eat cake.

'Don't you think she's too thin?' Auntie Pearl asks Stephen. 'They were both like that. Stand 'em sideways you couldn't see 'em.'

She takes frequent dainty little sips that never disturb her flow. Nothing will stop her now. Guns and wars and love affairs explode in bursts from time to time on the TV, loudly shouting in the sauna-heated room, but she flows over it all like a grand river. She takes off her apron and talks about the various merits of all the new shops that have opened up in the precinct, and where the nurse who comes to do her leg is going on holiday, and Claire's troubles at work with the dinner ladies, and Sandra's drain problems, and someone called Nor, whose husband's been on the sick for two years with depression.

I eat another slice of cake and start to feel sick. She'd have made a great drug dealer, Auntie Pearl, I think, watching her there with her tight blue skirt stretched over the sphere of her stomach, the sherry glass sitting on top like a lighthouse on a peculiar round rock. We are her prisoners, a couple of geese being stuffed for their livers. My gut lurches. She gets on to family stuff, tells the one about Veronica burning her bottom on the fire-guard, the one about me biting the dog, the time we fought over my Spanish Lady and Auntie Pearl took it off me and gave it to *her*: she scribbled all over the Spanish Lady's face. I watch this thing about magazine editors on the TV to take my mind off feeling sick.

Soon as it eases off, we'll go.

The Spanish Lady was *mine*.

'Of course, she was always very good at art at school, you know,' she's saying to Stephen. I think she's talking about Veronica Karen, then realise she means me. 'I don't know what she thinks she's doing working in a café. That's no job for a girl with a degree. Doesn't make the most of herself. Both of them, the same. You could never tell them any-thing.'

'That's true,' he says, turning to me accusingly. 'When are you going to write something again?'

'I'm not.'

'Well, what *are* you going to do?'

'What, when I grow up, you mean?' I laugh and a great swell of sickness runs up through me so that I have to get up at once and walk straight from the room. On the stairs I start running, collapse in the bathroom before Auntie Pearl's toilet and throw up all the vile cake and stew into the white lime-scaled bowl. I allow myself to cry a few stupid little tears while being sick because the feeling is so horrible and I want to die, then think: what about her? What does she feel like? I'm sorry, I'm sorry, I'm sorry, Veronica. I hang there for a while, flush twice, put down the lid and sit there with my back against the cistern waiting to see if I'm better or if it's all going to happen again. This is a nightmare. I feel like death. I won't get home tonight and I *want* to be home, I *want* to be home. If I were there, what would I do? Sit at my desk again. I could branch out. I could write something adult, or something that's neither. Could I illustrate it? They don't have illustrations in adult books, not unless you're Thackeray or some cleverdick. I rinse my mouth out again and again.

Something comes tapping at my memory: the mirage of sweet oblivion, so close, my lost hope, my insurance, the clear drip-drip of the water from the eaves like the dripping of the tap. I have to go back and stand on the edge of that cliff where I stood before he came, look down and see my foot about to slip.

I close my eyes. Please dear God, please get me through this.

I descend carefully, go carefully back to my chair and sit down. My head spins. Auntie Pearl's moaning to Stephen about Sandra: 'She comes now and then, but you know my nerves are all of a doodah after she's gone. Those kids are mad.'

'Still,' says Stephen, 'I suppose it's nice to see them.'

'Oh yes of course I'm always pleased to see them but I'm

glad to see the back of them too if you know what I mean. Emma's spoilt, you know, but you can't tell our Sandra. And I can't get over there with this leg.'

'I can't drive,' I get out.

They look at me.

'I was sick,' I say.

'Well, you'll have to stop here,' she says immediately, as if the whole thing was planned and she'd expected nothing else. 'You can have the box room, it's all made up, and this young man can sleep down here. That thing pulls out.'

'But I have to go home,' I mumble, panicked. 'I promised Veronica Karen I'd bring the photographs.'

'What photographs?'

'Just family photographs. All the old ones. I promised her I'd bring them in the morning.'

'Are you all right now?' Stephen asks, concerned.

'No,' I say, 'I don't think I am.'

'Oh, you don't want to go traipsing about tonight,' Auntie Pearl says comfortably. 'Why don't you just pop over in the morning while I'm down the hospital? Then you can see her in the afternoon if you want.'

I look at Stephen. He gives the faintest of shrugs. 'So long as I'm in London Tuesday afternoon for this interview,' he says.

'Fine,' I say, 'fine.'

I lean back and watch the antiques on the telly while the same old stories come rolling out, things she's said a million times. She gets so much wrong. If I say, No, Auntie Pearl, that wasn't Veronica, that was me, or, No, it wasn't there, it was at Rhyl, don't you remember, she cries me down as if we were in Parliament.

'I'd die for a cup of tea,' I say at last.

Stephen jumps up and dashes into the kitchen before anyone can move.

'Nice lad, isn't he?' she remarks flatly, scratching her nose, scarcely breaking the steady, complacent flow, from further back now, what Uncle Alan said to Uncle Vincent on the Lymm Fields outing, the Clitheroe Picnic, the time when Celia pulled Janet's hair. Then Auntie Pearl rises with a weary sigh and lumbers from the room with her sherry still clutched in her hand. I hear her groan slightly as she negotiates the stairs.

Stephen rushes in and falls to his knees. 'Aren't you going to talk to me?' he hisses urgently.

'What do you mean?'

'You've gone all funny!'

'I feel sick,' I say.

'It's not just that!'

'I don't know what you mean.'

He gazes into my face searchingly for a long time. Strange, I feel quite removed. I actually want to laugh. What a ridiculous life they gave me, after all. 'Stephen,' I say steadily, 'how am I supposed to behave? Tell me.'

But he just goes on looking and looking. 'Where have you gone?' he says.

'I'm here.' I laugh. 'I'm always here, it's everyone else who keeps going.'

Auntie Pearl's heavy descent can be heard on the stairs. He gets up and stands dishevelled, glaring malevolently at the door through which she enters wearing a long flowered nightie that bunches all around her and makes her look like Mrs Tiggywinkle. 'You don't mind me putting on my nightie, do you?' she says, plumping herself down on the flat black chair, 'I always get into my nightie at this time of night.'

'No, of course not.'

Oh bugger it, the poor old soul.

'Of course.'

She invites Stephen and me and all our friends to come and stay with her whenever we want to.

'Thank you,' says Stephen, 'that's very nice of you.'

'I mean, they'd have to understand, it's rough and ready like but they'd be very welcome, you know, just if they wanted a break somewhere.'

She's slurring her words now, just a bit.

'Rough and ready like,' she says, 'rough and ready.'

We have been here for a hundred years and we will never leave.

Auntie Pearl stands between us and the telly singing 'Yesterday', a bright round ball of a woman flinging her arms about slowly and heavily. Her wide face is uptilted to the naked bulb, her little eyes closed. Her voice throbs on the deep notes. I was thinking, wasn't I, I was thinking how nice it would be to go on the booze myself, Bessie Smith, Blanche DuBois, Edie Sedgewick and all that, although it wasn't booze with her, was it? All the sad glamour of it. But you have to be young. It can look good on you then. Don't grow old though, don't you dare grow old and be a drinker.

I look at Auntie Pearl and shudder.

Stephen lies back in his chair, one long hand draped across his bruised brow.

'You've not got a bad voice,' he says.

'Oh I have no illusions,' she says proudly, turning towards him with a small smile, 'I never had a voice.'

She sits down again on the high-backed chair and sticks her feet out in front of her. 'I'm not bad for my age,' she says. 'Look at those ankles,' rolling down her white popsocks for us to see better. 'You see,' she says, pointing out the way that her big toes turn in, 'all the women of our family, their feet go like that. Your mum had it and Grandma and Auntie Violet.' She rubs the red shiny knob on the side of one foot with the toes of the other. 'Veronica took after your dad, but you're like our side of the family,' she says meditatively. 'You'll get this. You'll go like me and your mam, you will.'

I want to fly up and scream at her: old hag! old bag! I will never be like you! I can't take any more. We are drenched in heat, our faces are red and shiny and Veronica Karen is out there dying.

'Auntie Pearl!' I jump up. 'Is it OK if I have a bath and then turn in? Have you got any hot water?'

'Course I have.' She sounds offended, as if I'd asked if she'd got an inside toilet.

'Oh good!'

I dash out, words echoing after me about towels and bath foam and such, but I don't wait to hear, I have to get away. She can talk him to death for all I care.

The bathroom is green and highly perfumed, so tiny it steams up in no time. A vast arched mirror fills the wall over the bath so that you can't help but see yourself undressing and getting in and out of the bath. Well, it's OK for me, look, the birth of Venus through the mist, one hand there – but I wouldn't want it if I was Auntie Pearl. Does she stand here looking at herself, I wonder? Anyway it soon mists over. On the tiles there's a shell containing a block of Imperial Leather, three little lidded pots wearing skirts, and a tall thin bottle of translucent purple bubble bath, which I drop in under the running water. It comes out in big blobs that sink like stones and cling there on the bottom of the bath like three vaguely anaemic purple molluscs, swishing about in a slow slug-like way as the water swirls past them. Wish I had my Clary Sage. I get the water really hot, then lower myself slowly down and ease back with the moisture settling on my face like mizzle and the warmth going through and through me.

Silence and drip–drip.

Sweet oblivion.

Rain dripping from the eaves, my quiet house ticking all around me. My parted legs lift in the water. I bring on an erotic fantasy about Stephen. I dream him coming up behind me and touching me all over with his big slow hands, the way he touched my piano that night standing there in my study, far away and long ago.

I dream on for a long long time. When I open my eyes I feel terribly lonely, and the water is cool.

The towel clings to me when I get out. I stand there looking at myself in the big mirror, assessing the effect. Smoothing my eyebrows, pulling the fleecy stuff tighter the better to define my buttocks, I think of going out there like this and encountering him on the small landing. I don't look anything like my mother or Auntie Pearl, thank God. I try to think of examples of women I know who don't look anything like their mothers, but all I can come up with are ones who look worse. Great. I gather up my clothes and cross the tiny landing in two steps to Auntie Pearl's box room, where I stand drying myself with obsessive, probing movements, thinking of his hands. It's like a berth in a ship. There's the old bedding chest with a crocheted cover on top, squashed in under the window, and an MFI bookcase for Auntie Pearl's dog-eared paperback library of violent pornography and slasher horror. Many a moment I whiled away amongst those pages, in my youth, on Saturday afternoon visits while Mum and Auntie Pearl nattered on about some family intrigue or other. Next to the bed there's a space of about ten inches where I stand naked combing through my wet hair and wondering what to wear in bed tonight. I'm running out of things. I open the chest and find a whole load of Veronica Karen's stuff on top, some letters and photographs and a couple of bashed-about exercise books, and my heart stops because I know I'll have to read them. There's a little jewelled bag with some old make-up dirtying up the bottom, and an old green dress which I remember she used to wear years ago, one of those things you always saw her in for a while, well loved. It's in photographs of a certain time when we were all down in London together, the lot of us. She was wearing it the time she came in with Alexander, that time in Frank's old flat, when Tonto was there, and she came running in and said: 'Look who I've found!' Alexander's eyes were sleepy and crinkled when he smiled, and my heart went pit-a-pat just like it says in the songs.

Lying on the bed like a lovely ghost, the dress shows thin and faded, the seams all frayed to nothing under the arms and bust. Oh, she looked lovely in it, she did, like a fairy princess. You could get away with looking like that in those days if you could carry it off, and she did, she did, she floated in this elegant green thing, the colour of faded moss, the softness of very old muslin. It showed off her narrow waist and the smooth beginnings of her cleavage.

I can't help it. I kick aside the towel and slip into the dress and it fits perfectly, falling into place upon me like Cinderella's shoe. There is no mirror but I know what I look like. I might give him a heart attack, I'll be like the second Mrs De Winter appearing at the top of the stairs in the first Mrs De Winter's dress. For one miraculous moment his heart will leap into his mouth, he'll think it is she, restored to health and beauty. Then he will recognise me and realise, with a small shock, the true depth of his disappointment.

I hurry it off. I can't wear Veronica Karen's things. I put everything back and poke about in the chest and find one or two funny old winceyette nighties and a very long white T-shirt with one of those awful Love is . . . things on it with that little fat boy and girl mooning about with hearts all round their heads. I put it on and get into bed thinking, this is where she slept. This is where she must have got sicker. Close my eyes. Slow breathing. No think, no feel.

There is a tap on the door.

'Yes?' I call, tight-voiced.

Stephen comes in and sits on the bed. 'She can talk, your Auntie Pearl, can't she?' he says.

'You're not kidding.'

He smiles, tired, shoulders drooping. 'And you,' he says, 'you've gone a million miles away. I can't get at you. Are you ever coming back?'

'I wanted to go home,' I say. 'We should never have stayed for tea, we should just have gone. This always happens.'

'What?'

'The sherry! That awful sherry! Where does she get it? It probably costs about two and six a bottle.'

He laughs. 'I know. I feel a bit weird myself. God knows what her liver's like. But sometimes, you know, you just have to go with the flow.'

'The flow! Trouble is, it's her flow, isn't it? No one else's.'

'Yeah, well . . .' he shrugs.

'How we can all sit around making smalltalk at a time like this.'

He fingers his bruise. 'Wouldn't do any good if we all sat around weeping and wailing, would it?' he says.

'I know, but she just goes on and on and on and . . .'

'She's lonely,' he says simply.

And I'm a cow.

'I think it's really good that she acts so natural when she's got people around,' he continues, leaning back with his hands behind his head. 'The way she just goes and puts on her nightie because she feels like it and puts the cake on the floor. No airs. I really like all that.'

'So what are your plans?' I ask. 'Are you coming back after your interview?'

'Of course I am.'

'So what are your plans?'

'Why do you sound so angry?'

'I'm not angry, I'm just confused.'

'What about?'

'It's you,' I say, 'I'm confused about you.'

His face is unreadable. The longer we don't speak the worse everything is. What I want, I realise, is for him to promise me everything, nothing less, promise his bloody soul here and now, but instead he reaches out and tries to pull me into a clumsy embrace.

'Not now,' I say, pushing him away, not roughly, 'not here,' but his eyes widen and he stands up.

'I'm not interested,' he says quietly, 'I'm just not interested, Cathy. You're just playing games. Do you think I'd have said all that about having a baby and everything if I wasn't dead serious? Do you? I'm sick of it, Cathy, I'm sick of it, I've had it all before. Life's too short.'

'I can't stand to see you slobbering all over Veronica Karen,' I say, regretting it immediately. 'I just can't stand it.'

His hand goes over his face and sits there like the thing from *Alien*.

'I'm a replacement, Stephen. I won't be it.'

He grabs my arm.

'I don't believe this,' he says, 'I don't believe this.'

For a moment I think he might go off into his Heathcliff-in-agony routine again, but instead he gets up and goes to the door and turns back again. 'Look, she's dying and I've got to say everything to her now before she goes, OK? She's the oldest friend I've got, that's all. Don't make me feel I'm looking over my shoulder all the time. Oh, Cathy!' He flops down on the bed again. 'You drive me up the wall, the pair of you!'

'What about me?' I say. 'You just talk about her all the time. What about me?' I'm going to cry. No, I'm not.

He grips my shoulders. 'Kiss me,' he says in a hostile voice, 'kiss me.' He shakes me. 'I need a kiss.'

We kiss. His face is big and hot and his breath smells stale. His tongue gives me shivers.

He pulls back and makes a small sound of exasperation. 'Don't force yourself,' he says, kissing me again on the mouth so hard it hurts, then gets up and goes to the door. 'It's not as if I don't love you,' he mumbles, grim-faced as he goes.

I flop face down into the pillow for a while. I think my lip is a little cut from his teeth; it is, I can taste blood. You know, he comes on all innocent with this oh–I'm-so-uncomplicated lark, but really when you think about it, what skill, what an exit. It's called leaving the tea to brew.

I open my eyes and see Veronica Karen's boots, wedged in between the bookcase and the wall.

They must be hers because they're certainly not Auntie Pearl's with her bunions and all. They're bent over tipsily at the ankles, with a tidemark turning white as if she's walked in mud or water and not bothered to clean them. They have pointed toes and flat heels and the leather's cracking over the toes.

I jump out of bed and dash to the chest. I have to do this. I have to take out all her things and haul them back to bed with me and squat on the pillow going through them.

Letters: nothing much, people I've never heard of writing from places like Turkey and Goa and Morocco about other people I've never heard of. An old valentine with a red silk heart. From Stephen, I know because of the stab in my heart, from Stephen when he was a boy. As I read, as I look, something smoulders and snarls, some mad mutant beast licking its flayed sides, offspring of fury and quaking guilt. It wants to rip and smash and tear these things. A couple of small dog-eared exercise books, blue, lined, a bit of Christmas sellotape stuck to one, bright green leaves, ruby red berries. Pages of gushy slop about people she fancies, as if she were a moony girl of thirteen. Cosmic ramblings about oneness, tarot spreads, lists (Kat Food again), names, recipes, lots of swirly pictures of romantic landscapes with winding rivers that get etched in again and again till they are shining black. Awkwardly folded, my letter: Dad's getting worse. He would love to see you. Sometimes I wonder how long he's got left.

She kept it.

Photographs: a bunch of people sitting round a campfire outside two tents; someone's flat, lots of people, one reading a book; black cat sitting on a chest of drawers; Camden Market, stall full of bric-à-brac, grinning black-haired woman in big winter clothes; Veronica Karen standing outside Desmond's Hip City in Brixton with a new spiral perm and very tight trousers. Nothing of me but this very old thing, she a baby in a bib, me a little girl in coat and bonnet. Nothing of Stephen. But look here – Veronica Karen and Alexander, hugging and laughing under a leafy green tree, she in a long black cloak. Lord love him, look at him, oh look at him then. He was good enough for anyone, my sweet doomed youth.

His soft, clear voice carries down the years:

Oh, Peggy Gordon, you are my da-a-a-arling,
Come sit you down upon my knee
And tell to me, the very re-e-e-eason
Why I am slighted so by thee.

Fury. Here she is sitting on a wall in a short skirt, legs all posed.

You know what she thought she was when she posed for those pictures, the ones Frank took? Marilyn Monroe spread out naked on red satin, greatness before her.

I put these things away, intact, turn off the light and lie down quivering in the dark she hated, the dark I put her in. I hear a faint disturbance from afar, sense the hollow rumbling, the trains going over Hog's Head Bridge.

Whoo whoo.

But the trains don't whistle any more.

Only the trains, Veronica, only the trains.

14

Last night and the night before I went to sleep early and woke at midnight and couldn't sleep then for hours, and here I am again. Must be nerves, I suppose, though I don't *feel* particularly nervous. Feel kind of nothing. Big day tomorrow. My brain turns this way and that. Well, it's nice to be back in my own bed again. You know, it's a terrible thing that my sister is dead and all I can think about is seeing him again tomorrow at the funeral. I don't know whether we will be strangers or not. I don't know anything. It's been two whole days. I could smell him on me all day going about Shugden with Claire, doing all the things that had to be done that day she died. I'm sunk now. I know it. I knew it as soon as he'd gone, because I started worrying about him straight away: before he'd even got out of the door I was thinking about him driving all that way alone with his load of shock, because he was white and silent and didn't know what to say or what to do with his eyes. He's never had grief before, poor baby, and it *was* a shock, her going so sudden like that, when we all thought we would see her again. No one told us her heart was going to give out. We hadn't even had time to get the pictures for the walls, maybe the one of Narcissus and the Nymphs, maybe the Desiderata, she liked all that hippie stuff. Hadn't had time to get the photographs, the one of Ambrose on the fence. She just died alone there in that pale room with the tubes and the silver machines, while we, polite and ill at ease with one another, were getting the breakfast at Auntie Pearl's.

When I got home to Moorcop I felt as if I'd been very far away, to the source of the Orinoco or a lost valley in Tibet, somewhere like that. Many years had passed since I had seen my house. I was standing in the hall feeling punch-drunk when the phone rang. It was a priest wanting to know about Veronica Karen.

'How would you sum up your sister?' he asked sympathetically. 'What are the sort of words that spring to mind when you think about her?'

I had to think hard, closing my eyes to do so.

I said she was very bright.

I said she was kind to animals.

I said she was very sensitive and imaginative.

I replaced the receiver, eyes still closed, put my hand out in the dark. 'It's OK,' I said. 'I'm here. I was here all the time.'

Then I got changed into my dark green T-shirt with the broken crotch fastening, my good leggings and my red chenille thing and went down town and bought some Wensleydale with apricot and a big jar of Garner's pickled onions and a bottle of Norfolk Punch, and went down Patacake Alley into Connor's and told them what had happened. They were very nice about it. I thought about saying it was her heart, which is true up to a point, and leaving it at that because you never know with somebody like Mrs Crowe how she'd react about a thing like AIDS. But then I thought, what's wrong with the truth? Mrs Crowe seemed OK. She came out from the back and patted me on the shoulder and gave me the rest of the week off work and made me sit in the corner booth and have a Costa Rican coffee of the week on the house. And after that word got around, this being Moorcop, and people have been ringing me up and sending me cards ever since.

People really are very kind.

It's funny, my house feels the same but I am not the same. I walk about it begging it to reassure me, but it just puts its arms around me without a word, refusing to deny that things are tough. But you've still got me, it says, and that's all that it can say. I must get back to normal as quickly as possible. Back to what? The past. These things have happened. You cannot get back to the past. My room is too silent. I can hear all the little voices of my thinking; I can lie back and observe their endless mirror regression into the cosmos. My own heartbeat is all I have. I must get some sleep. I have to put Veronica Karen with all the others, in the place where they go.

He hasn't rung. He didn't say he would. He didn't say much. He turned and shook my hand formally at the door, a curious, ominous gesture, squeezing, hurting, and when I looked down his hand was trembling. 'Was it us?' he whispered. 'Do you think it was the shock of seeing us?'

'There's always a question like that,' I said. Because there is.

Auntie Pearl was there; we didn't kiss.

Midnight.

A whole other day gone and I'm still here.

It's funny, when someone's gone, you still think of them in time and space, as if they're on a finite journey. I suppose she must be well on her way by now, you feel. Stopover at Singapore.

Dark in here. I put out my hand. How can I reach that far?

'It's OK,' I say.

Stopover on the rings of Saturn.

Well. People die on you, and that's a fact.

15

I've done my own flowers. Mixed roses. Oh, I do love mixed roses! It is the most perfect wreath I have ever done, a gorgeous riot of faded coppery and Titian tones with just the right sprinkling of small blood-red faces peeping through here and there. They are roses in a fairy tale, just right for the Princess Verona, taking pride of place on top of the palomino-coloured coffin that goes on before us in the big black hearse. We follow through the sun and rain of Shugden, crawling by the shoppers and the street of banks and the outdoor market and all the little roads running out to the high, bright crematorium.

Up here you can smell the air from the moors.

There he is.

He's not with me, he's with them, the London people. They come into the porch of the crematorium together from two cars. Bobbie smiles at me uncertainly and I smile back. I never really knew her. She's from the edge of Veronica Karen's life where it started blending away from mine into that other world. The others I don't know at all. There's a balding villain with red miserable roaming eyes, a little hippie man with long black hair and a brown velvet jacket, a tall gaunt woman with large hurt lips and brown cropped hair, and a solemn couple consisting of a pretty woman with too much face make-up and a heavy black man in a suit. And there's Stephen, still with his bruise, his badge of grief, though it is paler. Our eyes meet briefly but I can't bear not being able to read his and jerk mine away.

My cousin Sandra, a long, dark, spiky woman, takes my arm. 'Come on,' she says.

We go in and get into the flimsy pine pews, Auntie Pearl and Sandra and I at the front because we're closest family, with Uncle Alan and Auntie Violet behind with my cousins Claire and David. It's quite a good turn-out, lots of people I don t know, all kinds. Simon and Patch sent a card. Frank's here with Tonto. Russell and Patti have come. I sent Alexander a note but he's not here. Well, I didn't think he'd make it. As we stand here in this cold little hall, watching the coffin, which looks so small out there all alone, I am wondering where in the crowd is Stephen. Can he see me with my lipstick on and my hair taken back just so and this lovely black dress I always bring out for funerals? I'd wear a veil if I dared.

He should be here, at the front. He loved her as much as anyone.

Susannah told me years ago about when they told her her mother was dead. She was fifteen. There was a boy there that she fancied, and when they told her, all she could think was that she was special now, different from the rest, it would make her interesting to him. She said he was watching her and she started to cry, mechanical. I wonder if he's feeling sorry for me, she thought. But she hardly felt a thing.

Not then.

The priest, a tall young man with flat black hair and glasses, speaks from the lectern, his presence radiating a sense of nerves kept down by tremendous effort. He praises Veronica Karen's wit and charm and beauty and says what a good friend she was to so many, how she brightened up the lives of those who knew her. He cites her creativity, how she made jewellery and baked good cakes and excelled at playing the six-stringed dulcimer. Six-stringed dulcimer? What's he talking about? She did have one lying around once but she could never play it. Anyway, it doesn't have six strings, does it? And he speaks of her abiding affection for this place, for Shugden where she was born and grew up, how she always spoke with such warm regard of her early years here, and how sorely she would be missed by all her family.

I float somewhere above, a black widow in a veil, disconnected.

I wish we were in a church with Gothic windows, all dressed in heavy mourning with veils and things and pallbearers and mutes. More her style really, a bit of drama. And we would file out and process around the churchyard and they would lower her down under cedars and willow and we'd throw in handfuls of earth and possibly flowers and stand with bowed heads, the men fumbling the brims of their hats.

All gone into the world of light.

I click to attention. She's going. Her little yellow box with the lovely flowers on top is sliding away, the red curtains opening with a balletic ripple, whoosh!

She's taken my mixed roses away.

The flowers are all lined up outside in an odd little concrete walkway, tunnel-like. We roam along their line-up like the Queen inspecting the troops. I smell rain. Stephen's not looking at me. Patti and Russell and Tonto kiss me. My spivvish cousin David, a builder's merchant, says hello and introduces his girlfriend, Inge. Auntie Pearl looks very old between Sandra and Claire. He should be here, giving me support, not over there with those strangers. Did it all mean nothing then? Am I just someone in the crowd? We progress out into the car park, leaving the lonely bouquets with their wide silky ribbons coloured like small girls' party bows quivering in a little cold breeze that's springing up. Soon the wind will blow rain into their concrete tunnel, spattering the grey flags. I think of a mandala in the sand, seagulls on a rooftop, pavement art washed away by rain.

Sandra lights a cigarette in the car, musses her hair and

blows out smoke. 'It's a series of hurdles, Cath,' she says, turning to me in the back seat. The bones of her chin are chisel-edge fine, hard as metal. 'That's one more got through.'

Life, I suppose.

Stephen's red Fiesta, full of people, passes us going out on to the long sweep of the path. Sandra draws in a long sigh, straightens and drives. 'Are you all right, Mum?' she asks Auntie Pearl.

Auntie Pearl has carried a certain bitter stoicism about with her for years. She is armoured with it now, staring stony-faced ahead of her. '*I'm* all right,' she says queru-lously. 'It's this one here I'm worried about.'

She jerks a thumb at me.

'It's OK, Auntie Pearl,' I say, smiling, 'I'm all right.'

But she gives that disgusted sniff she does, the small toss of the head, dismissive.

Why didn't he come up to me? Why didn't he say any-thing?

At Sandra's house the double doors are folded back and the table is covered in sandwiches prettily arranged in brown and white circles, salmon and egg mayonnaise and stuffed chicken roll with cress and twisted cucumber gar-nish. Sandra and Claire and I pour drinks in the kitchen. Who gets the funeral they deserve? Where are the cakes and ale? Half of us are being careful because we're driving. I take an advocaat to Auntie Violet and Tonto accosts me on the way.

'She was special,' he says.

'Yes, Tonto.'

He smiles, a bashful, courageous kind of a smile. There is an echo of the romantic about his large handsome head, grizzling now with the years.

'Will we keep in touch now, Cathy?' he asks. 'I think we should.'

'We will, Tonto.'

It comes to me that I could probably have Tonto if I really wanted to, and what a mess it would be in the end.

'Here you are, Auntie Violet,' I say, bending down with the glass of advocaat.

She flounders about like a beetle trying to get off its back, a look of momentary intense anguish on her face changing to a smile. 'Thank you, pet,' she says wearily.

I smile. I wonder when all these people changed. I wasn't looking. How did they get so old? How did Auntie Pearl get so fat? Where's Mummy and Daddy and Veronica? Why is Sandra's face so haggard? Stephen's sitting with Bobbie and the tall shorn woman and the balding villain, an intense dangerous-looking man with a vulnerable wandering stare, who rubs his face with his hands from time to time. Another lover, obviously. His eyes look sore from blinking back tears.

Frank steps in front of me. 'Tilly sends her regards,' he intones, 'and says let bygones be bygones.'

'Oh, of course, Frank. Don't worry about it.'

He's wearing a suit and looks like a waiter. He should have a tea cloth over one arm.

'Look, Cathy,' he says, leaning close, 'I'm really sorry about all that scene at our place, you know how it is, things get out of hand.'

'That's OK, Frank. I know.'

'Tilly and me, we've got something for you, something we'd like you to have. Got your car, have you?'

'Yes.'

He beckons with his head, a shifty gesture suggesting intrigue.

I follow him out into the hall. 'What is it?'

'Come on,' he says, still head-beckoning, 'come on out to the car.'

Down the path to the gate, past the hydrangeas, Frank's solemn little figure leads me to his old black Beetle. Shivering, he lights a cigarette with one hand while fumbling with the boot with the other. 'Gonna rain later,' he says. The sallow skin around his eyes is crazed like very old china. Suddenly I'm convinced it's photographs. Probably even worse than the last lot, yes, these are the real filthy ones. We never really knew each other, me and Frank. We don't speak as he throws up the boot and hauls out a huge British Home Stores bag, the weight of which pulls his arms to the ground. The faint rattle of a snake breathes from its open mouth.

'Weighs a ton,' he says, bending down and holding it open so I can look in. 'Go and open your boot and I'll dump it in.'

It's the bead curtain, lying like a nest of white bones, coil upon coil, massive, soiled with the soiling of years. The Worm Ouroboros, sleeping.

'Oh Frank . . .' I palely say, as the pale serpent rears, rising in me as a possessing spirit, forcing up my gullet, 'the curtain!'

The boom of doom begins in my ears. I cannot speak.

'We thought you should have it.' He squints through cigarette smoke, hauling it up.

I run to my car and open up the boot. My heart shakes me down to the soles of my feet. The curtain stirs as he puts it down but settles back into sleep in a moment.

'I'm so glad you gave me that,' I say, hugging myself, grinning foolishly, biting off my words as my teeth begin to chatter. I am cold.

Why am I? Why am I so pleased to see this useless curtain, this folly?

'It's yours,' he says, and pats my arm.

She made that, she sought it out inch by inch along the foreshore, soaked and rinsed and poked muck. I see the writing on the stems, the makers' names. This cold is fear, feels like fear, deep-down fear of her in my head for the rest of time.

'What a time!' Frank says, pulling on his fag, looking up at the sky. 'What a bloody time, eh, Cath?'

A few spots of rain appear on the flagstones.

Back in the hall Patti comes up to me, looking bright and healthy as if she's just been striding over the moors in her old-fashioned sensible bottle-green dress, smiling her big smile. 'One good thing,' she says, her voice crackling, 'it's been really lovely to see you again. You *are* coming up to see us very very soon. You absolutely are. OK? I'm getting it straight now because Russell and I have to go shortly.'

How nice to be able to leave just like that whenever you felt like it. I wish I could just walk out of here when no one was looking, keep walking till I come up on to the moors, and then keep on some more, miles and miles and miles, all the way back to Moorcop.

'Of course I will,' I say, 'and you must come and see me too.'

These are the things you say at funerals. I'm OK. I'm fine. Handling it.

'You're coming to us for Christmas,' she says firmly. 'It's a date. If you can. If you want to, of course. And you can bring someone if you like.'

I think of the chapel snowed up, hot toddies and mulled wine and roaring fires; chocolate liqueurs, very expensive ones. Russell and Patti always do things in style.

'Do you know,' I say, 'I think that would be lovely.'

We go back into the living room. Stephen's nowhere to be seen though some of the London people are still about the place. Auntie Pearl has collared the big black guy and is telling him all about her days as a hat-check girl in Blackpool in the 1940s.

'Yeah?' he's saying in tones of deep amazement, '*yeah*?'

She grabs my arm.

'He's on the TV!' she proclaims.

The black guy grins.

'Are you?' I ask.

'Well,' he says, 'sometimes.'

'He's been in *Children's Ward*!' she crows.

People's glasses need topping up. I go into the kitchen to open another bottle of wine and it's just like a party, all the kitchens in all the parties I've ever been to in my life, all the bottle-covered tables and emergency stacks of plastic cups and dishes piling up on the draining board and the babble of voices. Stephen comes in while I'm struggling with the corkscrew.

'Bloody thing,' I say, 'bloody stupid corkscrew.'

He stands with folded arms, watching me. I get the cork halfway out and wrestle with it like Jacob struggling with the angel.

'Are you OK?' he asks.

'I'm OK.'

'I just thought I'd wait,' he says, 'and see how long you could ignore me.'

My heart jumps.

'I wasn't ignoring you. You were with all those people, I couldn't just walk up.'

'Why not?'

Russell appears in the doorway. 'Have you got a cloth, Cathy?' he asks with wet hands outstretched.

I look wildly about. This isn't my house, how do I know where a cloth is? I give him the one out of the sink.

'You haven't even asked me about the interview,' Stephen says.

My cousin Claire walks in with a plate of crumbs that was once thin slices of fine Madeira cake.

'So how was your interview?' I ask him.

'Fine.'

'Did you get it?'

'Just mind out of the way, lovey,' says Claire, moving him to one side with her hands as if he was a vase.

'Yeah,' he says grimly.

'Oh, that's good.'

Claire runs water into the sink.

'What do you want me to do?' he says bitterly. 'Get down under your window and serenade you?'

Is he mad?

Not here. Not with her listening back. I go out into the hall to get away from Claire so we can talk, but he doesn't follow me. How can he say I was ignoring him when it was the other way round? He doesn't come. Auntie Pearl heaves herself out into the hall. This is hopeless. I go back into the living room and sit down next to Auntie Violet. When he comes in he walks straight past me and sits with the balding villain, who is weeping openly now, desperate, unabashed, childlike tears. It's funny, you can never tell the ones who'll cry. I thought Tonto would have done, but he's been all dignified compassion and brave resolution. I wondered what she saw in the villain, but when I look I see that he has a nice face. Just the sort she'd go for in fact, soft at heart but seriously flawed and a bunch of trouble.

Poor man, poor hard man, he's done for.

Not me. I cope.

Stephen gets up suddenly and walks across the floor to get another sandwich from the side table near the back window. There is a terrible surge in me at that moment, a chronic lack of faith in love and happiness, a fatal disbelief. Just about all the couples I ever knew broke up. Think of the oceans opening their maw to swallow you. Think of the everlasting arms of loss. That's what it feels like, watching him walk across the floor and knowing it's hopeless, the will o' the wisp going on before across the benighted bog. For now I see without doubt that he is the Roc, the something big that now and then comes. He's a new party frock with ribbons and a sash, my first crush, a walk along an Irish strand, the plucked string of a fiddle, fireworks from the back window, the first time I got gloriously drunk, the best speed you ever had. He's a magnet. He's my treat, my sweet indulgence, Turkish Delight for the little princess. It's not possible that this should happen to me, and at a time like this. I've fallen again, fatally stabbed.

Oh God this time, this time, this time, says that little whiner inside, oh this time please, if you let me have him I promise you I'll never complain about anything ever again.

I go upstairs with Sandra and Claire because they want to show me some old things of Veronica's they think I might want. There's a dolls' house chair made out of matchboxes, an address book, my mother's golden wedding ring with a string tied round it, a child's silver bangle. And then they want to reminisce a while, about going to Lymm Fields and seeing frogs and falling in the nettles and taking Veronica for a ride round the flats on the handlebars of Uncle Vincent's old bike.

All these things, all these things I remember. Round and round in my fingers the silver bangle turns. A tiny wrist it once adorned, you'd never get that on your wrist now, would you? I'll keep it in my pocket perhaps, my fingers will touch it as I walk about.

And when I get downstairs again the London people have gone.

Panic hits, as if I were a child turning round in the street and finding itself lost. He's gone with them, he has, he has, oh the bastard, I hate him, he can't do this to me. My stomach drops a little more and a little more as I wander from the living room to the dining room, from there to the kitchen, even peering out of the window at the back as if it were not just Sandra's little square garden out there, with the grass and the dandelions and the clothes line, but the topiaried walk of a great estate where they'd all just gone for a turn about the grounds.

I meet Auntie Pearl in the hall. 'When did Stephen go?' I ask her.

She's had a few, her face has that slack look about it. 'Who?' she says, craning her whole head and squinting with the effort of hearing.

'Stephen.'

'Has he gone?'

271

David's new girlfriend squeezes past on her way to the toilet. I'm going to cry. I'm going to cry. How did I get this weak again? But I won't, they'll all think I'm overcome about Veronica Karen and they'll be ever so kind and I'll be stuck here with cups of hot sweet tea and Pearl's sherry for ever.

This is it.

While they're in there going round kissing everyone and saying goodbye. They'll be looking for me soon.

I grab my jacket and bag from the pegs and run.

16

The chippie's open for the evening; the smell of it mingles
with the rain that's pouring down as I reach home. My
street is shiny and soulful, the light from the shop falling
yellow over the wet pavement. Behind the swollen grey sky,
whispering like the rustling of silk skirts, a white light
shines. I get the bead curtain out of the boot, haul and
wrestle it in and turn on all the lights, draw the curtains,
put on the kettle for the safe sound of its crooning. I could
get pissed now, pop across the road for a bottle of Hardy's
Stamps. Oh dear me, the little lady of Ch'ing-Ch'i takes to
the wine. It's too warm for a fire. The light's flashing in
threes on the answering machine. I press the button. Sally
Wilcock wants to change her piano lesson to Monday.
Sandra asks if I'm OK. Give us a quick ring, she says, so I
can tell Mam you got back safe. Only me, says Susannah,
er, call you back later.

I dump the curtain under the stairs. God knows where I'll put it, I don't know if I'd want to be looking at it all the time. There's a feeling I have, like when you're seventeen and love's an intolerable weight you'll never bear. But you do, you bear it again and again all your life till you think that's it, you're immune, you'll never get it again, you think you're OK, you're jogging along then wham bam here it comes, terrible as ever it was. Isn't it funny? I was going to kill myself because I couldn't feel, and now I can feel and it's killing me. I'd never have done it. I know that now. Never in a million years. The dripping of the eaves is just too good to leave. In it there are symphonies, vast contained minimalist things, a series of oms.

I stand listening in the kitchen. Is there anybody there? said the traveller. Oh Lord, aren't there any sweets for me?

I get out the Wensleydale with apricot and my sharp knife and cut very thin slivers from the side, laying them in a perfect fan upon my old rose saucer. Good. Small things, small things, small steps, girl. You'll make it. I put on the coffee. Do it right. Better ring.

I get David. 'You just dashed off!' he says. 'No, it's all right, they was just a bit worried, that's all. Sandra's just running Mum home. Uncle Alan and Auntie Violet went . . .'

Claire calls something in the background.

'Oh God, no rest around here,' David says.

I should have stayed and helped clear up. Who do I think I am? This is what *she* would have done. 'Oh, I'm

sorry, David! You know, everyone seemed to be drifting off
and I just got a bit upset and . . .'

''S OK,' he says. 'Not a problem. You take care of yourself now. You get in touch with old Pearl soon, she's
worried about you.'

'OK.'

'Nice to see you again, kiddo,' he says. 'Probably catch
up with you again in about ten years.'

'Probably. So have they all gone then? All the people?'

I hear him draw on his cigarette. 'Yeah.'

A silence.

'Well, it was nice to see you again, David. If you're ever
in Moorcop, you and Inge.'

'Yeah, thanks. We could make a day of it.'

Click.

The silence of the house and the rain: I eat the cheese
with my fingers. Well, he knows where I am. He knows. I
go in and light a fire, take out the child's silver bangle from
my purse and smooth it round and round between my fingers should have been kinder. When the school board
came, she put her arm round me. She said, 'It's all right,
Cath, it'll be all right, it'll be all right, Cath.' I place the
bangle in my little box on the mantelpiece. Well well, Sally
Wilcock's become a regular. Now if she tells some of her
posh friends and I get a couple more regulars I might buy
some time to write my book. There's not a thing in my
head though. I drift back through to the kitchen, see my
sharp knife lying on the side and put it away in the cutlery

drawer, automatic. I always do that in case a serial killer breaks in, or even just a common-or-garden criminal in a panic. I put my hand into the darkness under the stairs and touch the sleeping coils of her pointless bead curtain. Now what kind of a bloody stupid thing is that to do, putting the knife away? I mean, how's that going to help? If you're a serial killer you bring your own knife presumably, and if you don't, where's the first place you're going to look? The cutlery drawer. Makes more sense to put it in the washing machine. I'll turn into a sad old lady in a nightie putting her knives in the washing machine every night before she goes to bed.

I put my hand into the darkness under the stairs and whisper: 'Sorry. Veronica Karen, I'm sorry.'

'It's all right, Cath, it'll be all right, it'll be all right, Cath,' she says.

I start to cry. She shouldn't be up there with the rain spattering into her concrete tunnel. She should be under cedars, listening to the trains going over Hog's Head Bridge.

Hugging myself in my chair, I let the long torrent quietly pour.

The doorbell rings and I jump. Quick! Quick! Give me the monkey's paw and I'll wish! It's my silly sister, come to play. It's the demon lover, oh where have you been, my long long love, these seven long years and more? It's the Angel of Death with a smile to say wait now, wait now, soft, you called and I came.

It rings again, insistent, so I go to the door with my heart in my mouth and fumble at the lock, opening the door on to Bluebeard's chamber.

Hallelujah.

He's leaning his shoulder against the door frame, arms huddled, wet hair dripping over his face. Oh take me in out of the storm, say his eyes. 'I'm parked just up the hill,' he mumbles. 'Can I come in?'

I stand back and he brushes past me.

Hallelujah. Hallelujah.

In the room we hover about each other. His bruise is yellow.

'Were you so very desperate to give me the slip?' he says tightly.

'I thought you'd gone.'

'Don't be stupid. Don't be *stupid.*'

He starts to cry. Oh, child, come to me. I take his big head in my hands and kiss his face and tell him not to cry, though I love his crying, the way it pulls at me. We lie down and weep together on the rug, close and warm, and when we are not crying any more we are kissing and there is nothing else left for us to do.

Three or four times now I've heard a cock crow from the gardens by the canal, out there in the dark. It's not raining any more. Soon I'll go back to sleep, but there's something I want to get down. Now, quickly, something I remember and want to get down. I rise from the warmth of the nest, his heavy slumbering balm, run a finger down his naked spine and feel around for my pink bathrobe and put it on, tiptoe out on to the landing and into my study and turn on the light.

I see my sister's first long brown stare when she was a baby, and think: I know what I'll do, I'll leave out Jem the Gypsy Boy and Giant Killyloo and Dame Doolily and all the rest and I'll just get this down, just this one thing. Ten tons of dust cover my desk, my word processor, my big dictionary, my little bowl of paper clips. Ten tons of dust, but never mind, I only need a pen and paper for this. It's just my first conscious memory, her first long brown stare, when my father in his uniform carried me from Auntie Pearl and Uncle Vincent's in the days when Auntie Pearl was really something with her thick henna-red hair and crimson lipstick. He took me back to my house, and we went in, and my mother was sitting in a chair with the baby on her lap, all resplendent in white lace, and they said: 'This is your little sister.' And she looked at me with her long brown unblinking stare, only now I know, of course, that her eyes would have been blue, slate blue, because babies' eyes always are. But I remember them brown because her eyes were brown, Veronica Karen's eyes were always brown.

There. That will do. It'll come clearer tomorrow.

THE CURE FOR DEATH BY LIGHTNING

Gail Anderson-Dargatz

'I loved it from the first page, she's fluent and graceful and there's passion and tension, in fact all I want from a novel. The writing is so powerful and yet shows a restraint that tightens the whole atmosphere. An excellent read – I was gripped' – *Margaret Forster*

The remote Turtle Valley in British Columbia is home to fifteen-year-old Beth Weeks and a community of eccentric but familiar characters. There, amidst a stunning landscape of purple swallows and green skies, strange and unsettling events occur: children go missing, a girl is mauled by a crazy bear and Beth too is being pursued . . .

The *Cure for Death by Lightning* is a rich and thrilling novel, as filled with strange deeds and dark fears as with beauty and magic.

You can order other Virago titles through our website: *www.virago.co.uk*
or by using the order form below

☐ The Cure for Death by Lightning	Gail Anderson-Dargatz	£15.00
☐ Alias Grace	Margaret Atwood	£8.99
☐ The Magic Toyshop	Angela Carter	£7.99
☐ Oyster	Janette Turner Hospital	£9.99
☐ Cowboys are My Weakness	Pam Houston	£6.99
☐ Impossible Saints	Michèle Roberts	£9.99
☐ Like	Ali Smith	£7.99

The prices shown above are correct at time of going to press. However, the publishers reserve the right to increase prices on covers from those previously advertised, without further notice.

Please allow for postage and packing: **Free UK delivery.**
Europe: add 25% of retail price; Rest of World: 45% of retail price.

To order any of the above or any other Virago titles, please call our credit card orderline or fill in this coupon and send/fax it to:

Virago, PO Box 121, Kettering, Northants NN14 4ZQ
Fax: 01832 733076   Tel: 01832 737520
Email: aspenhouse@FSBDial.co.uk

☐ I enclose a UK bank cheque made payable to Virago for £
☐ Please charge £   to my Visa/Delta/Maestro

Expiry Date ☐☐☐☐   Maestro Issue No. ☐☐

NAME (BLOCK LETTERS please) ....

ADDRESS ....

....

....

Postcode .... Telephone ....

Signature ....

Please allow 28 days for delivery within the UK. Offer subject to price and availability.